You'll Be Safe in My Arms

By

Kristina Thephachanh

ISBN: 1508429928

ISBN-13: 978-1508429920

ACKNOWLEDGEMENTS

To my Mom and Dad for supporting me in publishing this book and letting me write freely whenever I wanted to.

To Jonna Alonso, you will always be my best friend ever and thank you for encouraging me to write stories. If it wasn't for you, this book would have never been published.

To my sister, Melanie and my cousin, Sarah, thank you for being there to listen to all my crazy story ideas and for constantly hearing me blab on and on about this story.

To my writing teachers, Hilary Edwards, Maura Caley, and Brad Tonahill, for teaching me to be a better writer and bigger shout out to Mr. Tonahill for telling me you would, "read it right off the bat" if this book ever became a physical book.

To all my fans on AsianFanFics, thank you for making me smile everyday with your positive feedback on my stories and giving me confidence to write more.

BOOK KNOWLWDGE

Things to know before you start reading this story:

- K-Pop stands for Korean pop which is Korean pop music.

- Just like in America, having the same last name doesn't necessarily mean you're related. In Korea, the common last name is Kim, Lee, or Park because centuries ago when the royal families ruled many people name their children after them. That's why there are billions of Kims, Lees, and Parks.

- Unlike in American, Korean last names come first since it's the family names based on Korean society, the family name is more important than the individual's name.

- In America, high schools have 6 periods with different subjects and teachers while in Korea you have the same classroom and the teachers come to you instead of you going to them.

- "Yah" usually means "hey" depending on what the situation it's being used as. Usually used when angry/frustrated or to call someone over.

Chapter 1

BOMI

First day of senior year! Yippee... I hate school so much I just want to leave and never return to that foul place.

I only studied so hard for the past three years is that maybe I would be able to skip grades to end my misery but NOPE I guess it doesn't work that way at Junseo High.

Instead I was put in the Honors classes with a bunch of kids who aren't really that intelligent (in my opinion that is) but they are really clever on hiding lies and "accidents" they cause especially towards me.

Junseo is just like any other high school; they are all made up of cliques. You have the popular students who are basically queens and kings of the school, they even give themselves some ridiculous names to be called, then there are the nerds, the jocks, and many more. I don't fit in any category because I rather stay out of any these stupid sections, we shouldn't be categorized like some computer software file where the files only fit if it comes to its liking. We should be more like a library, where we are shelved as a specific category that fit different types of taste and style.

Anyway, the three and now four years I've been going to this high school I've been targeted by the whole school for no exact reason! Is it because I'm poor because that isn't my freaking fault!

Every night before bed I would think, *"Why wasn't I born to a different couple?"* I may sound like a cruel and disrespectful daughter but just wait till you meet my parents. I don't know why I even call them my parents they're more like demons sent from the devil himself to ruin anyone's' life they stumble upon and that would be me.

Well, the demons gave me a name, Bomi. Park Bomi but they never had said my name not even once. Well maybe when I was baby but once I started talking that's when the name Bomi never existed to them.

~ Flashback to Four Years Old ~

"Happy Birthday!" Bomi's mother said cheerily.

"Thank you Mother!" Bomi hugged her tightly.

"We have a big surprise for you," her father announced.

"Really?" Bomi cupped her small hands on her face, excited to hear what her surprise was.

"Yep!" They both cheered.

"We have a new name to call you," Her mother spoke.

"Wahh what is it?!" Bomi asked with excitement.

"Gaesaekki," my mother replied.

"Gae..gaesaeki?" Being the smart little girl she was Bomi already knew the meaning of the name.

Bomi's name was son of a bitch.

"Yes but don't worry you won't have the name forever," assured her father with a smile.

~ End of Flashback ~

After that they called me Gaesaekki for a year until my next birthday then I would get a new name to be called. For example, when I was six, I was Dong (poop), at age ten, I was Mangu (dumbass), and when I was thirteen, I was Ddorang (fag). Now at seventeen years old, I'm called Nappeun Nyeon (bastard).

Anyway, I woke up at six in the morning to avoid seeing my parents and to get to school early to also avoid the mass crowds of the student body. I did my normal routine which is brushing my teeth, putting on my school uniform (okay, I have to admit this has to be the most expensive thing my parents bought me).

Putting on my uniform is always the most time consuming part of my mornings. There's seven parts to my school uniform but you most importantly have to wear five parts of the uniform that include the black blazer, your name tag, the white dress shirt, the blue and black striped tie, and the tan skirt that goes a few inches above the knee. The blazer is sort of a weird one though, you can choose to wear your blazer or not but teachers prefer you wear it so you complete the sophisticated look of a Junseo High School student. The other two parts of the uniform are the white knee high socks and the sweater vest which are also optional.

It is very important that you wear at least the five parts of the uniform because if you don't wear your uniform properly you will be punished.

So I usually just wear everything except the sweater vest. I only wear that when necessary.

Afterwards I added lotion to my face and then Chap Stick to my lips. It was now 6:30 A.M. so I grabbed my backpack which was a weird rounded square or rectangle type thing with two back straps and a handle on top. I also picked up my pair of black converse (my one out of two pairs of shoes I have) off the floor and squished my feet into it.

Most of the stuff I have I bought myself since my parents are too selfish to get me anything.

"It's a waste of money, Mangu." My parents would say to me. Yeah, sure clothes are a waste of money; food is a waste of money, everything I own is a waste of money! Working at a restaurant on Tuesdays and Thursdays after school doesn't really help pay for a lot of stuff. Sure I get paid eight dollars an hour and that's good money but things nowadays are getting expensive.

I suddenly heard movement coming from one of the rooms.

Oh no, the demons are waking up, I better leave quickly! I quickly slipped out the front door and made my way towards school.

I stepped through the campus gates and bowed towards Mr. Cho, he's a teacher who stands at the school gates every morning with a large meter stick (he only carries the meter stick to scare us) to make sure everyone was wearing their uniform properly and so there were no tardy students because they will be punished for being late. He also works in the school office with all the student files and documents.

"Yah, yah, yah! Fix that tie of yours!" I heard him scold a male student.
I looked around the school campus and there was barely anyone to be seen. *Good.*

I trudged up the school steps and walked inside the warm building and stepped towards a set of tables where I would receive my school schedule.

"Hi Miss Park Bomi!" The nurse greeted with a rather large smile pasted on her face. She was in charge of the L-Y table.

She knows me pretty well because she's the school nurse and I always go in to treat my injuries.

"Hello," I bowed down with my usual straight face. I always try my best to keep a poker face on to hide my emotions from everyone.

"So how was your summer?" She asked rolling up her sleeves of her white doctor's coat and shuffling through files to find my schedule.

"It was a good," I lied. Summer was terrible I was forced to stay inside the house and just sit in my room all day and night except for when I go to work.

"Good to know you're having fun! Ah here it is," she pulled out my schedule and before she gave it to me, she takes a look at it. "Wow honors!"

"I study really hard every day," I commented and took my schedule from her. "See you around." I bowed down, turned around and left quickly before she started any more conversation.

"Okay bye!" She called out to me.

I hate all the teachers here, they keep annoying me. *Hmm what subjects do I have?*

COLLEGE HONORS –
1st: Math 2nd: Reading and Writing 3rd: English
4th: Science LUNCH 5th: Gym 6th: Free/Study Period

Yes! Finally a free period I can do anything I want! Wait a minute. What! Classroom 6B again! Why this classroom? I had this classroom for all the years I've been here. Out of all four honors classes it had to be this one. Well, at least I'll get my favorite seat.

When I got to the classroom I walk over to my favorite table. Each table fits at least four people and being the outcast, no one sits by me but I don't mind, no one is there to copy my answers or write awful stuff on my papers.

My favorite table is right by the window; I sit right on the corner where you get a good view outside especially since you get a view of the professionally decorated front campus of the school.

“I guess it's good to be back after all so I don't have to adapt to a new 'habitat'," I said out loud with a small smile. I sat down on the wooden stool and laid out my supplies to fit accordingly to my schedule.

JAESUN

"Yah you guys, come on hurry!” I called out to the others who were walking slowly behind me while I was keeping up a quick pace.

"Kid, slow down I don't know why you're so excited for school?" Minho said.

"I don't know why either but I just can't wait to see which class I’m in!" I replied walking backwards.

"Its 7:20 we better hurry up!" Alex announced starting to pick up his pace and the others started to walk faster as well.

Finally we reached school and as we walked in, some girls started to fan-girl over us. Yeah I guess we’re pretty popular around the school. We stepped towards a set of tables to get our schedule.

"I wonder if we will have the same class this year." Doyoon questioned as one of the office staff searched through the different files.

It must be really hard to find everyone’s schedule when everyone basically has the same last name, I thought as I watch the teacher rummaged through all the different Park files. Plus there’s not just one Park Jaesun or Park

Doyoon, there could be thousands of us with the same exact name!

"Yeah hopefully we do so we can hang out with each other all day!" Ethan commented and grabbed his schedule. After we were all handed our schedules, we gathered around and compared.

"Okay, I have class 5A," I said.

"I do too!" Joon said and we high-fived each other.

"Same here!" In the end we all were placed in classroom 5A.

"Come on, class is about to start!" Leo informed us as always. Leo is really into school and smart but I always wonder why he never makes it into the Honors classes.

We walked into class just in time before the bell rang when a girl with long wavy hair walked up to us.

"W-we set up the table for you guys, we even asked the t-teacher for permission to do so and he said it was okay," she stuttered a bit and pointed to the two tables in the back that were pushed together so that all seven of us could fit.

"Thanks," Kangdae said and ruffled the girl's hair which caused her to squeal and runaway to her friends.

"Good morning students! Please take your seats," Mr. Oh spoke in a weird way so definitely he was someone from the country side who never got use to speaking in a Seoul (city) dialect. "Now before we start anything fun, the school requires you to take a small test to see if you are in the right class. For example if you need to be put in honors or in a lower grade class." Mr. Oh passed out a two page packet to everyone in the class.

"That wasn't so bad," I said as I handed in my test.

"Ha-ha it was super easy I barely understood anything on that test," Minho laughed.

"Okay students I will check these tonight and be prepared to possibly move to a different class," Mr. Oh announced. "Let's start our lesson today, shall we?"

BOMI

Where the heck is the stupid teacher?! It's been twenty minutes since the bell rang and the teacher has not shown up yet.

"Well, well look who we have here isn't it Little Bomi," Hwang Dasom said in her annoying high pitched voice.

Dasom is a gaesaekki but even though I act like this, deep down inside I'm so scared of her. I worry in fear every day that I might get hurt really badly.

"Are you not going to answer me?" She fiddled with my hair and I scooted away from her. "Aww are you scared?" She grabbed a hold of the stool leg with her foot and dragged the stool away making me fall about three feet to the ground.

Everyone stopped what they were doing and started to laugh at me. I felt tears at the brim of my eyes but I refuse to let them fall. "How come you haven't disappeared yet? I'm surprised you survived all this time but I will only make it worse for you."

"Sorry I'm late kids all my files got mixed up with the class next door." Thank goodness the teacher came in and saved the day before anything else happened. I shuffled back onto my feet and picked myself up onto the stool again.

"We're like eighteen!" Some guy called out.

She dumped her bag and files onto her desk. Her heels made loud clacking noises as she hastily walked around the front of the classroom.

"Whatever. Please take your seats; the seats you are sitting in now, are your permanent seats unless I feel the need to move you. Okay? Well, I'm Mrs. Chan and so as an honors teacher for seniors I will be your teacher for all subjects except for gym that will be Mr. Kim."

Having one teacher for each subject, cool, at least I only have to deal with two teachers, I thought as she continued to talk.

"First things first, rules." Her voiced deepened into something serious and scary. Chills ran down my spine and I'm sure everyone was holding their breath.

"No unexcused absents or tardiness. There are no excuses why you are not here in class learning unless it is major. I expect everyone to be doing their part as a class to do their best to ace senior year!" She smiled widely at the class and everyone (I did as well) let out a sigh of relief

"For today, we won't do much since tomorrow we may get new students." My eyes widen in shock at the words "new students."

"But it seems we won't have many since I see only three seats left." Everyone turned around and stared at me.

"As if anyone is going to sit by you," I heard Dasom mutter.

I hope nobody gets into honors or at least be in this class, I don't want them harassing me.

Please.

Chapter 2

BOMI

"I'll see you guys after lunch," Mrs. Chan said.

All day long Mrs. Chan talked and just kept talking. She talked about her life, how she is half Chinese and half Korean, and that she was poor at first until her father invested in a company which got her family rich and blah, blah, blah.

She got to know a little about the students except me, of course, I tried to avoid any of the stupid questions she asked us like "When were you born?, Where were you born?, What do you want to be when you grow up?" Stupid questions are just meant to be unanswered.

I walk into the cafeteria and it was filled with deranged students running all over the place. Some kid pushed me out of his way ramming me into the wall. I quickly fixed up my wrinkled blazer and scan the room to find an empty table.

Bingo! Empty table in the corner, best place to be at! I walked in line to grab a tray of food and like always there are a bunch of people who cut in front of me but I don't mind as long as they aren't picking on me like their dinner plate.

When I finally grab my tray, I hurried over to my table and sat down. I was enjoying my turkey sandwich until someone had to come and ruin it.

"How's lunch?" Dasom came over to my table with her so called "crew" made up of Bang Sooah and Kwon Chanmi.

Sooah and Chanmi are always hanging around Dasom. Both Sooah and Chanmi are tall and skinny, Sooah always has the latest brand name accessories and Chanmi always has a different brand name purse to show off to everyone and always gets front row seats to concerts. She also likes to dye her hair a lot too. She should be lucky this school allows you to dye your hair different colors because not a lot of schools allow it.

"None of your business," I grumbled looking down at my tray.

"What did you say?" She questioned slamming her hand down on the table.

I stayed silent not wanting to say anything. She suddenly flipped over my tray; it splattered all over my uniform. I had kimchi and chocolate milk stains all over my white blouse and on the front of my skirt.

"Aww look Bomi had a little accident!" Dasom shouted out and everyone burst out into laughter.

Then I felt the tears begin to run down my face. *I sure will receive a beating tonight from my parents.*

I ran out of the cafeteria in a flash to hide in the bathroom.

I slammed my hands down on the sink and looked up at the mirror.

It's only been the first day and you're already making me miserable.

"I HATE YOU HWANG DASOM!" I cried out.

DOYOON

As we walked in to the cafeteria and sat down, everyone was laughing at something or someone.

"I wonder what everyone was laughing at." I thought out loud as everyone started to chat amongst themselves.

"Who knows," Ethan shrugged his shoulders and shoved some food into his mouth.

"I saw someone running out though," Kangdae added as he sat down with his tray.

"Was it a girl or a boy?" I asked out of curiosity.

"Girl," he answered with a mouth full of salad. "But it's none of our business anyway so just eat your food, Doyoon."

Kangdae is right, it's really none of our business but I hope nothing bad happened to that girl, I thought as I began eating my lunch.

UNKNOWN

I witness everything that happened and it hurts to see such a pretty girl get treated that way for four years straight. I sighed and thought about Bomi.

Why is she always on my mind all day and why am I being a bystander? I should do something but what?

BOMI

The bell for sixth period rang and gym was terrible as always. All we did was sit around, groaning on how much exercise we must do to pass and what not.

The stain on my skirt dried up but it still left a dark spot that was a tad bit noticeable since my skirt was not a dark color. *Why do the skirts have to be tan?*

As I stepped in class everyone started to laugh at me again. I put my head down and briskly walked to my seat but before I even reached my table I was tripped which made everyone die of laughter.

"Oh my goodness, are you okay?" Mrs. Chan walked in and quickly ran over to me. Everyone became silent of the teacher's arrival. I nodded my head and climbed up onto my feet and walked over to my seat.

"Who did this?" Mrs. Chan spoke up and eyed everyone in the classroom.

"I just tripped on my shoelace," I said quietly but enough to be heard.

"Are you telling the truth?"

"Yes Ma'am," I replied.

"Okay," She gave me an unsure look.

School finally ended and I raced out of that wicked school in hopes for someone not to kidnap me to beat me up.

"I don't want to go home, what are they going to do to me? This was so expensive," I look down at my stained uniform and deeply sighed.

I went into my home silently hoping my parents wouldn't hear me.

"Nappeun Nyeon!" My mother called out to me.

"Yes?" I nervously called back and rubbed the buttons of my blazer.

She walked to the front door where I stood from the kitchen. "Don't you have work–" She gasped. "How dare you! That is expensive!" She walked over to me and slapped my face.

I fell to the floor as tears unknowingly flowed down my cheeks dripping onto the floor.

"What's going on in here?" My father questioned stepping in the room.

"Honey, look at her uniform, it was her first day and she has ruined it!"

"WHAT!" He grabbed a magazine off the table, rolled it up and whacked me on the head repeatedly. "Do you know how much this cost? It was $250. You, stupid bitch I'm not paying for this shit!" He finally stopped hitting me. "Get up! And go to work!"

He grabbed a hold of my hair and pulled me up. I clenched my teeth to endure the stinging pain shooting around my head.

My mother gave me the last slap on my arm with a stick; she usually has to hit me with.

I lost strength in my legs and stumbled towards my room. I slowly shut the door closed, I look at my arm that was slapped and it was starting to feel sore.

I have to get to work soon so I have to get dressed quickly into my work uniform.

Our uniforms consist of a striped, short-sleeve dress shirt, a navy blue silk tie, a black skirt (the same length as my school uniform skirt), and a navy blue apron to go around my waist.

I work as a waitress at Yong Su San, it's a fancy restaurant but not too fancy sort of like Olive Garden in America.

I don't know how I'm going to hide this bruise from my co-workers or the customers with this short-sleeve shirt. I shook my head and stripped down out of my school uniform and into my work uniform.

After I finished dressing, I walked over to the wall closest to my bed which is on the floor and slid off the wood wall panel.

No one knows about this secret panel but me. This is where I hide all my personal items I don't want my parents to see. I have my stash of money, all my best report cards, pictures of my cousin and me, many math and science awards and my grandmother's expensive watch that she gave me before she passed, all of it hidden in this small little cubby.

Anyway, I pulled out a shoe box that holds my savings of money; I saved at least $6,000 since I started working in seventh grade. I took out $25 to pay for dry cleaning my uniform.

"Thank you," I bowed down to the worker as I left the dry cleaners.

It was about a fifteen minute walk to work while it's a ten minute walk to school.

"Hi Bomi!" Maybee waved to me excitedly. Her long, light brown hair bounced everywhere as she ran over to me.

Maybee is my Japanese co-worker; she doesn't go to my school though, she goes to an international school. She loves K-pop so much that she learned Korean in just three months then moved to Korea to study more Korean and to possibly meet her future husband. She can be very overly dramatic sometimes.

Although, I don't know why she is so nice to me or tries to get close to me I don't really talk to her a lot even though she's been here for maybe almost two years now, I guess she is the only one I can depend on being my one true friend.

"Oh my gosh! What happened?" She grabbed my arm and examined the bruise that began to form.

"It's nothing," I answered with no emotion in my voice.

"No, something must of have happened," she said rubbing my hand.

"Seriously, nothing happened, Maybee," I stated once more.

She said something in Japanese that I didn't understand. "Fine, be that way." She dropped my hand and left. She has a bit of an attitude too.

I walked to the back of the kitchen and checked in.

"A little late I see," I turned around to see Collin smirking at me.

Park Collin is my other co-worker besides having just Maybee being my only friend I guess I would say Collin is also my friend. I met Collin here at work during freshmen year, he also goes to Junseo High and he's also in honors. He usually with his group of friends they call themselves Warriors because they have sweet vocals but tough and powerful dance moves. Weird, right? But I guess it sort of suits them. They all wish to become a boy group in the K-pop industry someday.

Collin is a really good singer, he always sings when he is cleaning but he doesn't do it often, only when there is barely anyone around. He's a little of a shy guy when it comes towards his love for music.

"So what?" I questioned with a cold tone.

"Oh nothing maybe you might get fired because your always late," he answered nonchalantly.

I punched him in the arm as I walked by him. "Ouch! I was just kidding, you know we need you. I need you," he chuckled a little on the last part.

I smiled a bit and rolled my eyes. "Shut up!"

I guess Collin and Maybee are the only ones to make me smile.

"Bomi, table five needs a waitress," Maybee called. "And they are super cute!" I rolled my eyes once more. I walked out with my notepad and a few menus.

"Hello..." I froze when I saw who the customers were.

"Well, isn't little Miss Bomi," Taejoon said with a smile. "Look guys, it's Bomi!" Park Kyung and Aiden Ahn were also with him.

Taejoon. That cursed name. He also bullied me when I started High School and still does. To be honest, when we were freshmen I had a crush on Taejoon. He was in the honors classes and he was just so kind to me. He was my first friend. He hung out with me. He betrayed me. He became my enemy. I hate him. I became his victim.

Why did he have to come to this restaurant? Out of all the places in Seoul, he came here?

"Here are your menus," I said and turned around but before I left the table, I tripped over a foot. Taejoon's foot to be exact. He burst out into laughter and soon his friends joined in.

"Are you okay?" Maybee asked helping me up, I nodded. Tears started to build up.

"Are you crazy?!" Collin yelled coming over.

"What?" Taejoon scoffed.

"What did Bomi do to you?" He questioned with a serious look.

"What are you her boyfriend?" Taejoon smirked and nudged Kyung with his elbow.

"Yah Taejoon!" Collin stepped up and pushed Taejoon's shoulder with his hand.

"Don't touch me!" Taejoon said standing up.

"You are hurting my friend so I have the right to help defend her," Collin argued, my eyes widen a bit with shock.

I can't believe he said he would help defend me.

Taejoon pushed Collin down to the ground. Collin quickly got back up ready to fight back.

"Collin. Don't. It's not worth it, you might get fired," Maybee said pulling Collin back.

"They're not worth my time anyway, I'm getting Kiyoshi to serve these guys," he walked back into the kitchen angrily.

"Let's go," Maybee pulled me to the back of the kitchen following Collin. "Oh my," she started speaking in Japanese. At first she was talking in a soothing, comforting tone then she got angrier and angrier.

Maybe she's talking about Taejoon, I thought as she kept speaking.

"What are you talking about?" I asked laughing a little.

"Sorry, who was that jerk-face anyway?" She asked sitting next to me.

"Gu Taejoon."

"Well if I ever see him again he will be goo!" She punched a fist into the palm of her hand.

I laughed a little at her statement, even if I am a bit older than her and a bit taller, she's a tough one. Something I'm not.

"I heard we're turning Taejoon into goo count me in!" Collin jabbed his thumb at himself.

For the next hour they stayed here for, I stayed away from that table. Not even once have I set foot around that table.

While Kiyoshi gladly took my section, I took his section on the other side of the restaurant for tonight.

I wish Taejoon never existed or at least he was born a kind person.

I hate you Gu Taejoon.

Chapter 3

BOMI

I woke up at my usual time (6 A.M.). I glanced at my nice, clean, and *expensive* uniform. That word pinches my heart every time I say it.

I dragged myself out of bed and got ready to start another bitter day.

DOYOON

"Mom, Mom...Mom! Mom!" I shot up breathing heavily sweat dripped down my forehead. "Bad dream again."

It's been almost eight years why do I still have these dreams? They're gone. They're not a part of my life anymore.

"Are you okay, Doyoon?" Kangdae asked me rushing in to my side. I nodded. "Are you sure?" He gave me a worried look.

"Yes I'm sure, Mother," I joked.

"Ha-ha you're so funny," he scrunched up his face in annoyance and flicked my forehead.

He doesn't like being called mom even though he did take care of me when we were little so he was sort of like a mom.

"Hurry up and get ready for school or we'll leave without you." He got up and left the room.

Okay, Doyoon lets have a good day today. Maybe we will be in the honors class. Good luck! I pumped a fist in the air to get myself motivated.

I decided to add the gray sweater vest to my uniform so I look more professional or smart I should say. Plus this is basically the complete uniform set.

The boy uniforms at Junseo are basically the same as the girls except the skirt and the knee high socks. Well we, guys, do get long socks but they aren't that long, it stops maybe around the middle of the calf since we wear slacks.

Anyway, after preparing myself for a possibly good day, I grabbed my backpack and head towards the kitchen to make myself some toast.

Mm... toast.

BOMI

"Bomi-ah," people cooed as I walked through the hallways.

Shut up, shut up, SHUT UP! Please leave me alone.

Some people pushed me around the hallway as if I was some basketball being passed to the other team members. I picked up my pace shoving people away from me as they crowded around me.

"I heard you tried seducing Taejoon again," One girl said to me. I stopped in my tracks and turned around to look at her.

"What?" I questioned her as she giggled.

"Last night, you were seducing Taejoon. Come on, everyone knows you liked him and still do," she folded her arms and gave me an I'm-right-and-you're-wrong look.

"I never did and I never will!" I yelled before walking off.

Bomi why don't you just leave this wretched world? Because I want to show those stupid jerks I can become successful and be the bigger person. But you don't even have a future plan for yourself. True but I'll one day plan out how I want my future to look if I don't choose to leave. I bumped into someone which knocked me back to reality.

"I am so sorry, please don't hurt me!" I scrunched up my body and put my hands up to try to defend myself.

"Why would I do that?" He asked with a confused tone.

I looked up to see an unfamiliar face, smiling. His bangs weren't long; they almost cover eyes just a bit so he swept it over to the left side of his face.

He must be a new student, I thought as I stared at his face wondering how I should respond back to this new kid.

JAESUN

"Because everyone would," she answered. I looked into her beautiful brown eyes and saw sadness, loneliness and pain.

Those were the only words that could describe what I saw in her eyes.

"It's okay, I wouldn't hurt anyone. Okay maybe my brothers but I wouldn't hurt anyone. Umm hi I'm Jaesun," I put out my hand to shake hands with her but she just stared at me as if she was looking right through me.

"I have to get to class now," she swiftly walked pass me.

I pressed my lips in a straight line and put my hand down. I shoved both hands into my pockets and continued my way to class.

"Jaesun!" The fan girls cooed as I walk pass them.

BOMI

What a weird kid he didn't shove me when I bumped into him or hit me like everyone else would. I scratched my head as I walked into class and Mrs. Chan was not here yet.

Mrs. Chan please stop being late, you're only giving them an opportunity to hurt me.

"Bomi!" Dasom and her crew called. "I hope you're having a nice morning!" She flipped her one hundred dollar salon priced hair.

Why spend $100 on making your hair look nice when you can buy a ten dollar bottle of Pantene? At least it makes your hair shiny, soft, and smells good.

"You should really get your hair done it looks like a bird's nest." She giggled. She pulled her hair so they both show in front of her shoulders. "So then you can get fabulous hair like mine except my hair will always be better!"

At least my hair is natural and healthy!

Dasom's hair was probably bleached to get that color to show up. Her hair was brown with blonde tips and everyone knows people with dark hair have a harder time getting certain colors to show up in their hair.

"Are you even paying attention?" Chanmi whacked me with her workbook.

Dasom scoffed. "You will pay attention after this."

JAESUN

I couldn't sit still. I'm too excited. The thought of me making it into honors would just be an honor.

I studied so hard all summer or a week before school started but it would mean so much to be put into honors especially to get those credits for college.

"Yah stop shaking your leg, it's annoying," Alex whispered to me.

"Sorry." I smiled at him and started to the rub the buttons on my blazer.

"Okay class, I have your results and it looks like four of you guys made it," the teacher said. "And the four people are..."

BOMI

"Aww look the pig can't get it!" Some girl pointed out and laughed.

"I wish you would stop calling me a pig," I spoke quietly.

"Do you guys hear that?"

"Yeah, it kind of sounds like... Oink! Oink!"

They stole my pencil case and placed it onto of the tall cabinet and now I'm trying to climb on top of the lockers but it's too tall for me to pull myself up.

Where the hell is Mrs. Chan? I thought as I grew frustrated.

"Oh my gosh, it's Taejoon!" Dasom announced. I stopped and my eyes widen in shock.

"And Bangtan!" Some other girls squealed.

I turned around to see four guys standing at the front of the class room. Taejoon and... Jaesun? I shook my head and turned back around to fetch my pencil case.

"Taejoon, look the pig over there is trying to get her pencil case from the top cabinet," I heard Dasom say.

Then I heard shuffling and footsteps head towards me. A chair slammed down onto the ground. Someone stepped up onto it and grabbed my pencil case.

"Tae-Taejoon," I was completely shocked. He stuck out his hand with my pencil case in it.

I was just about to grab it but he quickly swiped his hand away, ripped opened my pencil case and threw it outside the classroom. Taejoon burst into laughter which caused everyone else joined in laughter. I glared at Taejoon as tears dripped down my face.

Those were expensive Taejoon!

"Aww is the little baby pig crying because her poor pencils are broken," he pouted at me then guffawed, holding onto his aching stomach.

"Her pencils are worth more than her!" Some boy pointed out.

I stood there with my mouth agape. Out of all the things people said to me that had to be one of the most abhorrent things someone had said about me.

I walked out quickly to go pick up all my writing utensils. A few pencils and pens were broken so now I only have two mechanical pencils to rely on for the rest of the school year.

As I crawled around searching for more of my pens, pencils, and erasers, someone else went down on their knees and helped picked some them up as well.

I looked up to see his face again.

JAESUN

I couldn't stand seeing her getting hurt again so I ran out and decided to help her pick up her stuff.

"Hey, are you alright?" I asked her and she nodded. I didn't want to bother her by asking questions so I stayed silent for a while.

"I think that's everything lets go back inside the classroom." I offered her a hand up from the ground but she stood up on her own and went back inside. Not even taking one glance back at me.

BOMI

Why is he even helping me? Sooner or later he's going to turn his back on me like everyone else.

"I am so sorry kids, my car broke down," Mrs. Chan said rushing in as Jaesun and I also stepped inside the classroom. "Okay where are my new students? Come on up!" Taejoon, Jaesun and the other two guys stood in front of the classroom.

"Introduce yourselves even if you already know most of the students in here," Mrs. Chan ordered.

"Hey my name is Gu Taejoon." He did forty-five degree bow. I can tell he thinks introducing himself is useless since everyone knows who he is. What a conceited prick.

"Hello, my name is Park Jaesun!" Jaesun did a ninety degree bow which shows that he is very respectful even to his fellow classmates.

His bangs got in his face again so he flipped his hair so it went back over to the left side of his face.

"Hi, I'm Park Doyoon," he was a tall skinny guy with black hair. His hair was perfectly in placed with not very many little hairs sticking out. I think he wanted to look smart because he was put in the honors classes.

He's probably not even that bright, I thought as I looked at him and then went back to staring blankly at the textbook held in front of me.

"Hi, the name's Lee Alex, so don't wear it out," he winked which got all the girls in awe.

I could only roll my eyes at his way of trying to be cool. He was short compared to Jaesun and Doyoon.

I don't know why but his hair reminds me of the top of a mushroom, it's like kind of roundish and it's just weird but it looks good on him. I guess.

"Okay so you can choose your seats. We might have to find another stool or desk for one of you," Mrs. Chan said, she placed a finger on her chin (probably thinking about the extra stool).

"I would like to sit next to Bom-" Taejoon started, I gasped that he almost said my name but he was cut off.

"The three of us would like to sit over there," Jaesun said pointing to himself, Alex, and Doyoon.

"Fine with me," Mrs. Chan smiled. "Now Taejoon I will call the custodian to bring in another stool." Taejoon folded his arms and huffed.

I looked back down at my book that I was "reading" as they walked towards me. Jaesun sat down next to me, that Doyoon guy sat in front of me and Alex sat next to Doyoon.

"Hey!" I looked up and it was Doyoon. I gave him a slight bow with my head. "What's your name?" He asked giving me a small smile.

Ring!

Saved by the bell. I got down from the stool and briskly walked out of the classroom.

Why are new students so weird? Always want to become friends with the first person they see. Don't they know they need to learn who to trust first?

DOYOON

"What a strange girl," I said tilting my head to the side. "Is she new because I haven't seen her around?"

"No, she's been here since like freshmen year," Jaesun replied.

"Really? I haven't seen her," I was utterly confused.

"I've seen her running around a few times," Jaesun tapped his pen on his workbook obviously uninterested in our conversation. Haven't even started a lesson yet and this kid is already doing work.

"Oh, well I don't think she knows us," I said scratching my ear.

"That's impossible! Everyone knows us!" Alex stated putting emphasis on "everybody" by spreading his arms out.

"But that doesn't mean we should know everyone," Jaesun said continuing to fill in answers.

"True. True," I said nodding my head. "She's pretty, isn't she?"

"Yeah but maybe if she smiles she would be gorgeous," Alex said. "I bet you I can make her laugh by doing this!" Alex crossed his eyes and had his mouth open like the scream.

Jaesun finally looked up from his book and started to laugh. We all then started laughing together.

BOMI

Finally lunch! I wish I could sit outside since I get less bullied out there but it's raining so I have to sit in the cafeteria.

I took my tray to my usual seat and began eating slowly. Then several other trays made their way down onto my table.

"Hey!" Jaesun smiled and sat down next to me. I nodded my head.

"These are my other friends or brothers, I should say. That is Kangdae, Minho, Leo, and Ethan," he introduced pointing to each boy. I slightly bowed.

"You never told us your name yet?" Doyoon asked sitting across from me. He kind of sounded annoyed since I completely ignored him the first time he asked for my name.

"P-Park Bomi," I stuttered looking down.

"Well it's very nice to meet you Bomi," that Leo guy greeted. He had dark red hair while the other boys either had dark brown or light brown hair or black hair, I don't usually like guys who dye their hair a different color but it actually suits him very well.

"Why are you sitting here?" I asked.

"Why not?" Alex questioned.

"Because no one ever wants to sit with me," I replied.

"Oh well umm... we haven't seen you around so I thought we get to know you," Leo explained.

I wanted to scoff at his statement. *How does he not know me or seen me I've been the school's target for four years now. Maybe these guys ARE new,* I thought as I slightly tilted my head to the side.

"We're pretty popular around the school though, how do you not know us? We've been here since freshmen year," Minho said. I shrugged.

I looked down at my tray. My head stayed down but my eyes looked up. I looked around and everyone was staring at me. I quickly stood up and walked away.

"Wait!" I hear one of the boys call out to me but I gave them the cold shoulder and continue my way to class to grab my stuff before gym.

I hate gym. They make me do stuff I can't even do sometimes I don't get to do anything since the coaches give up on me.

Today we have to see how many push-ups and sit ups we can do and with Mr. Kim I have do the activities.

He's been my substitute teacher many times last year since Mrs. Kwon got pregnant and what not so she couldn't come to school a lot of the times.

I guess I'll be paired with Mr. Kim since no else wants to be my partner and my class has an odd number of students.

The bell rang for fifth period as I made my way toward the locker room. As I walked in Dasom and a few other girls were looking at me and snickering.

I walk over to the closet bench and placed my gym clothes down on the opposite bench behind me. I stripped off my skirt, placed it on the opposite bench and grabbed my shorts; I then took off my blazer and blouse and set on the opposite bench as well.

Good thing I have a tank top underneath so I don't have to strip down all the way, I thought.

Before I grabbed my gym shirt, the strap on my tank was all twisted around my bra strap, I hate when this happens. After it was fixed I turned around to grab my shirt but all my clothes were gone.

"Those stupid bitches!" I yelled through gritted teeth.

Those girls must have taken it as I fiddled with my strap. This is too revealing I can't wear this! Oh yeah! The lost and found, I for sure can find a shirt in there. I walked around the locker room until I found the lost and found bin.

Are you serious! Why are there only jackets, what the heck! Fine, I'll wear this rain coat.

I walked out of the locker room and into the gym; everyone was standing around and chatting with one another.

"Everyone line up!" Mr. Kim yelled and everyone obeyed. "Park Bomi!"

"Yes," I answered, nervously.

"Why are you wearing a jacket, is it raining inside?" He asked.

I stayed silent looking down at the floor.

"Well..." he tapped his foot. "If you don't have a reason, please take it off." I took off the jacket, he gasped loudly. "Wow, I see you changed you look just like the girls over there," he said pointing to a few girls who were also wearing tank tops. I mentally face palm myself.

Well at least I'm not the only one.

"Well then... Everyone pick a partner please," Mr. Kim instructed.

As usual no one came to my side.

"Park Bomi, come here please," Mr. Kim ordered.

"Yes," I walked over to him. The feeling of embarrassment flooded through my body.

"Your partner will be Park Jaesun. You finally have a partner!" He said patting my shoulder. My eyes widen with shock, I backed away a bit at his sudden touch and that Jaesun was my partner. *Does it really have to be this kid!*

"Kay kids get ready for push-ups."

"You can go first," he gave me a small smile and gave him a slight glare because I did not want my partner to be a guy and if I hadn't mentioned before I was in a spaghetti strap tank top. This is too scandalous and I should be expelled for this crime that I didn't commit.

Okay, Bomi breathe in and out. Relax. The more you stress out about this the more panic you will be then you will go mad. I guess the self-pep talk helped calm me down.

I got down on the ground and waited for the call to go.

With heavy breaths, I finished my set of push-ups with a count of 35 push-ups in three reps but that didn't compare to Jaesun who did 68.

"How many sit-ups can you do in a minute?" Mr. Kim called out.

"You first," Jaesun said.

I lay down and positioned myself for sit-ups. Mr. Kim blew the whistle. Every time I went up Jaesun's face was really close to mine.

Man, this kid needs to back up and give me some space!

"What happened to your shoulder?" He pointed out as I made my 30th sit-up. I stopped and looked down at my shoulder.

An untreated, jagged scar appeared from my collarbone to my shoulder. A scar. That will never disappear no matter how hard you try to hide it and it will always remind me of that terrible day.

"I don't want to talk about it," I stated coldly and went for another sit-up.

"Sorry," he said and pressed his lips together.

"Let's go outside!" Mr. Kim waved his arm towards the double doors that lead out to the field.

I walked out to the field and I heard someone call my name.

"Bomi!" They called out to me in their annoying high pitched voices but there was only one I recognized.

I turned around and saw Dasom holding up a school uniform. My school uniform. I walked angrily toward them but before I got to touch the smooth fabric of the blazer, they dropped it on the ground.

"Oops!" Dasom giggled and walked away followed by her two minions.

"What an idiot," Chanmi giggled and pushed pass me even though there were plenty of room to walk around me.

I quickly went down on my knees to the ground and picked up my uniform.

I just got it washed! I checked around and wiped off any debris that stuck to it.

I let out a sigh of relief. *Thank goodness it's still pretty clean and luckily this is a turf field!*

I let out a few hot tears knowing I won't be hurt by my parents or have to waste any more money on dry cleaning this expensive uniform.

DOYOON

I was searching for Bomi all period long. I wanted to be her partner but Alex wanted to partners since all the other boys had partners and he didn't so I was forced to be his partner.

I finally found Bomi; she was on the ground on her knees. It looked like she was crying. I was about to go see her but some annoying fan girl stopped me.

"Doyoon, we're playing soccer, do you want to be on my team?" She asked cutely.

Being popular in all, I have to say yes. I don't want to be called as the jerk of the school. "Sure!" I gave her a fake smile.

"Let's go!" She dragged me towards the others of her team. I looked back to see Bomi and she was still on the ground with Jaesun at her side.

JAESUN

I witnessed Dasom and her friends drop Bomi's uniform onto the ground. She dropped to her knees and started to clean off her uniform.

I think she's crying, I walked over to her to see if she's okay.

"Hey, you okay?" I asked crouching down next to her. She wiped some of her tears and nodded. "It's okay Dasom's a bitch." She gave me a small smile that made butterflies flutter in my stomach.

"So we're playing soccer, you want to be on my team?" I asked.

"Sure," she gave a quick, short answer.

“Here I think you'll need this,” I handed her my thin hoodie.

“Oh thank you,” she smiled again at me. It may be cold out but her smile warms me right back up.

"And I'll put your uniform in a safe place, I promise it won't get dirty," I gave her an assuring look and placed it down on a bench.

"You're a pretty good runner," I complimented. "And a good soccer player."

She gave a slight bow. "Why so formal?" She just shrugs her shoulders. "We're friends now so we can be comfortable with each other!"

I can tell she stiffened a bit at my statement but I might as well be her first friend.

I've seen what they have done to her throughout our years in high school nevertheless I chose to be just a bystander. I feel so guilty for not helping her so now I get to make up for it.

BOMI

I really can't believe he said we're friends. He doesn't hurt me or doesn't harass me like everyone else but still he wants to be my friend. *Friend.* That word lightens up my heart.

A popular guy wants to be friends with a girl like me. I guess he's like my first real friend after my cousin, of course.

Anyway, what am I supposed to say like should I accept him? I could but could I really trust him so quickly like that?

Mr. Kim announced class was over and I raced to the locker room to change. Good thing I'm a "fast" runner according to Jaesun that is. I almost laughed at that statement because every single time I run away from Dujoon or Dasom or my parents they always end up catching me.

JAESUN

She raced out of the field with her uniform in hand when it was time to go. I must really be her first friend in the many years.

I wonder if she's happy or upset about it.
I shrugged. *Oh well, I hope she feels that there is someone who actually doesn't want to hurt her.*

AUTHOR

It's been a month and Bomi still hasn't fully open up to the Bangtan boys. She's actually been bullied even more for hanging out with them.

So Bomi tries to avoid them but they always come right back to her side just like a bad penny. Something that you don't want always reappears when you try to get rid of it.

Chapter 4

DOYOON

"Hey guys, we should do something after school!" Alex proposed as we walked to school.

"Like what?" Minho questioned.

"Bubble tea?" Alex shrugged his shoulders.

"Yes! I've been craving for bubble tea for ages!" Jaesun clapped his hands together.

"Can Bomi come along with us?" I suddenly asked.

"Why? She doesn't even talk to us, every time we talk to her all she does is nod, bow, or simply ignore us," Ethan pointed out.

His point is pretty accurate but...

"She's just different," I said in response.

"What! She's just a– Wait a minute, do you like her?" Kangdae gave me his ooh-someone-is-in-love look.

"What? Ha-ha you're funny! No but really I'm just trying to be nice plus I don't think she has any friends," I whispered that last part even though it was only just us walking to school.

"Okay I see your point, well its fine by me. I don't know 'bout you guys," Kangdae said. Everyone else nodded their heads.

Yes! Everyone agreed so maybe I can get close to her.

BOMI

After putting on my uniform, I ran the brush through my messy, tangled hair. I slid my backpack onto my back and headed out the front door.

Ooh it's a little chilly out. Wish I had a jacket, I thought as I stepped out into the cold October air.

Well, at least I have this blazer and sweater vest to keep me warm but this skirt does not help at all to keep the cold air out. With each step, I kept shaking as I made my way to school.

Finally when I arrived at school, I ran in to find warmth. I shook off all the cold off of me and let the heat engulf me.

"Look the poor girl is cold!" Some boy laughed. People around stopped what they were doing and focused on me. I stood there frozen not knowing what to do then I felt an arm slung around my shoulders.

Some students gasped, I looked up to see his face.

"Hey Bomi!" He greeted with a big smile.

Doyoon. I nodded and we started walking towards class. "Come on, I know you can talk. Can't I get a simple hi or hey?" He question waving his hand in front of my face.

"H-hi," I said quietly.

DOYOON

I got her to say something! Point one for Doyoon!

"So how are you?" I asked since it was getting a bit awkward.

She shrugged. I sighed. *You know what? I'm getting irritated of her ignoring us, I'm sorry if you're being bullied and don't have any friends but I'm trying my best to be your friend!*

I grabbed her shoulder and forced her to look at me. Her eyes widen with shock and fear.

"Why do they treat you like that?" I stabbed the question at her which made her cringed at the force of my words. "I'm sorry, I didn't mean to raise my voice on you," I softened a bit.

I let go of my grip on her shoulder and she immediately ran away from me.

"I didn't even have a chance to invite her to hang out with us," I stuffed my hands in my pockets and headed to class with my head hanging low.

I always regret the things I do and say to people but I can't help it, it just naturally comes out. But I hope she doesn't hate me or is scared of me.

BOMI

I ran towards the classroom even though I know he has the same class as me I just want to get as far away as I can for now from Doyoon.

He terrified me, the way he grabbed my shoulder and forced me to turn around, the way his voice deepened when he was angry. I really thought he was going to hurt me.

As I walked into class I yet tripped over someone's foot. He laughed the loudest out of everyone.

And there was Taejoon holding onto his stomach. Then everything got silent. I looked up and saw a hand: Jaesun's hand.

"Are you alright?" He asked with a concerned look. I nodded and took his hand.

His hand, warm and soft, a hand I would care to hold every day. I shook my head at the odd thought.

JAESUN

I really wish they would stop hurting Bomi, what has she done wrong? I may be popular but I'm not those other kids who bully other people like what is this? That one Korean drama, Boys Over Flowers? And Bomi is the school's target and instead of F4, it's F6 with Taejoon and Dasom with their little crew.

We're still holding hands as we walk to our seat. She quickly let go.

I wish it lasted longer.

"Thanks," she quietly said bowing down her head a bit.

"What did I say about being formal?" I gave a small smile. Her lips curved to a small smile as well.

The bell rang when Alex and Doyoon finally walked in.

"Hey Bomi!" Alex greeted Bomi happily.

She gave a small wave. While Doyoon stayed silent and sat down.

I wonder what's wrong with him, I thought as Mrs. Chan then walked in and the lesson started.

~ Lunch ~

BOMI

As I got up for lunch someone grabbed my hand which caused me to scream. I put my hands up to defend myself.

"Whoa, I'm so sorry Bomi I didn't mean to frighten you," He apologized and put my hands down.

I looked up and it was just Alex, I let out a sigh of relief.

"I was just hoping if... You know... We go to lunch together since we're going to sit at the same table anyway," he said rubbing the back of his neck with his free hand. He looked a little embarrassed as if he was asking me out on a date which I just found really strange.

"Oh okay and can you let go of me now," I said tugging my hand from his release.

"Oh he-he sorry," he laughed awkwardly. "Let's get going!"

As we walked through the halls I got a lot of death glares from their fan girls so I stepped away from Alex and picked up my pace.

"Hey, wait up!" Alex called out and ran up next to me.

"Fan girls," I whispered to him.

"What? Oh don't mind them," he said like everything will be okay but it won't.

When we got to the cafeteria, Alex and I were first in line but I was pushed and shoved all the way to the back. Suddenly I was pulled out of the line.

"I got you your lunch!" Alex said handing me a tray.

"You didn't have to," I said glumly, grabbing a hold of the metal tray.

"Hey, I at least have to treat you sometimes," he smiled as we walked to the table.

"Even if I ignored you guys for almost a month?" I questioned with an arched eyebrow.

"Well sure, plus I think I'm the only one you actually had a conversation with," he responded with a smile. "What's up, my brothers?"

"Hey Alex! Hey Bomi!" Minho greeted.

He sat down next to Ethan and I took my seat in between Jaesun and Doyoon. Not that I wanted to sit in between the two, it's just that, I wanted to sit next to Jaesun and Doyoon just nonchalantly slid down right next to me.

"Oh before I forget, we plan to get bubble tea after school, do you want to come along?" Jaesun asked me.

"I don't know," I bit my lip deciding whether I should go or not.

"Come on, I'm pretty sure you can spare some time for us," Alex said pouting.

"My parents might not allow it though...." I added.

"Please," Jaesun starting acting cute which I actually found adorable.

"I guess I can for an hour," I responded with shrug off my shoulders.

"Yay Bomi is coming!" Alex cheered.

I smiled at his childish actions

JAESUN

This is the most Bomi has spoken. I think little by little she's opening up to us but I would wish she would smile more.

I remember the first time she smiled at me. My lips curved up into a smile at the thought of it.

"Yah, why are you smiling by yourself?" Leo asked. I looked up at him.

"Huh I wasn't smiling," I said.

"Sure... you're having dirty thoughts!" He yelled out.

I looked over to Bomi who was trying hard not to laugh out loud. "Yah Kim Leo!" I threw my sandwich wrapper at him.

~ Gym ~

JAESUN

I saw Bomi walking into the gym and I waved my hand for her to sit next to me on the bleachers. She finally noticed my hand and strolled towards me.

"Oh I see Dasom gave back your shirt," I whispered to her, she slightly nodded.

"Okay students," Mr. Kim said looking at his clipboard. "Remember when we did all those activities last month like push-ups, sit-ups, and the mile." Everyone nodded. "Well I have everyone's results recorded and awards to give out to those who did the best." Everyone gasped; whispers were transferred to one another.

"Okay, settle down everyone. We will start with the boy who got the most. The boy who did 130 push-ups, eighty sit-ups, and five minutes and thirty-nine seconds on the mile is... Gu Taejoon!" Everyone cheered for that jerk especially the girls except Bomi of course.

"Now the girl who got the most did thirty-five push-ups, thirty-two sit-ups, and eight minutes and three seconds on the mile is..."

BOMI

"Park Bomi!"

My eyes widen with shock. *What! Me? Win an award no way!* If I show it to my parents they'll just rip it up and say it's useless.

Everyone stayed silent and then someone starting clapping. Jaesun was clapping for me. I shook my head at him but he just smiled and kept clapping.

"Come on Bomi, come get your certificate," Mr. Kim waved the piece of cardstock in his hand.

I slowly made my way towards Mr. Kim; he shook my hand as I grabbed the award. "Great job, see you're better than these girls!" He said.

I'm better than these girls in ALL subjects well at least the basic subjects like math, science, writing, and English. As I sat back down with Jaesun, he turned around and hugged me. I tensed up at the quick skinship.

"Congrats!" He pulled away from the hug and rubbed his nape. I'm guessing he's a bit embarrassed that he just hugged me.

"Thanks," I said. "But didn't you force me to run with you on the mile?"

"He-he yeah," he chuckled.

"This is my first award ever." I held it in front of my face. I ran my fingers on the shiny sticker placed on it.

"Really?" He questioned and I nodded.

“Well I’ve gotten many math and science awards before but nothing like this,” I held it up towards the ceiling to look at it in a different angle.

"Well then bubble tea after school now has a purpose." He put his arm around me and I smiled widely.

I feel somewhat protected under his arm; it felt normal like his arm has been there forever.

JAESUN

There's that smiled I was waiting for. I just hope that smile lasts forever.

DASOM

Jaesun has his arm around the poor girl and she's smiling. That should be me for god's sake! Of course I love Dujoon but if that didn’t work out Jaesun would be my second choice.

Bomi, I will make school like hell for you!

DOYOON

The dismissal bell rang and everyone immediately stood up, shoving all their materials into their bags and running out to make it on time to work or to private tutoring.

"Let’s go, Bomi!" I linked my arm through hers. She nodded and as usual her expressionless face.

I'll change that someday.

We met the others at the front of the school gates.

Once we were all there we walked to the cafe where they sold delicious bubble tea.

"What flavor do I want?" Kangdae questioned himself looking up at the menu.

"What flavor are you getting Bomi?" I asked her.

"I don't have any money," she replied sadly looking at the different price ranges from each drink.

"What?" I questioned with a confused look.

"I did say I would come but I didn't say I would get anything," she responded.

"Oh," that was all I could say. Of course I heard everyone say she's poor but I thought that was an exaggeration or something, I expected her to carry at least five dollars with her but turns out she doesn't have anything on her at all.

Before I could tell her I would pay for her, Jaesun was already one step ahead of me.

JAESUN

I overheard Bomi and Doyoon's conversation and it made me feel terrible to know she doesn't have any money and that it would selfish to drink something so delicious in front of her and that she couldn't get any. So I ordered two of my favorite bubble tea flavor which is Kiwi with litchi jelly.

"Bomi, here," I handed her the bubble tea and her face lit up.

"Are you sure?" She asked holding the drink.

"Of course plus I paid already," I gave her a small wink.

"Thanks, Jaesun," she smiled a bit. "You know to be honest I only had this once in my lifetime."

I nearly choked on the jellies. "What? Really?"

"Yeah, my parents wouldn't allow me to spend on such wasteful stuff plus I didn't have any money," she explained and I felt glad I did the right thing to buy her one.

"When was the last time you had one?" I asked.

"Umm... four, five years ago maybe," she answered and I almost choked on the jellies again. "My cousin took me."

"Your cousin?"

"Well technically, he snuck me out to go get it but almost getting caught wasn't so fun," she let out a small laugh.

"Why doesn't your cousin take you or shall I say sneak you out anymore?" I asked.

"Because... he's not here anymore, I don't want to talk about," she said.

"Oh yeah, of course I understand it's personal. Sorry for asking," I took a sip of my drink.

"No its okay it's kind of nice being asked about me it's like someone really wants to get to know me," she took her first sip from her drink and her eyes lit up. "Wah, this is so marvelous!"

"Glad you like it, this is my favorite flavor plus its fresh kiwis!" I said.

"Thanks again," she said taking in another drink.

"No problem," I said and she flashed a small smile at me.

BOMI

After an hour of chatting at the cafe, it was time to head home.

"You sure you don't want us to walk you home?" Alex asked me as we walked out of the cafe.

"No, I'll be fine plus it's not that dark," I assured them.

"Okay be safe!" Kangdae called out as I started to walk away.

"See you tomorrow!" Jaesun yelled out. I turned around and waved goodbye to the seven boys.

I walked into my house as quietly as I can but it was no use because right when I turned around one of the demons was standing in front of me with her arms crossed.

"Where have you been?" She asked angrily.

Why would you care anyway? That's what I would've said but that was a call for a beating.

"I had to clean the classroom today," I lied.

"Ha how pathetic when I was in high school I was so popular I didn't have to do that shit unlike you," she then walked back into her room.

Like I care if she was "popular", what does that have to do with anything?

I went into my room, laid on my bed and fell asleep with a smile plastered on my face remembering how good my day went.

Chapter 5

BOMI

I shivered as a cold breeze blew through the air. I looked up at the sky layered with dark, gloomy clouds.

I wrapped my blazer closer to me and took faster steps as I neared the school gates.

"Hey Bomi!" Doyoon greeted me as I walk into the building

"Hi," I was taken back at his sudden cheeriness. I proceed to walk, avoiding eye-contact with him because I knew people were watching me.

"How come you don't have a jacket, it's so cold outside?" He asked rubbing his arms pretending as if he were outside again.

"I don't own one but I can make do without one," I answered.

DOYOON

Stupid! Why do you have to ask such stupid questions? I face-palm myself, hopefully she didn't see me do it.

"Oh umm... Hey, let's go to the cafeteria that's where the other boys are at," I said trying to change the subject.

"Yeah, okay," she replied with a nod.

BOMI

"Bomi!" They all greeted me happily; I plopped down next to Jaesun.

I don't know why but Jaesun makes me feel safe and happy so I feel closer to him even though it's been a few days that I actually opened up to them. It just feels right.

"Morning Bomi," Jaesun greeted with a kind smile.

"Morning Jaesun," I greeted back to him. Then I started having a coughing fit because my spit went down my wind pipe instead. Jaesun started patting my back but it wasn't helping.

"I'm... Gonna... Go... Get... Water," I said in between coughs. I got up and went to the nearest water fountain which was just outside of the cafeteria.

DOYOON

Once Bomi was out of sight, I turned and faced the older boys.

"Guys, I think we should take Bomi out again today," I proposed. "Like to the mall or something."

"Why?" Leo gave me a confused look.

"Because did you not see her, she didn't have a jacket on and it's really cold outside," I explained. "Plus she said she doesn't own a jacket."

"So basically your plan is to buy her a jacket? It is the right thing to do for Bomi but you might make her feel burdened," Kangdae said.

"Why would that make her feel burdened?" I questioned him.

"Well one, we still barely know her and two, jackets are expensive," he responded and I agreed to his points.

"But still."

"But what, you like her don't you? Ha! What, you think buying her a jacket might make her like you?" Minho smirked at me. I clenched my fist at my sides.

Stay calm.

"Yes, I like her as a friend and I feel really bad for her," I lied at the first part, I really do like Bomi.

I get butterflies whenever she smiles; she has the most beautiful smile I've ever seen. Though, I've only seen it once.

"So you pity her?" Leo questioned with an eyebrow raised.

"What? No!" I crossed my arms. "Okay maybe but–"

"I think it's a good idea," Jaesun said.

"Thank you. See Jaesun agrees with me," I said smiling, trying to cover up what I was about to say.

"Fine, whatever but as long as you're paying," Ethan said leaning back in his seat; he struggled a bit since there was no backrest.

Finally after a long while Bomi came back. "Sorry for the wait, the line was long," she said as she sat back down.

I look like she had been crying and her cheek is a bit red but you know she was having a coughing fit so I just shrugged it off.

"No, its okay," I answered. "So are you doing anything after school?"

"Yeah, I have work," she replied.

No! My plan is ruined! I squeezed my hands together. *Relax, Doyoon. It's just one rain check; I can always take her sometime later.*

"Oh, where do you work at?" Alex asked her.

"I work as a waitress at Yong Su San," she replied.

"What! We love going there to eat!" I exclaimed. "How come we never see you?"

"It depends, where do you usually sit?" She questioned us.

"We sit on the left side where the big windows are," I responded.

"I serve people on the right side of that area," she said. “That’s probably why.”

"Can we come along with you?" I asked.

"I don’t know I guess," she said.

BOMI

Now they want to come to work with me. These guys must be trying really hard to be my friend and its working. I tilted my head to the side to rethink about my life choices.

"So you go to work after school, how long do you work for?" Jaesun asked.

"If we get out school at three and I end work at nine so I work six hours every Tuesday and Thursday," I answered.

"Guys, its 7:25 we should head to class now," Leo said getting up quickly and running off. “Bye.”

"Is he always like that?" I asked Jaesun out of curiosity since last month of hanging out with them every time it was five minutes before class starts Leo always runs off to class.

"Yeah he's been class president throughout middle school and still now high school so he's like really into school," Jaesun answered and I nodded. “But the strange thing is he is so lazy! And doesn’t give a crap about anything! I will never understand his laziness.”

Jaesun rubbed his face in frustration as I quietly laughed.

The bell rang right as we stepped in but if we were late, it would've been okay since Mrs. Chan wasn’t here yet. As always.

~ End of the Day ~

"Bomi, wait up!" I heard a familiar voice called out to me. I turned around and there was the boys walking up to me.

"Take us with you," Alex pleaded cutely which I didn't find exactly cute but it was funny.

"Why? Can't you meet me there?" I asked with an annoyed tone. "You know the place anyway."

"Because if you don't, we won't leave you alone," Alex crossed his arms.

"You do that anyway," I muttered.

"What was that?" Alex asked, smiling.

"Fine, whatever you can come along," I said.

I can't believe I just gave in like that! I mentally face palmed myself on the forehead.

This is the first time in two years that someone walked me home.

I remember when my cousin, Aaron used to come and walk me home every day even if we did go to different schools, he would walked that extra mile to my school from his school just to walk me ten minutes to my house but sadly he had to move someplace else so I never got to see him again. It was my entire fault that he had to go.

"It was my fault," I thought out loud.

"What's your fault?" Jaesun asked.

"Nothing," I answered quickly and shook my head.

As we got closer and closer to my house, I stopped in my tracks.

"You have to wait here," I said to boys.

"Why?" Ethan asked.

"Because my parents will freak out seeing me bring seven boys to my house," I explained.

They might call me a slut or something worse; I thought waiting for their response.

"We understand," Kangdae said.

"Thanks, so just wait here by this tree my house is just right there," I pointed to a dirty light blue one story house that stood fifty feet away from the tree we stood at. All the boys nodded, I turned around and walked towards my house.

My parents were talking about bills in the kitchen as I walked in.

Sometimes they try to make me pay for the house bill since I make $96 every week for those two days of work but my parents work at some large company so they get paid $30 dollars an hour for seven hours and that's every day for the both of them unlike me, only going to work for two days. In the end they always pay for it anyway.

I quickly stripped out of my uniform and into my work uniform.

As I was leaving the house, my father stopped me. I stood outside of the door facing my father.

"Nappeun Nyeon, can you explain to me why the electricity bill is so high?" He asked me with his arms crossed and a magazine rolled up underneath his armpit.

How the hell would I know! I thought as I looked up at him with a confused expression.

The only electricity I use in the house is the light in my room since I don't own any electronics whereas my parents who have smartphones, tablets, desktops, laptops, three flat screen TVs, and two Canon cameras.

"I don't know," I responded.

"You're a liar!" He yelled at me and whacked me hard on my head with the magazine multiple times.

I cringe at the pain but I try to hold up my stance. A tear rolled down my cheek as I held my head up.

Be strong, Bomi! You must endure a few more hits.

AUTHOR

The boys witness Bomi being hit; their faces were full of shock.

"Did you guys see that?" Jaesun asked the other boys and they nodded.

"Why... Why would anyone do that?" Minho said anger was felt in his words.

"Even our parents weren't like that," Ethan crossed his arms shaking his head.

"Let's not bring those people up, for Doyoon's sake." Kangdae whispered firmly, he spoke quietly so Doyoon wouldn't hear but his focus was all on Bomi.

"Quick she's coming act like you didn't notice anything," Leo turned around and scratched his head as he looked up at the sky looking confused.

Tears dripped down Bomi's cheeks. *Why would he hit me for no damn reason I didn't do anything wrong!* Bomi thought. She wiped her tears as she got closer to the boys.

"Sorry for taking a long time," she apologized sniffling.

"It's okay," Jaesun said giving her a comforting smile and placed a hand on her shoulder.

He must of have hurt a lot to make her to cry, Jaesun thought as Bomi returned him a small sad smile.

"You didn't see anything weird right?" She asked with a worried look.

Maybe they witness my father hitting me, Bomi thought as she bit her lip, waiting for an answer from one of the boys.

"If you mean by weird like Minho trying to dance to a really girly and cute dance then yes I witness something weird," Jaesun responded jabbing a thumb towards the older boy.

"Yah!" Minho yelled angrily, stepping close to Jaesun.

"Sorry but I just had to say it," Jaesun said putting his hand up and let out a small laugh.

"Let's get going," Bomi said giggling.

BOMI

"Bomi!" Maybee ran over to me and gave me a hug. "It's been so lonely without you!"

Maybee works full time here since she lives alone and needs to pay for rent and her game design classes. So she always gets lonely working here without me and Collin around.

When she lets go of me, she notices the boys standing behind me. "Oh, who are these lovely boys?" She whispers to me but I could tell the boys were listening in.

"Just some boys who keep stalking me," I said with a small smile.

"Yah!" Jaesun shouted crossing his arms. "We're her friends."

“Bomi, go check in and I'll sit your friends in your section," and before I could say anything Maybee was already escorting them to a table.

I walk to the back of the kitchen to find Collin fiddling with his tie as always.

"Late as always," Collin said his attention still on his tie.

It irritates me how he always fixes his tie all wrong. I walk over to him, slap his hands off his tie, and fixed it myself.

"He-he thanks," he said rubbing the back of his neck.

"Whatever," I said punching in my worker ID into the computer when I finished fixing his tie.

"So who are the guys out there? Is one of them your boyfriend or are all of them yours? Dang, girl I didn't know you had it in you," he patted my head and I swatted his hand away.

"Yah, do you want die!" I threatened slapping his arm.

"That was the most threatening thing you've ever said to me," he said wiping fake tears away. "I'm so proud!"

"Just shut up already! You guys are like a married couple," Kiyoshi said walking in.

"Looks like I have to dig a bigger grave for the both of you!" I barked at the two as I walked out while Collin followed closely behind.

"So who are they anyway? They look familiar," Collin questioned.

"I don't know, they just started hanging out with me for no reason but supposedly they're popular at our school," I responded. "Why don't you take a look at them yourself?"

We walked over to their table with a few menus.

"Because I don't check out guys, I check out girls," he answered and I whacked him with the menus: the hard-covered menus.

"Ouch! Park Bomi!" Collin rubbed the head and glared at me.

"Park Collin?" Leo snapped his fingers.

"Bangtan?" Collin smiled. I looked over at the two boys.

So they know each other? Well, of course, they know each other; I thought and shook my head.

"It's been a while hasn't it," Ethan said.

"How come you never told me you were close buddies with these popular idiots?" He asked me, I shrugged.

"Hey, we're not that stupid, these little munchkins got into the honors classes," Ethan pointed out.

"Wow, what an improvement!" Collin clapped his hands.

"Okay so are you going to take their order or am I going to?" I asked him.

"Whoa ho, someone wants some time alone. Don't worry, I got chu," he nudged my side and growled at him.

The boys stayed at the restaurant the whole time as I worked, for some reason they made work more comfortable and I was a little embarrassed working in front of them.

I really don't get these boys. It may seem like I talk to them a lot but that's when I'm really interested in the conversation or when they're asking me a question. But what I really do to them is shrug, nod my head, or simply ignore them.

Maybe they just pity me.

Of course, why haven't I thought of it earlier? They might just be like this now but sooner or later when they think I trust them, they will stab me right in the back.

Or maybe just maybe things might actually be right. I'll just have to wait and see.

Chapter 6

~ November 20 ~

AUTHOR

Another month has passed and the days have been getting colder and school was nothing but hell for Bomi. She's been kicked, encircled by Dasom and her crew in the bathroom only to be harassed and hit, different students writing abhorrent things on her stuff, tripping her, and making everything seem like an accident, however, Bangtan was there to help her but none of that was helping since it only made it worse.

Bangtan felt that maybe Bomi was actually trying to open up to them but she's still locked up in that shell and not wanting to come out, nevertheless, Bomi wants to come out of that shell but she can't. She feels as if right when she comes out, her world will be shattered and so forever she will be in that shell.

Today was a big day for Bomi. It's so big and important day that she took some time off work.

Even if Bomi was so excited, her heart will always still be broken up and she still hates herself for what had happened that day.

BOMI

I rolled out of bed a little earlier than usual and did my normal routine.

Afterwards, I headed outside with a shiver and made my journey to school but I made a few stops along the way.

First stop the bakery. When I walked in, the smell of the freshly baked bread, pastries, and whipped cream frosted cakes decorated with an arrangement of fruits was so magnificent I can't even describe the smell. I walked over to the display to look at all the delicious breads.

That one is $5, $7, $10. I mentally said pointing to each packaged bread pastry.

Why so expensive I remember them being like $2, $3. I sighed and left the bakery in disappointment but I will come back later to purchase them.

Second stop the flower shop. I skipped over the large bouquets to the smaller bouquets of flowers.

One bundle is $6 but another is $11, $15, and $20. All my favorite bouquets are expensive.

It's okay, it's worth spending money on you since you spent so much on me, I thought as I left the flower shop and quickly made my way to school.

JAESUN

"Where's Bomi?" I asked myself as I waited in front of the school gates. I look down at my watch. "Come on Bomi, class starts in six minutes!"

Finally, I see her walking towards the school. "Bomi, hurry we have six minutes till class!" and with that she came running towards me.

“Made it just on time, Bomi,” Mr. Cho waved his stick at us as we walked through the gates.

"Did you wait for me?" She asked breathing heavily; big puffs of condensation clouds escape her lips.

"No, I also just got here and I saw you walking," I lied, walking towards the school building.

"Oh, I lost track of time so if you haven't just gotten here I would probably be in trouble. Thanks." She bowed her head down.

"No problem, how come you didn't check the time?" I asked.

"I don't have anything to tell time with. I don't own a phone nor a watch," she replied which made my heart ache.

"Oh I'm sorry, I didn't know....how do you keep track of time?" I asked as we took our seats at our table with Alex and Doyoon.

"I studied a bit of the sky and the sun so I guess the time by looking at the sky or I basically look at any clock close by," she replied.

"Oh," that was all I can say. I was speechless; this girl has been playing survival for a long time. She only relies on her resources in order for her to survive.

I've seen her every day, every year without a jacket. The days will only get colder, how does she survive the rough winters? How does she stay warm? All these questions just flooded my brain.

"Park Jaesun!" Mrs. Chan yelled which knocked me back to reality.

"Yes," I replied nervously, I was so sure she saw me blinking out.

"Would you like to solve the next math problem?" She asked with a small grin and pointed to the white board.

I sat there freaking out not knowing what to do since I don't know what problem we are on or the lesson to be exact.

Then I felt a tap on my shoulder, I looked over and it was Bomi. She pointed to the page on her textbook and showed me the problem we were on. I mouthed out a "thank you" and she nodded.

"Ye Ma'am," I got up and started to solve the problem on the board.

AUTHOR

Doyoon, Alex, and Jaesun went out of the classroom to use the bathroom even Mrs. Chan got out the classroom to use the bathroom too. So Bomi was left alone.

She was preparing to start the English lesson even though she really didn't need English lessons since Aaron was born in America and every time they were together he would teach her English so that maybe someday when they were older he could take Bomi to America again but this time to get away from her awful parents and get away from his unsupportive parents as well but that day never came.

BOMI

"Bomi-ah!" those evil witches cooed my name.

Clack! Clack! The sounds of her heels inched closer and closer to me, I tried to ignore it but they echoed around all around the room.

I took out my English workbook and place it on the table but it was soon swiped off the table and onto the floor with a smack.

I looked up and there Dasom was glaring down at me. She was at least a foot taller than me with those tall heels on.

"Answer me when I call you!" She spat out. "Have you not been paying attention to my warnings? You must stay away from Bangtan especially Jaesun!" Her hands smacked hard against my shoulders pushing me off the stool and landed right on my hip.

I began to cry from the pain. Hard tile and my fragile body mixed together is not a good combination.

"Ha-ha look she's crying, what a baby!" Dasom laughed and everyone else gathered in.

I wanted to get up off the floor but the pain was unbearable. I started to crawl up to my stool but it was kicked away and so my hands snacked right down onto the hard floor. The stool spun a couple times before it fell to the floor with a thump.

Ring!

Everyone scattered to their desks while I was left sitting on the floor on all fours. Tears splashing onto the floor.

"Bomi, are you alright?" I looked up and there was Doyoon and Jaesun.

DOYOON

I walked in hearing the bell and I see Bomi sitting on the floor on her hands and knees.

"Bomi, are you alright?" I ran over to her and asked her even though I knew she wasn't okay.

She gave a slight nod; I lifted her chin and wiped her tears with my thumb.

"It's okay," I said to her. I helped her up, she stumbled and almost fell but Jaesun caught her before she fell back onto the floor.

She winced in pain as Jaesun helped her to find her balance.

Anger shot through my veins. I turned around grabbed Bomi's chair and slammed it on the ground which got everyone attention.

"Who the hell did this?" I asked angrily, my voice deepened.

"She fell on her own!" Dasom called out. "She's just a baby and doesn't know how to use her own feet."

"You shut the fuck up; no one cares what you have to say, Hwang Dasom! You were probably the one who did this to her!" I yelled at her.

"But Doyoon," she whined stomping her feet on the ground.

And she's calling Bomi a baby. I rolled my eyes at her stupidity.

"Don't Doyoon me, you need to stop bullying Bomi, she hasn't done anything wrong," I started to calm a bit but then that witch just had to ruin my mood once again.

Dasom scoffed. "Ha, friend, you got to be kidding me Doyoon, who wants to be friends with a poor girl?"

"I'm friends with you aren't I?" I crossed my arms and smirked.

Ooh burn, point two for Doyoon! I mentally high-fived myself and smiled widely.

"Sorry kids, there was an incident that I had to deal with– why's the atmosphere so strange in here?" Mrs. Chan questioned as she walked in. "Anyway, let's start the lesson today shall we!"

AUTHOR

Little did they know, Doyoon's little warning only made it worse for Bomi.

The bell rang for Lunch and everyone ran out the door even Mrs. Chan. While Bomi sat still on her stool staring blankly at her workbook that has been untouched with no answers filled in nor any work shown.

BOMI

I refused to leave my seat due to the pain on my right side. So I sat there staring at my science textbook as everyone left. After a few minutes I finally decide to get up.

As I limped towards the cafeteria, I was stopped by some guy I did not know but then again I don't know many of the people here at school.

"Hey," he greeted with a smile that could be mistaken as a kind smile. I gave him the coldest look ever.

"Stand here right here will ya," he then ran off, leaving me standing there dumbfounded.

Then SPLAT! One by one then all at once, eggs splattered all over me. I hear laughter all around me. A large amount of a white powdery substance was dumped over my head my best guess that it was bucket of flour; I looked up to see a few male students sitting on top of the beams with empty plastic buckets.

I tried running away from the scene but they encircled me so I couldn't escape. No matter hard I tried I would be pushed back into the middle. I slipped on the slippery mess and fell on my butt and they proceeded to throw eggs and flour at me.

After all their eggs and flour was gone, I felt sticky and powdery all around even in places you don't want eggs or flour to be in.

Everyone who attacked me scattered before any teacher came by but these teachers are happy to be on break since they don't need to be in class or watching students.

"Bomi!" I hear a familiar voice call me and I left running towards the locker rooms. No matter how excruciating the pain was I couldn't let him see me like this. "Bomi, wait up!" He continued to call after me.

Once I got there I lock the door so no one else can get in and disturb me. I undress and stepped into the locker shower room.

All that running made my side hurt even more but at least the hot water will soothe it. I turned the knob and let the hot water run down my skin and wash off all the egg yolk and flour.

Since I have nothing else to dress in I have to wear my gym clothes the rest of the day.

"This will cost more than $25 to get this uniform clean. I'm sorry but you will go through a lot this year," I spoke to my uniform as I picked at the dried flour on my blazer. "This is the only nicest thing I have, now what am I going to wear when I see Aaron?"

JAESUN

Bomi wasn't in the cafeteria yet, it kind of made me worried so I got up to go find Bomi.

When I got out a see a group of kids with eggs and bags of flour that's when I saw Bomi in the middle covered in flour and eggs, I called after her but then she started running I called again, she continued to run without looking back.

What the hell is wrong with these people, did they not get Doyoon's warning. Do they even know how scary Doyoon gets when he is angry?

After everyone cleared, I ran around searching for Bomi but she was nowhere to be found

Hopefully she's okay, I thought. I walked back to the cafeteria with my shoulders hanging low.

"Jaesun, what's wrong?" Ethan asked me.

"Bomi was attacked again but with eggs and flour," I explained.

"What!" Doyoon shot up but Leo made him sit back down. "Well did you help her?"

"I couldn't, when I came all their ingredients were gone and when I called her she ran away, she was too quick for me to follow her," I said.

"Where the fuck is all the teachers?" I heard Doyoon grumble. Sometimes I think Doyoon needs to control his anger issues and learn to watch his language.

"Hopefully she shows up to class," Alex said then began eating again.

Yeah, hopefully, I thought. Every now and then I would poke my head, hoping Bomi would walk through the double doors.

I angrily got up and walked out of the cafeteria. I'm done with this cruelty towards Bomi. What has she ever done to deserve them?

~ Fifth Period ~

BOMI

Just about two more hours till I'm out of this school then I get to see Aaron! I mentally jumped up and down; it's been such a long time since I've seen him.

I quickly changed into my gym clothes and headed out into the gym.

Maybe I'll opt out today since my side hurts too much and maybe just not go to sixth period. Wait! But all my stuff is still there or maybe Dasom threw it out already. I sat by myself on the bleachers in the gym waiting for everyone to come in after changing.

JAESUN

I walked in the gym hoping to see Bomi and there she was sitting on the bleachers but before I could go talk to her Mr. Kim called me over.

When he finished the attendance and talked about how skinny I was. I turned around to see Bomi gone.

"Huh, where'd she go?"

BOMI

"Can I opt out for today?" I asked Mr. Kim once everyone filled the gym and onto the bleachers.

"Why?" He questioned looking at me, thinking there is nothing wrong with me.

"I fell and hurt my side badly," I answered.

"How about I send you to the nurse but first let me take the attendance," he said and I nodded and limped back my seat on the bleachers.

Afterwards, Mr. Kim gave me a thumb up and I left for the nurse.

"Hi Bomi, I'm surprised I haven't seen you in a while," the nurse said as I walked in.

It's not like I want to be here. You're like the most annoying person at school. I respectfully bowed to her.

"So what brings you here?" She smiled widely and stood up from her computer.

"I fell off my stool so I'm here to get better," I stated.

"Oh and may I see this injury of yours?" She asked.

I had to take a moment to think about it because the injury is on my hip.

"It's on my hip..." I my eyes wandered over to the right.

"Oh and you'll feel uncomfortable," she said nodding her head. "Okay how bout you go in the bathroom right here and tell me what it looks like." I did as I was told.

Oh my gosh! It was the biggest bruise I've ever seen on me, it covered basically my whole right hip and it was a mix of dark black, deep blue, and purple. It was disgusting to look at.

I explained everything back to the nurse and came out.

"Well you probably want to ice that." She handed me an ice pack. "Just put this on your side and you can rest here if you want then just leave whenever," she turned back around and faced her computer screen.

Cool, I can leave whenever I want maybe I'll go in the middle of 6th period. Okay, sounds good to me as long I don't get to see those people.

I picked out a K-Pop magazine on the table out of the many magazines and began reading it.

I just can't wait to get out of school and see my utmost favorite person in the entire universe!

Chapter 7

JAESUN

Where is Bomi? It's already half way through sixth period and almost the end of the school day.

"Yah Park Jaesun," Alex flicked my forehead.

"What!" I said rubbing my forehead.

"Were you not paying attention to my story about the whales?" He asked.

"What the... Obviously if you had to get my attention," I said sarcastically.

"You're thinking about her, aren't you?" He narrowed his eyes at me.

"Who?" I asked even though I know the answer to his question.

"Bomi of course!" he waved his arms in the arm, I pushed them back down since people were staring. "Come on its so obvious, the way you look at her and the way you treat her."

Was I really being that obvious? I thought and scratched my head.

"So what if I like her, she's the first girl I've ever laid eyes on and she needs a friend, everyone here treats like trash except for us. Plus remember eight years ago," I tried to whisper that last part but I can tell Doyoon heard since he quickly looked away. It's been hard for Doyoon ever since that moment.

"Plus she was the only one to open my heart." I tried not to laugh since it sounded so cheesy but it's the truth.

"True but there was that one girl um.... Jung Emily!" Alex snapped his fingers.

"Yeah but she debuted with Cheonsa (Angel) and she's dating Kim James too, plus I liked her for her appearance, her personality was eh," I explained. “But Bomi she’s...”

That’s when I saw her– Bomi– my eyes lit up. She slowly limped back to her seat, she struggled a bit trying to get on top of the stool but she preserved and sat down.

"Where'd you go?" I asked her and she showed me the nurse's pass she got. "Was it because of this morning?" She slightly nodded her head.

The bell rang to announce school was over and she quickly limped out of class.

AUTHOR

"Guys, I'm really worried for Bomi?" Jaesun said to the other boys of Bangtan.

"She was pushed, egged, and floured today, ah! I feel so bad for her," Alex ruffled up his hair but then quickly fixed it before anyone saw his messed up hair. "Hey, maybe we should follow her in just in case if something else happens to her."

So with that the boys slowly began following Bomi close behind. Bomi had no idea that she was being followed she was more focused on getting home so she can see Aaron.

Finally when Bomi reached her house, the boys stopped at the tree and watched Bomi go through her room window instead of the front door which confused the boys.

BOMI

I went through my room window instead because I did not want my parents to see this messed up uniform.

I quickly got out of my gym clothes and slipped on a knit sweater that Aaron bought for me, and my only pair of black jeans.

I crawled over on my knees to my secret wall panel and took out at least two-hundred dollars from my shoebox.

This is so much money I'm going to use, I thought as I shoved it in my pocket, then I grabbed the small picture of me and Aaron when he took me to Lotte World for the first time in freshmen year.

Once I had all my things I shimmied out of the window again and made my way to the dry cleaners.

AUTHOR

"My goodness sweetie, why is your uniform so dirty and covered with flour and eggs?" The dry cleaner owner lady asked Bomi as she examined the sticky school uniform.

Bomi just shrugged. *Maybe I won't make up an excuse this time because there is no way you get this much flour and egg on you during cooking class.*

"Well, it might take a long time to clean this," she gritted her teeth, thinking of how much time she will have to spend trying to clean the uniform back to its original state.

"Do you think you can do it soon since there's school tomorrow?" Bomi asked playing with her fingers.

"Possibly I can get it done tonight maybe nine o'clock so in six hours since this is a lot to clean off so this will cost $150," She replied picking at hard dried flour on the blazer. "Sorry if that's a lot more than usual."

Bomi let out a huge sigh. "No, that's fine as long I have it for tomorrow," Bomi said as she paid the owner and turned to leave.

"Park Bomi," the owner said rubbing off crusted on flour off of Bomi's nametag.

"Yes?" Bomi turned back around.

"Oh, I was just reading your name tag... I think I remember you," she tapped her chin trying to remember where she had seen Bomi's name.

"You do?" Bomi questioned.

"Ah! You are the number one student of your school!" She pointed out.

High schools in Korea always compare students' grades and test scores to the rest of the student body so every month or so they post up the top one hundred students on the school board. It's just ridiculous!

"Yes, that's correct but how do you know?" Bomi asked.

"Oh, my son Park Kyung, he's a stupid little boy even if he is in honors, he is always in 20th place, he always hangs out with those bad boys but I guess since he hasn't been to the police station yet he is still my good little boy. Do you know my son?" Mrs. Park asked.

Oh I sure know him alright, he is always with Taejoon and I remember seeing his face during my flour and egg attack this afternoon, Bomi thought.

"Yeah well I have to go now, I have to meet up with someone special," Bomi said.

"Oh yes of course, go on I'll see you later," she waved goodbye.

Bomi bowed down and left. Bomi trudged on to the bakery which was just a couple doors down from the dry cleaners.

"Why, the bakery?" Leo questioned, scratching his head.

"Alex, go inside and see what she's getting," Doyoon ordered and pushed him towards the bakery.

"But she'll recognize me," Alex said, dragging his feet to stop Doyoon from pushing him.

"Here put these on," Doyoon grabbed Minho's sunglasses and put it on Alex.

Alex shook his head and placed the sunglasses on his face.

“This is a stupid idea,” he mumbled then walked into the bakery and sat down at a table near Bomi and pretended to play on his phone.

BOMI

"Hello Miss, what would you like the get today?" A male worker asked me as he bowed. I’m guessing he wanted that K-Pop look since he his hair is blond. I think dying your hair blonde to look like a westerner is weird but I don’t think it looks that bad on him.

“I would like to get this bread right here," I pointed to barbeque pork filled buns that were nice and golden brown. "I would like two please."

"Yes, of course," he smiled and opened the display; he grabbed the two buns and placed it into a small pink paper bag. "And will that be it for today?"

"Yes," I answered.

"That'll be six dollars please," he said, I handed him the money. "Say... what school do you go to?"

"Junseo High," I replied.

"Really, I go there too. My name is Choi Cheolsu,” He jerked his head to the right so that his bangs swept to the side. "I've seen you around sometimes but how come I've never really see you?" He asked me and I just shrug.

I somewhat remember seeing Cheolsu around with his group of friends. They call themselves, Velocity for their fast-pace and skillful dance moves.

"I'm Park Bomi by the way and you probably don't see me a lot because I'm in the honors class," I answered rubbing the back of my neck. I always feel embarrassed when I tell people I'm in the honors classes because I don't want it to seem like I'm bragging about it.

"Which class? I'm also in honors," He questioned me more; luckily there wasn't anyone behind me.

"Classroom 6B, Mrs. Chan's class," I replied.

"Oh, I'm in the classroom next door I have Mr. Yoon, he's bit weird but he's a cool and relaxed guy," he said. "Anyway, did you see that girl get egged today that was too funny! I didn't throw anything at her but I stood around to watch."

"That was me," I looked down at my feet even more embarrassed.

"I am so sorry, I didn't know," he bit his bottom lip which I actually found cute, I don't usually call people or even boys cute but Cheolsu is very attractive.

"No, it's okay," I turned around to leave.

"Well, maybe if you come by again or if we see each other at school, we can hang out some time!" He called out and I smiled a bit.

AUTHOR

After seeing Bomi leave the store, Alex ran out of the bakery to tell the others what just happened.

"You guys know Choi Cheolsu, right?" Alex asked. "From um... Velocity," They all nodded. "Well I guess he sort if asked Bomi out."

"What!" Jaesun yelled out.

"Shh! Well, okay, maybe it wasn't like that but he did say if she came by they should hang out," Alex explained as they continue to follow Bomi. "And oh, she bought two barbeque pork buns which are my definite favorite."

"She better stay away from that kid," Doyoon muttered angrily.

As Bomi walked on to the flower shop, she stopped when she a particular little store came into sight: a clothing store.

BOMI

I stared at it for what seem like hours: A jacket. Something I had always wanted. I have money for it but I feel I'll need the money for something more important than clothes.

I sighed sadly and walked away to my next stop.

JAESUN

So this is the jacket she wants. I smiled to myself. *Hopefully your birthday is nearby.*

I took out my phone and snapped a photo of it.

"Jaesun, let's move before we lose her!" Ethan called out to me.

"I'm coming!" I shoved my phone back into my pocket and ran towards the others.

AUTHOR

"That'll be fifteen dollars," said the old lady at the flower shop.

Bomi handed the old lady the money and grasped the bouquet of white roses.

"Sweetie, why aren't you wearing a jacket it's very cold out there," the old woman questioned Bomi before she left the shop. "Testing is coming up soon for you so you cannot be sick when they do come up. It'll be bad for your college application."

"Oh I was in a rush to get out of the house," Bomi answered.

"Oh, you meeting someone special with those flowers," she questioned.

"Yes, I'm going to meet my cousin, I haven't seen him in a while," Bomi replied with a small smile.

"Well then, I won't keep you long have fun and remember to put on a jacket," she said once more.

"Yes, thank you!" Bomi bowed and left the shop.

Finally Aaron I will finally see you, I got your favorite snack and your favorite flowers! Bomi radiantly smiled as she walked along the busy sidewalk.

"Guys, I've never seen Bomi smile like that," Doyoon pointed out.

"Yeah, whatever she is doing must be real special and excited to make her this happy," Minho said.

They followed her towards a very unusual place.

"What she doing her?" Kangdae questioned scratching his ear.

They walked around the big water fountain placed in the middle of the roundabout.

"This place is creepy and she comes here alone," Leo said, rubbing his arm as an eerie breeze passed by.

"The place may be creepy but it sure is fancy," Minho added as they all ducked behind the sparkling water fountain.

"I think she's here to visit someone, I think she's starting to say something," Jaesun whispered as the seven boys crept a bit closer to Bomi.

BOMI

Hmm let's see 221, 222, 223, ah 224!

"Hi Aaron, I haven't seen you in such a long time!" I bent down and placed the flowers down leaning against the grave stone.

This stone was very expensive to buy but I had just enough to pay, I thought and I sat down next to it.

"I see your parents still haven't visited you yet like always but I doubt they ever will. Anyway, I got your favorite flowers, they were a bit pricey but it's okay and then I got you your favorite bun!" I sat down beside the stone and placed the wrapped bun right beside the flowers; I grabbed mine and started eating it.

"School been a bit rough for me like always, today I got egged and it's going to cost $150 to clean it but it's only going to get worse for me. You know there was this one day where I had this stupid coughing fit so I went out for water and when I went out Hwang Dasom grabbed me and slammed me against the wall, she then slapped me and yelled, *"Who the hell are you to hang out with Bangtan, don't you ever hang out with them again!"* I was so scared and no one was there to help me. I wish you were there to help me, I remember you said, "*When you become a senior, you were going to come to Junseo to protect me*" but I guess you know... it won't happen but look I survived haven't I? But I don't know if I can any longer," I sighed and shoved the plastic wrapper into the pink paper bag.

"I have some good news!" I said trying to brighten the mood a bit. "I made some new friends, I know I might sound crazy but yes, they are all guys. They're actually really nice to me and they care about me, and they call themselves Bangtan since supposedly they were bulletproof through their hardships when they were little. They are quite the boys and I guess they make me happy. Nevertheless, I don't think I can trust them, I'm not really sure why but I feel once I open up to them they will turn their backs on me. It happened once and I don't want it to happen once more." I sat in silence for a second or two thinking about the questions Aaron would probably asked me.

Ah-ha definitely he would ask me about how my financial hardships are going, I thought.

"Money is going down more and more. I still haven't bought a jacket yet. I know what you're probably thinking but I can't buy it, jackets are just way too expensive and maybe someday I can move out of my stupid parents' house so I need the money. My parents, yeah they abuse me and call me bad names. Nothing has changed ever since you left me. Aaron, I'm so lonely in this world without you," I leaned against the granite stone and took out the photo of us out of my pocket.

"If it weren't for me you would still be in this world..." Tears dripped down my cheeks falling onto the photo. "I'm sorry Aaron this is my fault, I'm sorry," I cried.

"I should of been the one to go not you, you could of been successful and happy but no. Maybe I should I go, maybe I can be happy with you. I know you left for me to go on a different path to be happy but I'm not. I'm sorry. I wished you could come back to me. I wish heaven had a phone so I can hear your voice one last time. I miss you dearly." I closed my eyes and cried.

The sky grew darker and I knew I had to go. "Aaron, I have to leave now I'm sorry for leaving so soon, happy birthday." I traced my fingers along his engraved name on the stone. I got up, wiped away my tears and walked all the way to work.

JAESUN

I wiped away my tears and I looked at the others who were also wiping their tears away as well.

I never knew Bomi felt this about things that happen through her life, she has too many negatives events happen in one day.

So this is how you felt this whole time, I thought. I walked up to the grave and the others followed in suit.

"Aaron Yang Nov 20, 1996 - August 15, 2012. Beloved Cousin of Park Bomi," I read out loud.

"So this is what she meant when she said her cousin is not here anymore or he moved away," Kangdae said and I nodded.

Then Doyoon sat on ground next to the grave stone where Bomi sat and started talking.

DOYOON

Sadness flooded my body and I couldn't help it but I just had to speak and say what I felt or I'm pretty sure what we all felt.

"Umm Hi Aaron, I'm Park Doyoon and these are my brothers Kangdae, Jaesun, Alex, Minho, Leo, and Ethan and we're known as Bangtan and we're also Bomi's friends. We just want to let you know that we have no intentions on wanting to hurt Bomi at all, we want to help her. And we don't pity her either. The moment we met Bomi, we immediately started to care for her like she's one of us. So I hope this clears things up." I got up and dusted my uniform pants.

"And if Bomi ever needs help, we will be right by her side," I then got back down once more and did a big formal bow which then the others did as well.

Chapter 8

BOMI

"Bomi, where have you been I heard you took some hours off and where is your uniform?" Maybee asked as I checked in for work.

She always forgets that I go see Aaron and she's the only one I told about Aaron besides my boss, he needs to know why I'm not showing up at work.

"I went to go see Aaron today and Mr. Hyung says I don't have to wear it for today, remember?" I answered.

"Oh yeah I'm sorry," she gave me a hug.

"It's okay," I said returning the hug.

"Bomi, my tie needs help again," Collin said walking in, fiddling with his tie. I sighed and walked over to him and fixed his tie.

"When will you learn to fix your own tie? How do you even fix your school tie?" I questioned him.

"Easy, it's a clip on," he said with a smile.

"Whatever," I rolled my eyes.

"You know this is the most I heard you talk before, something has finally opened you up," he narrowed his eyes and smiled at me.

"Maybe," I shrugged my shoulders.

"Bomi, table four needs a waitress!" Kiyoshi shouted out. "There are seven people!"

"I'm coming! Geez, only been here for thirty seconds and I already have to work," I grumbled after fixing Collin's tie, I slapped him on the chest then grabbed seven menus and my notepad before heading out. "Hello I'm Bomi..."

"Bomi?" One of them said.

"Cheolsu?" I recognized the same blonde hair and cute baby-face from the bakery.

AH! What am I saying? I began to fiddle with my fingers underneath the menus which I then handed them to the group of boys.

"Hey, you remember! I didn't know you worked here," he said with a smile.

"Well, we don't really know each other so," I replied. “And we kind of just met so...”

"Right..." He said as if he just made it awkward for the both of us (which he did). "These are my friends; you perhaps have to have seen them around."

I bowed a bit and they bowed back. They then ordered and I turned around to leave.

"Hey, hopefully you think about my offer so then we can get to know each other," Cheolsu called out before I left.

"Yeah maybe," I said back to him and left for the kitchen with a small smile.

"Ooh someone's flirting," Maybee said and poked my side.

"You, flirting, that’s hilarious!" Collin guffawed.

"I was not," I said and hung up the order to the kitchen.

"Of course you weren't but the cute blonde kid was," she said and pointed to Cheolsu.

"Really?" I questioned her, raising an eyebrow.

Wow, first time I've ever heard someone was flirting with me, I thought and the scratched top of my head.

"It’s pretty obvious," she nodded her head.

"Or maybe he's trying to be nice and wants to be friends with Bomi," Collin said. "You girls just think every guy that talks to you is flirting with you."

"Ha, what do you know about flirting?” She crossed her arms.

“More than you, little girl,” he patted her head.

“Anyway, but still his eyes lit up like Christmas lights seeing you and Bomi is the perfect ideal type every guy wants; she has flawless white skin, has a cute innocent baby face, beautiful long brown hair, big brown eyes, plump pink lips, is five feet and two inches tall, has nice long legs like K-pop girl idols, and a kind, sweet personality," Maybee explained, I was touched, she described me as someone I never even seen when I look at a mirror.

"Are you guys talking about me?" Kiyoshi said, popping his head around the corner from where we all stood.

"Ew, why would I?" Maybee said folding her arms and rolled her eyes.

Maybee and Kiyoshi actually have a thing for each other but they won't admit to it to each other.

"Why wouldn't you, I'm just too fabulous for you girls," he said flipping his nonexistent long hair.

"Whatever," Maybee turned her attention back to me. "So I think you should take his offer."

I turned to look at table and they were all talking to each other. "Plus the cool guy you're looking at now, he was acting like a total goof ball before he saw you coming," she said, walking away.

Does he really like me after just meeting each other for a few minutes? I thought.

CHEOLSU

"You're kidding right; she's the school's target?" I was dumbfounded, I've been at Junseo since freshmen year and I just now met the girl the school has been targeted by everyone.

I guess the word doesn't get around fast through our large school, I thought.

"I know right! She's like so pretty, prettier than most of the popular girls at Junseo. I don't understand why they bully her," Lucas said. "And everyone says she poor but I can't tell for all I know she could be filthy rich!"

"I feel horrible now," I ran my fingers through my hair. "When I first met Bomi at the bakery, I asked her if she saw that girl that got egged and said it was funny then she responded by saying that it was her."

"But hey, you're doing the right thing by getting to know her. I heard she doesn't have any friends," Hansol pointed out to me.

Hansol is right plus ever since she left the bakery, I couldn't get Bomi out of my head even though I somewhat just met her, she was just stuck in there; it was like we already knew each other, I thought as I rubbed my head.

"Bomi's coming," Yeoshin said and I quickly sat up straight.

"Okay here is your food, please enjoy your meal," she said with a smile and bowed. Her smile is making me go crazy right now.

Gosh! Why is she so pretty? I smiled back at her.

After our meal, we paid and started heading back out to our dance studio.

"Oh um... guys wait, I think I left something inside," I stepped back inside the restaurant and saw Bomi cleaning our table. "Hey Bomi."

"Oh Cheolsu back so soon," she said with a small smile. *Geez, please stop with your beautiful smiles. Okay, don't stop but still.*

"He-he yeah, I came back to um... give you this," I handed her the folded piece of paper; she slowly grabbed it and unfolded it.

"Is this your phone number?" She asked with the small paper in her hands.

"Yeah," I rubbed the back of my neck from the embarrassment.

"I'm sorry, I can't take this," she said, handing me back the paper and my heart dropped. She walked away with menus in her arms.

"Why?" I questioned, following her.

"I don't have a phone, so it would be useless," she answered, she turned back around and stared to wipe down the table. I then remembered Hansol mentioning me that she's said to be poor.

"Oh," I grabbed her hand, opened it and placed the paper inside and smiled. "Keep it so when you do find a phone just call me if you need anything."

"O-oh okay," she stuttered a bit.

"Hopefully I see you tomorrow at school," I said leaving.

"Bye," she said, standing there with a bit of a shocked face. I smiled.

BOMI

I froze at the quick skinship, I looked down at my hand Cheolsu touched; it was a forceful but gentle touch.

"You okay Bomi?" Collin asked as he stood in front of me waving his hand in front of my face. “Hello? Earth to Bomi.”

"Yeah, I think so," I said. I shook my head and shoved the paper in my pocket then went back to cleaning the table. "Why is there so many people that go to Junseo and they do not know who I am?"

"Maybe you need to get out there, you know get attention," he replied and I glared at him.

Of course, I know bragging about being the school's target is the weirdest thing to do but maybe; I guess the whole school isn't attacking me.

"Bomi, you should go home now, it’s getting dark outside," Collin said, wiping down the last table.

"Are you sure?" I questioned.

"Yeah I can take care of the rest, I'll see you at school," he answered with a nod of his head.

"Okay then, get home safely," I patted his shoulder.

“Girl, you get yourself home safely,” he lightly tapped my nose and smiled.

I smiled back and left running back home.

"Nappeun Nyeon, did you see that stupid cousin of yours today?" My mother asked as I walked in and I nodded afraid to say anything else. "When are you going to stop, he's gone, never coming back!"

"No," I murmured, looking down at my feet.

"Excuse me?" My mother narrowed her eyes at me.

"No, I won't stop seeing him," I started to tremble. "And you can't stop me."

"You disrespectful girl!" She yelled with a raise of her powerful and frightening hand.

I froze. Too afraid to move. Her long fingernails roughly scraped across my cheek.

"Fine, do what you want! Just get out of my fucking sight!" She yelled. "Ungrateful bitch," I hear her mutter as she walked off.

I walked quickly into my room. *This will leave a mark.* Long red streaks were imprinted on my skin; some of my skin has been scraped off as well.

I woke up and looked in the mirror and gasped. "I don't even own any make-up to cover it," I said, touching my cheeks where the red streaks would have been but is now replaced by scabs.

I put down my hand and sighed; I grabbed my bag and headed out the door.

"Bomi!" I hear his familiar, sweet voice.

I looked over my shoulder and there was Jaesun walking towards me. "Bomi, I was just about to... Whoa what happened to your face?" He cupped my face with one hand and lifted up my face; his finger traced along the scratches that were etched in my skin.

Even if I can't see what position we were in, I could already tell it looks like he was about to kiss me. I could feel the death glares burning through my skin from the fan girls.

I quickly push him away from. "I'm sorry," he apologizes.

"Its fine, I just accidently scratched myself," I said hoping he bought my lie.

JAESUN

Lies. I don't believe this girl at all. A scratch like that it had to be made by someone with long nails and looking at Bomi's fingernails they were really short.

She quickly hid her hands behind her back; I guess she saw me looking at them.

Must of have been her mother. I sighed, and shoved my hands in my pockets

"Let's go," I gave a kind smile and she nodded.

DASOM

I can't believe that ugly, poor girl was about to kiss Jaesun! I stomped my feet against the tile floor.

You will pay for this. Then and idea popped in my head and I smiled to myself, I turned to Chanmi and whispered my idea to her.

"He-he let's get Taejoon on this maybe he can help carry her," she giggled.

I hope you never return after this, I thought.

BOMI

Once we walked into the cafeteria, all the guys kept asking me what happened to my cheek but I just shrugged off their questions.

"So today is Friday and all..." Alex started off after a period of awkward silence. "Would you like to go skating with us, Bomi?"

"Today? I don't know," I had to think about it for a bit, I hadn't been to the skate deck since seventh grade, obviously, Aaron took me but I probably can't skate well. Plus my side is still in pain and it's still the ugliest bruise ever.

"Well, if you can't go today then how about next week?" Jaesun suggested.

I wonder if my parents would let me out of the house. Wait, who cares anyway because they don't, I thought.

"Sure," I responded.

"Okay, cool. Let's head to class now guys," Leo said.

"Let's go," Jaesun said, lending his hand to help me up and I happily took it. His hands were warm and soft.

I wouldn't mind holding a hand like this every day. I thought as we let go each other's hand.

CHEOLSU

Ugh where is she? I don't see her, I thought as I waited impatiently outside my classroom door to see if Bomi came to school today.

"You waiting for your girl?" Yano asked, leaning against the door frame.

"Yes and for your information she isn't my girl," I said in defense.

"Not yet that is," he smirked and I shoved him back into the classroom.

"Go away, Yano," I shouted at him but he just stuck his tongue out and laughed at me.

Then there she was walking gracefully down the hallway but her expression is way different than when I saw her.

Is she always like this at school? She looks upset and her eyes are full of loneliness. Oh my, are those scratches on her face? I wonder what happened to her beautiful, precious face, I thought as she walked closer to her classroom.

I noticed she was with Jaesun, Doyoon, and Alex. I wanted to say something but she was already in her classroom.

I sighed of disappointment and walked back into the classroom.

BOMI

The days quickly go by and once in a while, I get looked at by some girls and Dasom too. Though their looks are more devious, I try to shrug it off but I'm curious why they give me that look.

The last bell of the day rang for the day and everyone quickly got up and packed their belongings before racing out the room to catch their rides back home or to private tutoring or going out with their best friends unlike me who is walking home alone.

"Wait Bomi, can you come here for a bit?" Mrs. Chan asked, before I stepped foot out of the room.

"Yes," I said walking over to her desk.

"You're smart right?" She asked.

What kind of question is that? I'm the top number one student in the whole school and in honors, obviously I'm smart! I thought.

"Wait, sorry let me rephrase that, do you know how to grade papers?" She asked.

"Yes, I do," I answered.

"Can you do me a big favor and stay after school to grade these math tests? My sister is in the hospital so I don't have time to grade these test before tomorrow?" She asked.

Well, I couldn't say no so I gladly accepted her requests.

"Thank you so much, I will repay for you this good deed!" She said and left me in the room with a stack of tests.

"Okay well let's get started," I said and sat back down with a red pen and starting grading.

Wow, I wonder how some of these people get into Honors? I thought as I gave someone a 30% on their test.

DOYOON

"Where is Bomi?" I asked myself as I waited for Bomi.

I wanted to walk her home but she hasn't shown up yet. "I'll just keep waiting." I said to myself and leaned against the stone pillar.

DASOM

Where could that girl be? I thought.

Bomi still has not shown up yet and it's making me pissed. Then I see Mrs. Chan walk out the building with her car keys in hand.

"Oh Mrs. Chan, have you seen Bomi?' I asked kindly.

"She's in the classroom grading tests," she replied.

"Oh really, thank you so much! Have a good evening," I said smiling and bowed down. I turned my attention to my girls and Taejoon. "Should we just wait for her or go in and attack?"

"Let's wait and let her do her good deed," Taejoon said, closing his eyes and leaning back on the pillar.

Ah he's so hot! I fanned myself down before I overheated.

DOYOON

So Bomi is grading papers I see, I thought. I heard all this from Dasom and Mrs. Chan but why would Dasom be worried about Bomi?

Then I heard them talking about going in and attack. I don't know but something weird is going on.

I watched them go back inside the school and so I followed them closely behind just to make sure they aren't planning anything sinister.

BOMI

It's been almost an hour until I finally finish the grading the test. "Ugh why is grading so tiring?" I asked myself, stretching my arms up.

"How about you take a break?" I heard a familiar voice say. I looked up and saw Dasom, I immediately stood up.

"Don't be frightened it's just me and a few other friends," she walked towards me and I stumbled backwards. She took one big step towards me and I ran towards the window, she laughed at my cowardliness.

I need to get out of here! I thought and ran towards the other door but it was blocked by Chanmi.

"Ha, you're not going anywhere!" She laughed. I couldn't go to the other door since Dasom is over there.

I stood there frozen. Fearing my next move will be a mistake. All of a sudden, I was lifted off my feet and was in a bridal style position. I screamed and squirmed to get out of his strong gripped.

"Do you want to be thrown off the building instead?" He asked angrily. I stopped moving and looked up. It was Taejoon. "That's what I thought, let's go."

"Let go of me!" I said, hitting his chest but he just ignored me and he walked on with Dasom and Chanmi walking in front.

Clack, clack, clack! The sounds of their heels bounced off the walls and banged against my eardrums.

"Where are you taking me?" I asked frightened.

I then noticed where we were headed. *No.* I violently squirmed around in his arms, hoping to be released but it wasn't any help his grip just got even tighter.

We walked in and it was moist and humid feeling, the smell was full of the chlorine.

Taejoon stopped walking when we were only feet away from the pool.

"Bomi, what did I tell you about staying away from Bangtan?" She asked in her high pitched voice. I come to school seeing you and Jaesun almost kissing, what's wrong with this picture? You've ignored me Park Bomi and now it's time to pay." She says and nods to Taejoon and he starts walking towards the pool.

"I hope you never come back!" I hear her yell before I was engulfed by the icy, cool waters of the pool.

Chapter 9

DOYOON

I watched as Taejoon carried someone out of the classroom. It took me a moment to realize whose long brown hair belongs.

"Bomi? That's Bomi!" With that I took running off.

BOMI

I flailed my arms around not being able to swim and having to be dropped in the deepest part of the pool.

Maybe this is my time to go. Maybe I'll be happy when I'm gone and I won't have to wash this damn uniform again, I thought.

I stopped moving and let myself sink to the bottom.

I'll finally be with you. Please wait for me.

DOYOON

I watched as the three left the pool laughing.

What were they doing in the pool and where's Bomi? Where's Bomi... I thought as the questioned drifted around my brain. I gasped.

"Bomi!" I burst through the pool doors and searched around for Bomi but she was nowhere in sight.

I heard a ripple in the water and quickly walked over and looked into the pool and there was Bomi slowly making her way to the bottom.

"NO!" I screamed and jumped in (despite, me being in a two hundred-fifty dollar uniform that was freshly ironed this morning).

As I swam closer to Bomi, I reached out and grabbed her hand to make sure she doesn't drift any farther.

When I had a tight grip on her I grabbed her by the waist and swam up to the surface. I pulled her out of the pool and laid her head on my lap.

"Come on, wake up!" I shook her but I knew this wasn't going to help. So I started to push onto her chest.

After a long while she started to cough up water. I sighed in relief.

"Doyoon," she said in a weak voice.

"Don't worry, I'm here for you," I said as I moved hair away from her face.

"Why'd you save me?" She asked as she sat up.

"Huh, why did I save you?" I repeated the question and she just looked at me with a confused look. "Well, because you're my friend."

"Lies," she said in a cold voice. "You only kept me alive so you can just get entertainment which is me being bullied."

What is this girl talking about? I've been with her whenever she was in trouble; I thought.

I was getting a bit angry for the fact that I just saved her and now her telling me that I shouldn't have saved her.

"What?" I questioned my voice shaking with anger.

"This was a perfect moment for me to be happy, not to be here anymore you don't know what pain and misery I go through every day," she answered, tears trickling down her face.

"And leave me! How could you? All I have been doing is being nice to you, I became your friend. I really care for you and this is how you treat me after saving you. I saved you because I can't think of a day without you!" I snapped.

Her face was covered with fear and with that she took off running.

I know I have frightened her but she made me mad and I couldn't hold it in anymore. I know I did wrong, I know I wasn't supposed to say those words in this situation.

I probably made her more depressed knowing that now she thinks she doesn't have any more friends.

BOMI

My body trembled with shock and fear when Doyoon snapped so I took off running. And I kept running. Not looking back.

Tears dripped down my faces, I wiped them away but they kept returning.

Doyoon scares me so much when he is angry, I don’t know what happens to him when he’s mad but it’s like a demon just takes over him and there’s no stopping him until he realizes what he has done wrong.

Finally I stopped running to take a breath; I looked up realizing where I was.

Why did my feet take me here? I thought looking up at the sign decorated with pinks and brown swirls and stars.

I guess he's my only hope and friends. I wiped more of my tears away and stepped inside the warm shop.

"Hey Bomi... What happened to you, why are you wet?" Cheolsu asked as I stepped into the bakery.

I realized that even from running, it did not help drain much water and so I was dripping wet.

He leaned over the counter and swept away wet strands of hair away from my face. I blushed.

"I fell," I answered.

"In the pool?" He let out a small giggle and I nodded.

CHEOLSU

"In the pool?" I giggled because it sounded so ridiculous. She nodded in response, looking down at her feet.

What if she was pushed by one of the students? I thought and I bit my lip.

"I think I'll take your offer," she said and my eyes lit up. I eagerly looked at face to find some truth in her words.

"Really?" I questioned and she nodded once more. "I leave in thirty minutes but let's see if I can leave early today?" I climbed over the counter and walked to the back to talk with my manager.

"Jonathan!" I called out. Jonathan, the manager of the place, his father actually owns the place and other cafes around the area. So Jonathan plays a big part in the business.

"Yes Cheolsu," he said looking at his clipboard. He was doing the inventory which was actually supposed to be my job right now but I kept dropping stuff so he said he would do it himself.

"Can I leave a bit early today?" I asked.

"Why?" He questioned with a sigh, looking up at me.

"I promised my friend I would take her out today," I answered.

"Your girlfriend?" He asked with an interested tone.

"No, she's not my girlfriend but can I go please?" I asked, cutely and pouted my lips (this method of acting cute actually helps me get me what I want).

"Fine but she better turn into your girlfriend soon," he said and gave me a wink.

"Thank you so much," I said and bowed. "Let's go!" I ripped off my apron and tossed it over the counter.

"So where do you want to go?" We walked along the side walk to who knows where we were going.

“I don't know," She responded. I glanced at her and I got an idea.

"I know, this way," I took her to the bus stop and we waited for the bus to arrive.

Once the bus arrived, we quickly hopped on. We stood up holding the handlebars. I watched as water dripped off her clothes.

The bus violently swayed to one side and she let go of the bar. I caught her just before she fell to the ground.

“Thanks,” she said and curled a piece of hair behind her ear.

“No problem,” I smiled at her and she smiled back. I leaned over and curl a lock of hair behind her other ear. We both flushed a bright shade of red.

Once we arrived to our destination, Bomi gave me a weird look.

"The mall?" She raised her eyebrows.

"Come on, I love the mall," I said and took her hand. “This is the number one hang out place besides my dance studio.”

We walked inside and her eyes lit up. "Wow, I never been to this mall before," she said and looked around.

"Come on I'll show you around," I said, our hands were still intertwined and I didn’t want to unravel them.

BOMI

Cheolsu took me around the mall and I had to say, it was pretty fun being with Cheolsu.

We went to a bunch of Cheolsu's favorite stores and I helped him pick out clothes for him. I chose a lot of button-front shirts for him since I like guys who have that preppy look.

Then we went an arcade and played a bunch games. He helped me steer my way to the finish line in a driving game then, obviously, being the dancer he is, he beat me in a game of Dance Dance Revolution but I can't dance and I never played the game before.

"Are you hungry?" He asked as we exited the arcade and I nodded.

We went to a small shop where they sold pretzels and ordered two. Afterwards, we strolled over to a nearby cafe and ordered hot chocolate since I'm not much of a fan of coffee.

"They have everything in this mall," I said, sipping my hot chocolate.

"Yep, you've missed out on all the fun," Cheolsu said as he brought out his phone.

Suddenly, Cheolsu's phone began to ring. "I'll be right back, I need to answer this," he then left the cafe.

CHEOLSU

I wasn't actually receiving a call, I played a ringtone I have on my phone to trick her into thinking it was a call.

After I left the cafe and stood outside, I dialed my cousin who works here at the mall.

"Hello," my cousin said on the other line.

"Hey Tiffany, my friend umm... well... fell in a pool, don't ask why and so she's all wet, do you think you can prepare an outfit for her? I'm already at the mall, make it quick please, I'll be on my way to pick it up soon," I explained to her and hung up. Sometimes, I have a habit of explaining something to someone really fast and then walk away or hang up without giving the person a chance to respond.

I quickly ran all the way to the clothes store that my cousin works in. "You have it?" I asked her.

"Yeah here," she handed me a bag. "So is this girl your girlfriend?"

"No, she's just a friend," I replied as I slid my card through the card reader.

"Okay and she fell in a pool? How?" She questioned, tapping the computer screen.

"I said don't ask why ugh, I don't know when she came to me she was soaked but I guess now she's a little dry but she's still pretty wet," I answered.

"Okay then, you better get back to her before she wonders where you're at," she said and handed me my receipt.

"Thank you, Tiffany," I said, waving bye to her.

“Whatever,” she said and returned working. Tiffany can be really caring sometimes but she just has that attitude of not caring which really bugs me sometimes.

Anyway, I made my way back to the cafe where I found a confused Bomi.

"Where'd you go?" She asked.

"I had to use the restroom and had to make a quick stop somewhere," I responded. "Here take this," I placed the plastic bag on the table.

"What's this?" She asked.

"Look for yourself," She took the bag curiously, opened it and gasped.

"Oh my, are these clothes for me? I can't take this, it must've been expensive," she said, placing the bag back on the table and pushed it towards me. I smiled and grabbed her hand to grab ahold of the handles.

"No, take it you're still wet and you reek of chlorine so please take it as a token of our friendship," I said. "Come on, I'll take you to the restroom to change." I took her free hand and walked her through a hallway that leads to the restrooms.

"Oh and anything that's in there, I didn't pick out it was my cousin, she works in a store here," I said. "Don't worry, I'll be out here when you come out," she nodded and went in the restroom.

BOMI

I can't believe he is doing this for me; he really is a sweet guy.

I dug through the bag and there's pair of blue jeans, a cute gray wool sweater, even a bra and underwear, and shoes too! I'm just astonished that he would so this for me and we haven't been friends for a long time too.

After I finished, I placed my wet uniform inside the bag and left the stall. Before I left the restroom, I took a moment to look in the mirror.

Wow, this is just amazing. I fixed my hair up a bit and pushed the door opened.

As Cheolsu said he was waiting in the hall, I guess he didn't notice me come out since he was busy with his phone.

"Ahem."

CHEOLSU

"Ahem."

I looked up and there's Bomi dressed up. I swallowed down some saliva since my throat was feeling dry.

"Wow! You look good and dry," I joked. She suddenly engulfed in a hug, my eyes widen with shock.

"Thank you so much, you don't understand how grateful I am," she said with her face buried in my chest. My shirt getting a little damp, I can tell she was crying. We parted and I wiped her tears with my thumbs.

"This is seriously the nicest thing someone has ever done to me," she said and let out a few more tears.

"Don't cry," I said with a smile and ruffled up her hair. She smiled at me and we walked on through the mall talking about whatever and getting to know her more.

Maybe the two of us could work out well but I want to know your relationship with Bangtan first. I can't really ask right now since we are still in the process of becoming closer but I think that ended with the many skinship moments and that we hold hands, I thought as I admired Bomi's flawless white skin.

She's so beautiful in so many ways. She may have a few scars here and then but they doesn't catch my attention when I look at her.

She turned her head to look at me and I quickly looked away. She silently giggled as she flushed a light shade of pink and I did the same.

BOMI

Today was so much fun; I never thought I could have such a fun day in my life ever since Aaron left and never smiled so much or even laughed.

Cheolsu was as kind as ever, he spent so much money on me considering he works at a bakery.

Most of the time, I admired his cute face. He some acne scars on his cheeks but he was just so perfect looking.

The day was almost at end and he offered to walk me home. When we arrived, I gave him a well-deserved hug before I went inside the house.

Now I have to decide if I will be going skating tomorrow and face Doyoon or stay home and ignore them.

As I walked to my room, I bumped into my mother. "Useless girl coming home late," she grumbled as I walked by. I grimaced at her words and shut my door tightly.

Now I deserve a good hot shower after all this craziness today. I thought and walked into the bathroom.

Chapter 10

JAESUN

"Why isn't Bomi here yet? I told her to meet us at the skate deck at two and it's now three," I looked down at my phone again.

We waited outside the building even though there was actually barely anyone at the skate deck today; we decided to wait for Bomi outside.

I wish you had a phone or a way where we can keep in contact; I thought and gripped my phone tightly in my hand.

"Maybe she's mad at us for something we've done," Doyoon said, sadly looking down.

"What?" I narrowed my eyes at him. “What did you do, Doyoon?”

"I lied that day when I was all wet. I was actually in the pool," he said.

"Why were you in a pool?" Leo asked.

"Because I was saving Bomi," he said.

"B-Bomi? You were saving Bomi?" I questioned him.

He nodded. "Taejoon threw her in the deep end and so I went in to save her."

"And how does this explain why she might not be coming?" Kangdae questioned folding his arms.

"I kind of yelled at her after I saved her," He said.

"And why was that?" I asked, balling my fist.

"Because she asked why I saved her and she was prepared to die and be happy and I snapped at her. Why she would leave me? She was going to leave and leave me alone just like how my mom left me!" He raised his voice and tears dripped down his face.

"Well our parents were cruel as ever but they never died!" Kangdae said.

"I loved my mom but she hated me and she left me!" He screamed. "That's how everyone solves their problem, isn't it? When someone hates you, they runaway and never return." He then fell to his knees and crumpled into a ball and cried.

AUTHOR

Doyoon was the most affected when all of their parents abandoned them.

All their parents were the best of friends and so when they were only eighteen years old they decided to live with each other. After living there for a while, seven little baby boys popped into their lives but their parents were only in their 20s meaning they were still teens. They would go party and get drunk, they were liked that ever since Bangtan started to walk.

They would leave Bangtan at home all by themselves which left them to take care of themselves or at least Kangdae did being the oldest in all. So even if they aren't blood related they considered themselves brothers for sticking together and being there for each other.

The boys hated their parents very much even at a young age. People don't understand that children can hate things. They think they just dislike it for a short period of time but for Bangtan it was real hate except there was Doyoon, who loved his mother dearly but his mother hated him.

She would ignore the little boy or yell at him to go away; nevertheless, Doyoon would go running back in hopes to jump into his mother's arms.

Then came that one day where he just fell apart and he couldn't bear to hear the mention of his parents.

They were only ten years old at the time; they arrived to an empty home and a note that read:

Dear stupid kids,

We have left, don't miss us or worry about us cause we sure aren't going to worry about you. We have figured out that you kids are ruining our freedom even if we are 30-years-old now, we still can have our youth without you. So do whatever you want and don't come find us either.

After Leo read this, everyone was shocked especially Doyoon who was already on the floor crying for his mother. Some of the boys started to tear up because they all wondered who was going to support them. How were they going to pay for rent?

"Hey, guys what's this?" Alex picked a rather large yellow envelope that was stuffed to the max. Kangdae took it out the little boy's hand and read a second note that was written.

So you kids don't starve or when the rent comes in, we've been saving this for the ten years you've come and ruined our lives. Use it wisely or however you useless kids want to use it for.

Inside contained bundles of cash, even though it was a great amount of money, they found a good restaurant to work at to earn even more money.

Despite scrubbing dishes for almost five hours every day for three months, they still did not have enough to pay for the rent since their parents never paid the rent for eight months so the bill was so high it was enough to buy a motorboat. They were soon kicked out by the landlord and were left on the streets to fend themselves until an old women found them and took them in with her.

As nature took its course and the old women passed way two years later and the boys were left with her house and belongings. Not knowing what to do with her items, they sold it to make a little extra cash. They felt terrible for selling her stuff but what else could they do.

During all these years Doyoon was never the same, he cried every day locked up inside his room and only came out for the bathroom and for his plate of food but he rarely ate due to his depression state.

This also meant he did not go to school but to keep him from being held back, the old women (before she passed) came up with an excused that Doyoon was very ill and that he was not able to go to school and that his brothers will be able to take the work to him and back so with that the boys all took turns doing all his homework and tests.

Doyoon successfully finished elementary school despite not going at all. In middle school, Doyoon finally decided to go to school but he would just stay close to his older brothers and stay silent. He was the quiet one, didn't meet any friend or say hi to anyone. Doyoon just wanted to be alone.

In seventh grade, he started to forget about his parents and he got back to his happy and crazy self, once in a while he would get back into his depressed self. But everyone was happy that their youngest brother was back to normal.

But one day in eight grade year, Jaesun, Leo, and Doyoon went grocery shopping when they spotted Doyoon's parents. Sadness took over his body again but in a totally different way. He started being a total player in eighth and ninth grade. Bringing girls home with him or even sneaking out to the clubs to go meet girls. He never drank though but he still was taking this situation the wrong way. The boys soon learned that Doyoon was only doing this because he felt no one loved him even though he had Bangtan, he still didn't feel it. A big hole was in his heart that needed to be filled up but it couldn't be seal so he dated many girls to feel love again.

The boys explained all this to Doyoon which caused Doyoon to be furious so he locked himself in his room once again and became violent.

The boys banged on the door, yelling, telling him to stop. He trashed the room, he ripped out the bed sheets, curtains, papers, and books lay everywhere, it was as if a tornado hit. As he was ripping out books from the bookshelf, one book in particular caught his attention.

Back in elementary school, Leo used to share a room with Doyoon but Leo couldn't handle being in a room with him since Leo couldn't do anything at all. All the lights had to be off since it bugged Doyoon. He couldn't play music since it was too noisy for Doyoon. Everything Leo did bothered Doyoon so he packed up his belongings and moved into a room with Jaesun.

He picked up the flimsy notebook and ran his fingers against the wrinkled up cover. Doyoon found one of Leo's song books; he rapidly flipped through the blank book until he found a page with random drawings and squiggly lines.

"Doyoon, please open up the door!" Minho screamed.

"Are you okay? Doyoon, please tell us you are okay!" Ethan cried.

Doyoon ignores their calls for answers. "Tomorrow by Bangtan Boys," he leaned against the wall and began reading the lyrics neatly written, although, having scribbles decorating the border of the page.

Same day, same moon
24/7 every moment repeats
My life is in between
Jobless twenty-something's are afraid of tomorrow
It's funny, you think anything
is possible when you're a kid
When you feel how hard it is to get through a day
Keep feeling like the
"Control" beat, keep downloading it
Every single day is a repetition of ctrl+c, ctrl+v

I have a long way to go but
why am I running in place?
I scream out of frustration
but the empty air echoes
I hope tomorrow will
be different from today
I'm just wishing

Follow your dream like a breaker
Even if it breaks down, oh better
Follow your dream like a breaker
Even if it breaks down,
don't ever run backwards, never
Because the dawn right before
the sun rises is the darkest
Even in the far future,
never forget the you of right now
Wherever you are right now,
you're just taking a break
Don't give up, you know
Don't get too far away, tomorrow
don't get far away, tomorrow
don't get too far away, tomorrow...

After reading this Doyoon realized that he is fighting a useless war and he should just stop and take a step towards his dream, he doesn't know what his dream is but it's there somewhere, waiting for him to reach up and touch it.

The next following school year, Doyoon took this chance to start as a whole new person. He was happy, crazy, and very cheerful and he turned out to be a very popular student at school alongside his brothers.

However, there were some days that he didn't stop thinking about his mother no matter how much he despises her now.

So from then on, the boys called themselves Bangtan (after the boy group who inspired Doyoon to return to normal) which means bulletproof. They were all being bulletproof throughout their sufferings. They didn't let their hardships bring them down.

DOYOON

I couldn't hold any of my feelings in anymore so I let them out by curling up into a ball and cried as hard as I could.

"It's okay, Doyoon," Kangdae said trying to comfort me by rubbing my back.

"Mom, Mom!" I cried, I wiped my tears away but the tears kept flowing.

"Come on, let's go home. Obviously, what Doyoon did probably scared Bomi and she won't be coming any time soon," Leo said.

I slowly got up and we made our way back to our home. When we got back I dragged myself into my bedroom and crawled under the blankets and cried again.

BOMI

There was no way I was going to face Doyoon today. I felt too scared to see him. I was also afraid he might yell at me again so I stayed back but I'm worried I hurt the others' feelings since I didn't show up and I might as well just try to ignore them so I don't get more hurt myself.

But how long can I keep it up? I thought. *Or maybe, I should hang out with Cheolsu more, I'm pretty sure Dasom doesn't care about Velocity, hopefully she doesn't?* I nodded to myself.

Starting on Monday I will hang out with Velocity instead of Bangtan. I'm sorry; I thought sadly and returned to the dry cleaners to pick up my clean uniform.

"Thank you so much again," I said with a smile.

"Ah it's okay, you keep this business running," the male worker joked.

"Ha-ha you're welcome I guess," I rubbed my nape in embarrassment.

"You should get home soon, it's already 9:30, I'm sure you have school tomorrow and it's almost time for finals so you better get studying," he informed me.

"Okay, thank you," I bowed and turned around and opened the door.

As I stepped out, a cool breeze blew through the air making the trees and leaves rustle around me. I looked over to my left and a couple doors down I see the pink and brown sign.

Should I see Cheolsu? No, maybe he's not working right now. I shook my head and turned to leave.

"Bomi, is that you?"

I turned around to see Cheolsu closing the door to the Bakery and locking it up for the night. "Oh, hey Cheolsu!"

"Hey, what are you doing up this late with your uniform?" He asked, walking over to me.

"Oh, just picking it up at the dry cleaners since I fell in the pool as you know," I pointing up to the dry cleaners sign.

"Oh I see, shall I walk you home or something?" He asked me.

I thought about it for a moment. "Oh no that's okay," I gave me a small smile even I actually wanted him to walk me home.

"Okay, well I'll see you at school then," he said.

"See you later," I nodded and we left heading in different directions.

"Wait," he called out to me.

"Yes?"

"Never mind, goodnight," he smiled and I smiled back.

I wonder what he was going to say, I thought as I bit my lip to keep myself from smiling. *Well, I just see him tomorrow and see how things work between us and his best friends.*

CHEOLSU

Oh my goodness Cheolsu! Why must you get so nervous that you can't even ask a girl if she wants to have lunch together tomorrow at school! I thought as I pushed the door open to my house.

My phone rang right as I stepped inside. "Hello? Mom?"

I walked into the kitchen and opened up the fridge to find, of course, nothing. "Uh-huh I'm eating well, yes three meals a day. Mom, why do you tell me to eat three meals a day and then tell me not to gain weight?" I shut the fridge door closed and rolled my eyes.

"What? No, I don't have a girlfriend ugh, Mom, can you listen to me for just once!"

Chapter 11

BOMI

"Ah, what am I going to do?" I asked myself as I walked to school. I would have to start ignoring Bangtan and start hanging out with Velocity starting today.

Would they even accept me? Of course, Cheolsu would but what about the others? I thought as the school gates came in view. *If they don't I'll go back to being a loner and I don't want that.*

DOYOON

I waited in front of the school for Bomi hoping to get a chance to apologize to her for my actions. I absolutely feel terrible for what I've done but I couldn't help it for what happened throughout my life, my mind just took over itself.

Finally, I caught a glimpse of Bomi and she's walking right towards me. She looks up and her eyes are filled with sadness.

"Bomi, I just wanted to say sorry-" She walked right pass me, not even looking back.

I sighed as a tear rolled down my cheek, I quickly wipe it away. "It's okay, next time I must say something."

BOMI

I walked through the school gates, taking a moment to bow to Mr. Cho and into the school campus and there he was, Doyoon, waiting for me.

Right when I get to school Doyoon (someone I need to avoid) is standing around trying to look all cool with his hands in his pockets.

He starts saying stuff to me but I just silently pass by, giving him the cold shoulder.

I'm sorry, Doyoon. I walked on, making my way towards the classroom.

As I walk through the halls, many students are hanging around with their group of friends. Some of the groups of guys start smirking at me making me feel uncomfortable; I hug my textbooks closer to my chest.

"Ah!" I tripped over someone's foot and all my textbooks scatter across the floor but luckily I didn't crash down on the floor as well. I bent down and started collecting them.

"Oops," some guy laughed and kicked away my book before walking away.

"Hey, are you okay?" Cheolsu asked me as he bent down and helped me pick up my books.

"Yeah, I'm okay," I said, standing back up and he handed me back the rest of my books; our hands touch for a moment and I quickly pulled away. "Thanks."

"No problem," he rubbed the back of his neck. "I see you're wearing your new shoes."

"My other shoes were still pretty wet and I might as well just throw them away, I've been wearing them for some time," I said and he nodded.

"So... My friends and I want to know if you want to hang out with us at lunch." He questioned me.

Good. I don't have to ask him but did his friends really agree to have me hang out with them? I thought.

~ Before Cheolsu went to go see Bomi ~

AUTHOR

"Can we please have Bomi sit with us at lunch?!" Cheolsu pleaded.

"What if we get picked on too?" Lucas questioned. "Just having her with us, it could ruin our reputation."

"Ha! What reputation?" Hongbin scoffed. "We aren't that popular here at school."

"Come on, she's not that bad and maybe we won't get picked on," Cheolsu responded. "Plus we're doing a good thing, adding more friends on her friend list."

"I guess it wouldn't be too bad," Hansol agreed. “We never know until we try.”

"Fine, lets invite her to lunch," Yeoshin said.

"There you go, that’s the spirit!" Cheolsu cheered with a big smiled.

"Look there's Bomi," Yano pointed out.

"Where?" Cheolsu asked, turning around scanning the hallway.

When he finally spotted her, he witnessed her being tripped and he quickly ran over to her.

BOMI

“Well, that is if you don’t have anyone else-“

“I’d love to sit with you and your friends at lunch,” I answered with a smile

"Really? I'll come get you at lunch, wait for me," he said, turning around to leave.

“Okay, see you later," I bit my lip once again to keep myself from smiling.

I walked inside the class and sat down on top of my stool

"Hi Bomi," Jaesun greeted me as he sat down next to me; I also gave him the cold shoulder.

JAESUN

I greeted Bomi but she ignored me. I tilted my head to the side in confusion.

Why is she ignoring me? Shouldn't she just ignore Doyoon, he was the one doing wrong not me! I thought and looked over at the younger boy with a face of hatred.

I puff of steam escaped my lips as I opened up my textbook.

BOMI

My heart started to ache when I ignored Jaesun but it's for the best for the both of us. I won't get bullied as much and I won't be a burden to him.

When the bell rang I ran out of the classroom. Although I heard Jaesun call my name, I didn't look back and kept walking.

JAESUN

The bell rang and I thought it was the perfect time to talk to Bomi.

"Bomi-" I started but she raced out of the classroom.

I understand Doyoon's actions could not be controlled but still now his wrong doings are going off to me too. I shouldn't be the one to be ignored by Bomi; she should be coming to me. Maybe what happened to her with being thrown into the pool and Doyoon yelling at her was too much for her and she thinks if she stays away from us it'll be better for her.

Bomi, you can't just ignore your way out of this, I'll be the one protecting you, not Doyoon but me! I thought. I was about to get up to find Bomi but I was stopped by someone I didn't want to see right now or anytime soon.

"Jaesun," Dasom said, trying to act all cute. It's obvious that she likes me but I have no interest in her. She's just some bratty girl who wants the spotlight all on her and only her.

"Jaesun," she said once more. "Stop wasting your time with that poor girl?"

"Huh?" I raised my eyebrow.

"She already found someone else," she said, crossing her arms. "Just look."

She walked outside the classroom and pointed in the direction she wanted me to look at. I looked over and there's Bomi with Cheolsu and they're both laughing.

I haven't seen Bomi like that before; I can't make her smile or laugh like that. Maybe I am wasting my time on a girl I can't get. I look down at my feet and walk back into the classroom.

DASOM

Maybe you'll finally have your freedom after all but I don't think it's over just yet. I smiled. *Now that I have Jaesun all to myself you can hang out with that loser kid, Cheolsu.*

I walked back into the classroom and started talking to Jaesun. I don't know why he's playing so hard to get, he keeps pushing me away but I just know he wants me.

BOMI

As I rushed out of the classroom I bumped into someone.

"Aren't you in a rush," Cheolsu said, smiling.

"He-he," I moved pieces of my hair out of my face. "I'm sorry."

"No it's okay so how was your day so far?" he asked.

"Umm it was okay, I didn't fall in the pool again," I joked with a small laugh and he laughed too.

"Well hopefully you don't fall in ever again," he said. "Besides hanging out at lunch, you busy after school?"

"I don't think so," I replied.

Why did I reply like that? Of course, I don't have anything to do after school. Maybe I didn't want to sound too desperate or give in so easily, I thought.

"Would you like to come with me to my dance studio?" He asked me.

"You want me to go?" I questioned, pointing to myself.

"Of course, I'm your best friend and I must take my best friend to my dance studio," he said.

"Best friend..." Those words ran around my mouth and snaked its way into my brain.

I only got friend from Bangtan, I thought for a moment debating whether I should go or not but it might be fun so might as well go.

"I would love to come!" I answered.

"Great and you can help sort of judge us since we have a dance competition coming up really soon, you can come to that too if you'd like," he offered.

"Sure," I smiled at him.

He's offering so many chances for me to hang out with him. I can't figure out what this feeling is that I have every time he smiles or laughs, it was like the feeling I had when I was with Jaesun.

I touched my face in just in case if I was daydreaming but it was real; my icy cold fingers trembled as they tapped along my warm face.

The bell ran and students all around started to scatter back to their classrooms where they would spend another tedious hour taking notes.

"Whoops better get to class, see you later," Cheolsu said and clapped my shoulder

"See you," I said.

We both turned around and walked back to class in different directions.

~ Lunch ~

JAESUN

I was going to ask Bomi is she wanted to go with me to lunch but once the bell rang she got up and left without saying a word.

The boys and I walked out and there Bomi was with Cheolsu again. Smiling again.

I turned to look at Doyoon; I glared at him and walked off by myself.

I'm done with this! I shouldn't be treated like this by Bomi this was finally my chance to get to Bomi, I thought.

Then I stopped. *Wait, maybe I'm blaming the wrong person, I should be blaming Dasom and Dujoon instead since they were about to basically murder Bomi but still if only Doyoon kept his mouth shut or at least said, "I saved you because I care about you" and "come on lets go put you in some dry clothes" that would of been better then yelling at her,* I thought angrily and continue my way to the cafeteria, ignoring any fan girl trying to talk to me.

BOMI

Instead of having Cheolsu coming to get me, I would just go meet up with him myself since I did not want to wait in class while Jaesun or Doyoon or Alex try to get my attention. I looked over to see Jaesun hastily walk away from the two boys, he looked a little angry.

I sighed. Just thinking about mistreating Bangtan kills me, I'm pretty sure I should just ignore Doyoon but it's for the best, maybe Taejoon or Dasom would go a little easy on me since I stopped hanging out with them unless Dasom has a thing for Velocity too.

I swear if Dasom has a thing for every person I get close to I'm going to kick her-

"Hey Bomi, you okay?" Cheolsu asked, waving his hand in my face.

"Of course, I am," I said with a small smile and shook my head.

We grabbed our food and as I walked along side Cheolsu, someone tripped me but before I landed face first on the ground Cheolsu caught a hold of me but he then lost his balance and so we both fell. I landed on top of him.

"Are you okay?" He asked with a worried look. Whispers can be heard all around but I ignored them, I looked into his eyes and it was full of worry.

He must really care for me, I thought and nodded. I got up and straightened out my skirt.

I lend a hand out to help Cheolsu up and he gladly took it. "Are you okay because I landed on top of you," I said.

He laughed a bit and rubbed the back of his neck. "Ha yeah I'm fine, you know you're not that heavy."

"That's because I don't eat much," I muttered.

"Huh?" He raised his eyebrow.

"Nothing," I said quickly.

"Well at least these sandwiches are in wrappers and our chocolate milk is in cartons," he picked up our food and handed mine to me.

"Thanks," I said with a smile and we both went back on our way to our table.

CHEOLSU

When I caught Bomi and she fell on top of me, my heart was beating so fast I swear I thought she could feel it, even though, I was so worried that she might have been hurt.

Surprisingly, she was super light so she didn't really hurt me. It was like having a memory foam pillow being thrown at you; they look heavy because they aren't filled with feathers but they are super light and don't really hurt.

I picked our lunch back up and she smiled at me. Every time she smiles my heart just beats faster and faster.

JAESUN

I just saw Bomi fall on top of Cheolsu. I closed my eyes in frustration.

This was my only chance and you ruined it, Park Doyoon!

"Jaesun," I heard that annoying voice call my name again. I turned around and there's Dasom. "Can I sit next to you?"

And I had to say yes so all through lunch I had little miss clingy next to me at our table and I was sure that the others were annoyed as well.

Bomi, please come back to us.

BOMI

During lunch, I got to know the boys of Velocity more and they seem very cool guys but not as cool as Bangtan was to me. All the boys were older than me (by months that is, we all are in the same grade) and taller than me like really tall. Anyway, Cheolsu wasn't the only blonde one in the group.

Yoon Hansol is the oldest boy of all of them but sadly he is the shortest but still taller than me. He might want to consider about it getting his blonde hair fixed since his roots were starting to show. At first, I thought he was a cold guy because of his harsh eyes but he is actually really funny, he doesn't really look an approachable guy unlike Cheolsu but after getting to know him he's a cool guy.

Lee Yeoshin is the second oldest. He seemed like very chill and relaxed guy. He has light purple hair that suits him very well. Anyway, he was the one who actually tried to get to know me. He didn't dwell on himself, like most people would do, and he asked lots questions about me instead. I could tell he probably helps stop conflict whenever the group gets into one and he is very quiet too.

Jang Lucas turns out to be the tallest and I think he acts like he's some big hotshot that can get all the girls. He also cracked a lot of funny jokes and rapped a little here and there so he pretty much tried to get my attention. It got annoying how much he was showing off, the other boys were also getting irritated of him and so they started to hit him a few times or told him to shut up. Geez, my head hurts just talking about him.

Cha Yano stayed pretty silent throughout lunch, it was probably a bit awkward for him but it's okay, we're in the same club it was bit awkward for me too so I stayed quiet as well. He had gray hair that layered just the top of his head and underneath was his natural black hair or at least I think it's his natural hair.

Kim Wonwoo smiled a lot and started the conversation when things got into an awkward silence. But I couldn't help but just star at his orange hair; it didn't work on him at all, well maybe, when you look at his side profile it looks nice but orange is just not his color.

And finally Oh Hongbin, the youngest of them all, but still older than me by seven days, he told a lot of jokes and laughed a lot.

They all asked me questions like when is your birthday, do you have any siblings, do you want to hang out with us every day, and did you ever date anyone? These boys made me laugh at their silly questions.

"I think you might make her feel uncomfortable with your questions," Yeoshin said. "We can talk about something else if you like, Bomi?"

"No it's fine, it feels nice that people want to get to know me," I said with a small smile.

Those were the same words I said to Jaesun. I thought sadly. *Stop, Bomi! You can't be thinking Jaesun because every time you think of him your heart is only going to hurt even more.*

"I have one more question," Lucas said, knocking me back into reality.

"What is it?"

"Do you like our Cheolsu?" He stared intently into my eyes.

I was a bit flustered at his question. "Umm..." I rubbed the back of my neck.

"Ay you're making her too uncomfortable," Yano said. "You don't have to answer, Bomi."

The bell then rang saying that lunch is over.

CHEOLSU

"I'll walk you to class," I said.

"But were walking the same way," she replied. "And they're walking the same way too."

"I know that silly," I said and ruffled her hair and she quickly slapped my hand away and she brushed her hand over her hair to straighten it out.

"Anyway, sorry for that awkward question earlier, my friends can be weird and awkward sometimes especially in front of a pretty girl."

Her cheeks turned a light pink, I smiled at her blushing.

She's so adorable.

We stopped in front of her classroom and she turned her head to look up at me.

"Well I'll see you after school then," I said. "I'll wait in front by the gates."

"Okay, I'll see there," she waved her hand and I left with a smile.

I walked back to class happily with a wide grin plastered on my face.

"Yah, yah, yah!" Mr. Jeon hit me on top of my head with a rolled piece of paper. "You're late!"

"But Mr. Jeon, we still have a minute until the bell rings," I said.

"Oh really?" He nodded his head and crossed his arms behind his back. "Continue on then."

I bowed down and rolled my eyes. This will be a very long two hours.

Chapter 12

~ Sixth Period ~

BOMI

During the rest of the periods, Jaesun kept trying to get my attention, I stayed silent.

"Did I do something wrong?" He whispered.

I slightly shook my head and he sighed. "I miss you," I heard him whisper and I looked at him but he went back to finishing his notes.

"I miss you too," I unknowingly whispered back to him and then returned writing in my notes as well.

The bell rang and so I packed my belongings and headed out to the school gates.

I walked to the front of the school and spotted Velocity waiting for me. As I walked closer to them, a hand grabbed my wrist. I screamed.

"Whoa, it's okay, it's just me," Doyoon said, holding my hand. "Look I just wanted to say, I'm sorry about what happened on Friday, my actions took over and I couldn't control it-"

"I forgive you," I said cutting him off, he looked up at me.

"But I didn't finish," he said.

"I know and it's okay, sometimes people's minds cannot be controlled and accidents happen so I forgive you," he looked at me still a little confused.

"So does this mean you'll talk to us again and come back and hang out with us again?" He asked and I bit my lip then I saw Dasom walking this way and my eyes widen with fear.

I'm sorry but you yelling at me aren't the only reason why I'm ignoring you, I thought and tugged my hand free from his grip.

"I have to go," I started to walk away but Doyoon held on tightly to my hand.

"Why?" He whined. "Why can't you stay?"

"I just have to go," Dasom was creeping closer and closer by the second. My heart was beating faster. "I'm going somewhere today and I have to go."

I can't be seen with Doyoon, the only bad thing that happened today was when I fell on top of Cheolsu.

"No, don't leave please," he desperately pleaded.

"I'm sorry but I can't stay I have to go," I tugged harder but he was too strong. "I can't stay."

"Promise you'll come back to me... back to Bangtan," he said.

"I promise, now let go. Please!" and he finally let go, I took off running to Cheolsu.

"Bomi, are you okay?" I had a few tears running down my face and I quickly wiped them away.

"Yeah I'm fine, let's just go," I said with a weak smile.

"Okay then," Cheolsu grabbed my hand and gave it a light squeeze. "Let's get going."

JAESUN

I stood in the background and watched as Bomi desperately tried to get away from Doyoon and run ever so fast towards Cheolsu; she left happily smiling at him.

"Will I ever get my chance?" I muttered to myself as I walked towards Doyoon who stood frozen like a statue.

"You okay?" I asked, putting my hand on his shoulder making him tense up but then he relaxed.

He nodded. "She forgave me."

"Good, let's go home," I slung my arm around his shoulders and we walked home in silence.

BOMI

"We're going to make a quick stop first before we head to the dance studio," Yeoshin informed me.

"Okay, where to?" I asked.

"To the hair salon," he answered.

"Gotta get a new hairstyle before our competition," Lucas says running his fingers through his hair.

"Hmm, what hair color should I get?" Cheolsu tapped his chin. "What do you think, Bomi?"

"Me? I think blonde hair suits you but maybe try going to your natural hair color, I'm fine with either one just don't do some crazy hair color like Wonwoo," I giggled and he started to laugh as well.

"I heard you," Wonwoo said, sneaking his orange head in between Cheolsu and me. I giggled and pushed away.

We shortly arrived at a hair salon. As when we entered Yano started shouting. "Shorty!" He shouted and a bunch of customers started staring at us. I hid behind Cheolsu embarrassed.

"It's okay Bomi, he's always like this when we come here," Cheolsu assured me.

"Yah! Are you trying to destroy my business," a girl about my height started walking towards us. She had black hair layered with blue streaks if I weren't mistaken I'd think she was a celebrity.

"Ha business, how are you going to run a business if you can't even run your own school project by yourself," he joked and hugged her. "How's my older sister, Melissa doing?"

"Better without you," she said and poked Yano's side.

Oh, so she's his older sister! I mentally clapped my hands for figuring out why Yano started shouting like he owned the place but then again he sort of does.

"Ouch that's hurts! How's Dongjin doing?" He asked.

"Stupid as ever can't even do a simple calculus problem without my help," she answered.

"Geez, ninth graders these days," Yano shook his head.

"But little brother is doing well," she added.

"That's good," he said.

"So I'm guessing you need a new hairstyle for your competition this Saturday," she questioned, looking at the boys and then she pots me and we make eye contact for a moment. "Oh and who is this? Cheolsu, you didn't tell me you had a girlfriend."

"Oh no, we're not dating," we both said at the same time.

"Sure... I never held my best guy friend's hand before," she said with a smirk and walked away.

We both look down at our hands and we immediately let go of each other hands. The other boys began to snicker.

"Come over here please!" Melissa called out to us. We all walked over to a secluded area where there were eight hairstyling stations.

"This area is specifically for us unless a K-pop group or idol comes here then they use this area," Cheolsu whispered to me. "For example, Super Junior came here once."

"No way, you're lying," I narrowed my eyes at him.

"Nope, look for yourself," he pointed to a small Polaroid taped on the wall with all twelve members of Super Junior, Velocity, Yano's sister and seven other hairstylists in the picture.

"Oh my goodness! Which one of these chairs did Donghae sit in?" I asked.

"Um, that one," he pointed to the first chair on the left. I walked towards and slipped inside and wiggled around in the plastic seat. "You're so weird."

"Oh yeah, what if Miss A came here, I bet you would sit in Suzy's chair all day," I argued.

"That is so true except I like Min better but I would still do the same," Cheolsu said.

"Okay, let me go get your hair stylists," Melissa said and left.

She then came back with six other female stylists and they got right to work. "Let's get to work ladies; these boys need a competition to win!"

AUTHOR

"What kind of hairstyle would you like, Cheolsu?" The hairstylist asked Cheolsu.

"I was thinking of staying blonde but I also want to go back to my natural hair," Cheolsu answered, still unsure of how he should impress Bomi with his new hair.

"I think I know what you're looking for," she said with a smile and turned him around.

"My hair is starting to change back to its normal hair color, can you fix it up a bit and give it a trim please," Hansol requested.

"I'd like to go back to brown, purple it's too much for me," Yeoshin explained.

"Ah, brown so boring, I like Cheolsu's hair so change it to blonde but don't bleach it, I like the whole dirty brown look I think I can get more girls this way," Lucas said as he touched and picked at his hair. "Maybe cut up the sides so I can have this beautiful top hair thing like um... Like Yano!"

"I'll see what I can do," she rolled her eyes and spun him around.

"Melissa, turn me back to my natural hair color, don't cut up too much either, my hair is still pretty short," Yano said which he received a slap on the forehead from her.

"You better keep your hair black, too much dye can damage your hair," she said. "Maybe I'll just shave it all off."

"Don't you dare," Yano stared intensely into his sister's eyes and she did the same.

"I was reading a westerner magazine and it showed many different styles so I want a hipster hair style," Hongbin requested. "Hair shaved on the side and then this top part swept over to the side."

"Blonde and that's it nothing else, don't you dare touch those scissors either," Wonwoo said firmly.

Geez, what a bunch of girls. Bomi rolled her eyes and continued to wiggle around in her seat.

"I'll be back," Bomi got up and left the room.

BOMI

I walked around the salon a few times and drank some water from the water fountain.

"Bomi, what do you think?" I hear Cheolsu say.

I turn around to see seven boys with fresh new hairstyles. "You guys look amazing, are you sure you should be entering a music competition?"

"I do make a good model, don't I?" Lucas started doing some model poses.

"We don't know him," all the boys muttered and walked away from Lucas.

"Ha-ha, so now there's four blonde guys now?" you pointed out.

"I won't be blonde for long," Cheolsu said. "It's just hair chalk, it'll stay on for two weeks so I'll be back to being brunette in no time."

"Everyone else is in their natural hair color," Yeoshin pointed out and rubbed his hair.

"Well you guys look amazing," I said.

"Don't you guys look fabulous," Melissa touched Yano's face, he slapped her hand away.

"So Bomi, are you sure you don't want to do anything to your hair?" She asked me.

"No, that's okay. Maybe next time," I said with a kind smile.

"Do you have a boyfriend?" She asked.

"Yah Melissa!" Yano shouted at his sister.

"What? If you don't then what do you look in for a guy?" She asked. Her questions were weird and unusual but I didn't mind answering them.

"You're making her uncomfortable, don't you have a business to run," Yano pushed his sister away.

"It's okay, I would say I look at their hair, they have to have nice soft hair, just nice looking hair, good personality, good looking, and smart," I answered.

She took a step towards me. "I think we'll get along just fine because I look at guys' hair as well," she whispered to me. "And that's why I own a hair salon!"

"Well, we must go now. Bye Melissa tell Mom and Dad hi and Dongjin," Yano said, pushing us out the door.

"I'm texting you later tonight," she said.

"I'm busy tonight and tomorrow and the next day, maybe the whole week or month," he said and closed the door. “Sorry my sister can be odd sometimes, she’s always trying to set me up with girls.”

“Ha-ha,” I awkwardly laughed. “That’s okay, first time someone tried to set me up with their sibling.”

“Oh my, there’s the bus, run!” Hansol yelled and we all went racing towards the bus that was just about to close its doors.

“Geez, kids these days can’t be on time for anything,” I hear the bus driver mutter.

I dug into my backpack pocket for some change to pay for the bus fee but I couldn’t find anything.

“Don’t worry I got you covered,” Cheolsu said and took my hand; we stood next to each other holding the handlebar to keep us from falling.

After a while, we got off the bus and walked towards a small building. It looked pretty sketchy if you asked me but walking inside was a different story.

"Wow so you guys practice here," I walked around looking at all the mirrors.

Wow, I've haven't seen so many mirrors, I only use a small tiny mirror at home, I thought as I fixed up my hair a bit.

"Yeah, we come here ever so often to dance and sing a bit," Cheolsu said, starting to stretch his legs.

"We enter a lot of music competitions," Lucas added and I nodded.

Cheolsu got up and walked over to me. "Come here, I have something to show you." He took my hand once more and we walked through a door which held a display with a variety of ribbons, trophies, and certificates.

"Oh my, did you guys win all of these?" I questioned looking at all the first and second place prizes.

"Yeah," He said and I was truly amazed. "Can I ask you a question?"

"Yeah, go ahead," I said still admiring the display.

"What's your relationship with Bangtan?" I looked up at him.

"Umm they're my friends," I said. "Nothing really much to it.

"So Jaesun is just your friend right?" He asked.

"Yes, of course," I raised my eyebrows. "Why do you ask?"

"Nothing, I just wanted to know since before you hung out with them a lot," He said.

"Oh," I was still confused. "Well, we're not in good terms at the moment."

We then left the room and joined the other boys who started to practice their dance.

"Okay, lets run through the dance once and then afterwards, we'll fix parts here and there," Hansol said and everyone nodded. I sat in the corner watching them dance and sing.

They are truly amazing, I wonder if Bangtan sings and dance? I know Leo and Minho rap and Jaesun and Alex sing, what about the others? I thought. *What did I tell you Bomi, you can't be thinking about them! I'm sorry I can't help it, it's like everything I do I'm reminded of them.*

After a short but tiring hour, they took a break. They all slumped down onto the floor with heavy breaths. Their chests heaved up and down rapidly as beads of sweat coursed down their faces.

"You guys are really good," I gave them a thumb up.

"Thanks," Cheolsu said, sitting down next to me and taking a swig of water. "You wanna learn the dance?"

"Me? I don't know, I don't really dance or at least I never tried dancing before," I answered.

"Come on, it'll be fun," He stood up and grabbed my hand and dragged me to the middle of the floor. "This move is easy so you are going to spread your feet apart right in front, left in the back then put your right hand where your heart is and your left by your right hip, turn your upper body to the right and at the same time slowly pull your right hand away so comes down like this."

I followed exactly what he showed me and then we went through it at full speed. I don’t know if I did it correctly but I know I did a terrible job.

"Perfect, see I did say it was easy," he said with a smile. "Okay I'll teach you the chorus so the next move is going to be a bit tricky since it works more with the feet."

I tried my best to calculate it in my head how it works but I failed at it since I couldn't do the feet part.

"Here," He bent down and moved my feet. "Okay so moved your feet in a crisscross motion. Good, good now try to move backwards while you move your feet in and out."

I did as he said and I did it. "Amazing, who knew you could dance!" He smiled.

"I didn't even know myself," I said with a laugh.

He then taught me so other moves that were a bit tricky. "I'm sorry see I'm not good at this," I said after trying for the fifth time.

"No it’s okay, it’s your first time, don’t worry I'll help you," he said and put his arms around me and moved my arms around to the moves; I blushed at the sudden skinship.

CHEOLSU

I put my arms around Bomi and helped do the dance moves. She felt warm and I just wanted to keep her in my arms forever.

I notice Bomi blushing so I smiled. For some reason, I let go of Bomi, though, I wanted to keep her there in my arms. "You think you got it now?" I asked and she nodded.

"Yeoshin, can you turn on the music and put it at the chorus," I ordered Yeoshin who was by the speakers.

"Okay," He turned on the music and Bomi and I both danced together. I was so amazed how perfectly she had done it and she only learned it in a couple of minutes.

After we danced together, we all clapped for Bomi. "Thank you," she said smiling. "You know Cheolsu; you're a really good teacher."

"Really, thanks this my first time teaching someone," I said.

After another hour or two of practicing, it was time to head home and so I told the other members that they could head home first and that I would walk Bomi home.

The cold air made our breaths into small clouds. I notice Bomi shivering in the cold, she was wearing only her school uniform and I could tell that skirt wasn't really helping her keep warm so I took off my jacket and placed it around her shoulders. She looked up surprised.

"Oh thank you," she said and wrapped it closer to her.

BOMI

Cheolsu gave me his jacket and I blush a little at his kind actions.

Thank goodness it's dark so he can't see my face. I wrapped his jacket closer to me and I could smell his scent on it. He had a sweet but strong scent; it reminded me of Jaesun's scent and a little bit of Doyoon's but it was more of Jaesun since Doyoon had a strong scent probably because of his cologne.

When we reached a safe distance away from my house, I turned to Cheolsu and said my thanks.

"Umm thanks for taking me out today, it was fun," I said.

"Oh no problem it was fun hanging out with you," he smiled. "We should hang out some more sometime."

"Oh and here's your jacket," I gave him his jacket and he gladly accepted it.

"I'll see you tomorrow," I said but before I left I gave him a tight embrace and he tightly hugged me back. He then kissed the top of my head.

"Bye, Bomi," he said when we let go of each other.

I walked into my home and smiled to myself then a slipper hit me right in my face.

"Coming home late, eh? Why don't you study instead of playing around, you're so stupid," my mother said and left to her bedroom.

Why does she even care and she doesn't even understand that I'm in the honors classes for Buddha's sake! I just don't understand her at all! I thought as I walked into my room.

UNKNOWN

I watched as Bomi and Cheolsu hugged each other and Cheolsu kissed the top of her forehead.

I wonder what's their relationship is now. Are they dating? Does she know my feelings for her? I thought as I walked away from the scene.

Or does she even like Cheolsu? Of course she does, she let him kiss her. I sighed in defeat.

"Someday," I said and walked home.

CHEOLSU

I walked home cheering to myself. *I can't believe I kissed her! You did an amazing good job on keeping your cool! She seems so happy, why is she being bullied? Well, I'm glad I'm doing to the right thing to keep her happy.*

I smiled widely to myself as I walked into my home.

"Looks like someone is happy," someone said.

"AHH! Wonwoo what are you doing here?" I questioned him. "And inside of my house."

"Long story short, my sister brought over her boyfriend and my parents won't allowed them to sleep in the same room so he must sleep in my room but either way in the middle of the night my sister sneaks into my room to sleep with him," he explained. "So my room is occupied."

"Ugh, fine you can stay here but you're paying for food," I said, throwing myself onto the couch.

"I already got you covered," he said, pulling out a box of pizza from behind him.

"Maybe you can sleep over often," I nudged him with my elbow and smiled.

Chapter 13

~ Thursday, December 4 ~

JAESUN

"Happy birthday to you! Happy birthday to you! Happy birthday, dear Jaesun. Happy Birthday to you!" All the boys sang to me as they walked into my dark room with a cake. The glowing candles illuminated my room.

"Thanks!" I said with a wide grin and blew out the eighteen candles scattered around the cake. *I'm finally eighteen-years-old!*

"So how does it feel to be eighteen now?" Kangdae said. Kangdae is older than me by ten months so he'll be nineteen next year in February.

It must be nice to have a birthday really early in the year like that.

"Um I feel the same actually, I just feel a bit older I guess," I responded with a smile

"Are you sure? Because when I turned eighteen I felt like I evolved into something amazing!" Alex explained.

"Are you a poke'mon or something?" Minho questioned, slapping Alex's head. "Well, at least now you're old enough to go to the clubs!"

"We don't even go to any clubs," Ethan said.

"I know but still if there were a day we were to go," he said and crossed his arms.

"Oh please, the only club you'll be getting into is Club Penguin. I don't want to see any one coming home with some slutty girl or coming home drunk," Kangdae said firmly.

"Yes sir," everyone said in response.

"Anyway, let's turn our attention back to our birthday boy," Leo said. "Ready for some cake?" He handed me a piece of the cake and it had strawberry ice cream in the middle with real strawberries bits in it, it was a beautiful cake especially since it's pink which is my favorite color of all time.

After eating, Ethan announced it was time for presents to be opened.

"You guys, I told you I didn't want anything," I said as I sat down on the couch and presents were placed in front of me.

"We know but do you ever listen when we say we don't want any presents," Kangdae pointed out.

"Yeah but you're the eldest and I'm the second youngest so I shouldn't expect anything," I said.

"Why are you so damn respectful cause I don't remember teaching you any of this," Kangdae said and ruffled up my hair.

It is true, Kangdae didn't teach me anything about being respectful but I did help the old women a lot so I spent most of my time with her. She helped me learn some valuable things about life and why we shouldn't be bounded to the laws of society and that we should break through them.

"Open mine first!" Doyoon waved the pink box in my face.

"Okay, calm down," I laughed. I opened the box up and found a new leather jacket.

"Wow!" I held in up and touched the leather sleeves.

"Yeah, I thought you needed a new one since the other one looked tight on you," Taehyung explained.

"Thank you," I placed the jacket neatly back into the box.

"Sorry Jaesun no present for you since I bought the cake," Minho said.

"Or he thinks he bought the cake," I hear Leo mutter and I could only laugh.

"Here," Alex handed me a big bag with cute characters on it and I took it with a confused look.

"Oh my goodness, it's so cute!" I said as I took out a giant mushroom plushy.

"Well, we all know you have this weird obsession with cute plush things and I was just walking by a store when I saw this and it reminded me of you," Alex said.

"Thank you," I said.

"Now this last one is from me, Leo, and Ethan," Kangdae said and handed me a small box wrapped in gold wrapping paper.

"And Minho," Minho coughed and looked to his side as if he didn't say anything.

"Sure... I thought no present since you "bought" the cake," Leo said as he put emphasis on bought with his fingers.

"Just open it," Ethan said, smiling.

I carefully un-wrap the gift and my eyes widen. "H-How?" I was speechless.

"We're not poor, Jaesun. We can afford this stuff and we still have a lot left," Kangdae said with a small laugh.

I held the phone in my hands: A Samsung Galaxy Note 3. It's so big in my hands.

Does it even fit in my pocket? I thought to myself.

"The boys and I were thinking, you shouldn't be using that lame flip phone and plus the rest of us has a smart phone and you don't," Ethan added.

"Is this why my phone didn't work yesterday?" I asked as I messed around with the applications.

"Yep," they said and I nodded.

"Thank you," I said once more and gave everyone a hug.

"Now, let's get ready for school," Leo said with a clap of his hands.

~ *Saturday, December 6* ~

CHEOLSU

"Are you ready?" I asked Bomi.

"Come on; let's go, you guys have a competition to win!" She jumped in excitement.

We piled in our van and made our way to Sejong Center for the Performing Arts. We knew we arrived when the center came in view. It is a rather large building.

"Oh my, it's such a huge building," Bomi had her face pressed up against the window.

"It's really nice inside too. We've been here a couple of times for different other competitions," I explained. "It's the largest arts and cultural complex in Seoul."

We came to stop and we all exited out the vans and started walking towards the entrance.

BOMI

"Wow!" I turned in circle looking at the very modern designs and colors decorating the inside.

"Come on, our dressing room is this way," Cheolsu said. "Lucas already signed us in."

"You want me to come in the dressing room with you guys?" I raised an eyebrow.

"It's okay there's a different room, we can change in," he explained.

"Okay then," I said still unsure.

"You can turn around now," Yeoshin said.

I had to turn around as they changed because their "different room" was actually just one of those bamboo screens.

They were all wearing black– Their outfits weren't eye catching as I thought they were going to be but they work really well with their song.

Knock, knock!

"My goodness, luckily I made it here on time!" Melissa walked in with a bunch of make-up boxes and three other girls with her.

"The competition hasn't started yet," Yano said.

"Oh well actually the competition starts right about now," she said, looking at her watch.

"Ladies and gentlemen, welcome to our annual music competition!" A male announcer was heard from a speaker. "All performers must be in their dressing rooms preparing for their performance." He went on explaining what was going to happen and so on.

"Let's start this show shall we. Please welcome our first performance, The Dazzlings!"

"Okay we are performance number ten," Hongbin informed us.

"So we still have time, let's get to work," Melissa stated and opened up her boxes filled with make-up and hair supplies.

I sat in the corner watching the boys get all dolled up. I couldn't help but laugh. Some of the boys were warming up their voices as their hair and make-up were being done.

"What's so funny?" Yano asked me, looking through the mirror.

"You guys are just like a group of girls," I giggled. "Getting your make-up done and what not."

"When we're K-pop idols, this is how it's going to be so don't judge us," Lucas said, poking my sides.

I quickly grabbed his wrist and twisted it. "Yah touch me again and you'll never use this hand again." I threatened.

"Okay, okay just not today I need to hand," I let go of his wrist and smiled.

"Performance number ten, please make your way back stage, any guests please head to your seats in the auditorium," a women announced through the backstage speakers.

"Break a leg," I said before following Melissa out to the auditorium.

"You sure you don't like my little brother?" Melissa asked me.

"Oh my goodness, just keep walking," I pushed her forward and down into a seat.

"He's not that bad of a kid," she went on.

"Look they're up!" I pointed up on the stage.

"Next up we have Velocity!"

As they performed I cheered for them as loud as I can as well as other people were. Their dance moves were in sync and their singing was perfect.

When their performance was finished, we headed back to their dressing room.

"You guys were stupendous!" I hugged each of the boys.

"Whoa, big words," Lucas said and I punched him in the arm.

"Let's go watch the rest of the performances," Melissa said and we all followed her out again into the auditorium.

"That's was just an excellent show with many talented boys and girls, wasn't it? Now we will announce the winners, when I call your team name please make your way up onto the stage," The MC informed the audience.

"Third place goes to... The Dazzlings with their beautiful performance of contemporary dancing," he announced. Five beautiful girls in bright blue sparkling leotards walked up onto the stage with high postures.

"Second place then goes to... Seoul Quartet who performed River Flows in You by Yiruma." Four people went up onto the stage with a different instrument. One girl had a cello, another had a violin, a boy had viola and another boy had a violin as well.

"Now first place goes to..." I held Cheolsu's hand and gave it a light squeeze. "Velocity!"

We all cheered and clapped. They received a golden trophy once they got up on stage.

"Congratulations, and I hope you continue on doing well in your music career"

"Congrats on your win today!" I said to them as we walked through the parking lot.

"Thank you," Cheolsu said to me with a smile.

"Who's hungry cause I know I am," Melissa said. "How 'bout some pork belly?"

"Yes please!" I called out and everyone looked at me. "What, I have cravings too!" I said and went inside the van.

AUTHOR

As everyone was enjoying their meal, everyone suddenly became silent as Bomi munched on loudly picking at every single dish with her fork even though this food was more meant for the hands.

"I've never seen a girl eat that much," Cheolsu said, slowly shoving a lettuce wrap in his mouth.

"How can she shove that much food in her mouth?" Wonwoo questioned

"Not even Melissa eats that much," Yano said.

"I'm not fat Yano and I never was!" She shouted at Yano.

Bomi then realized the sudden silenced at the table. "What?"

"Nothing," Hongbin answered.

"You guys better eat before I eat it all," Bomi said placing another piece of meat in her mouth.

"Okay before anyone else take another bite let's make a toast," Melissa announced, taking a glance at Bomi who yet put an eighth lettuce wrap in her mouth and continued to happily munching on it.

"This is a celebration!" Melissa lifted up her glass of alcohol while the students lifted up their glass of sparkling apple cider. "This goes to Velocity for their first place win today and for Cheolsu's birthday tomorrow!"

Bomi gasped nearly choking on her food. "It's your birthday tomorrow?"

"Ha-ha yeah," Cheolsu face reddened from embarrassment.

An idea popped up inside of Bomi's head. "Get up," she ordered Cheolsu as she stood up from her seat.

"What?" He looked up at Bomi with a confused expression.

"Get up! We'll back soon," Bomi told the others and they nodded.

"Have fun on your date!" Lucas called out them.

Bomi scowled at the boy and ever so calmly walked over to him and whispered into his ear. "You better keep that mouth of yours shut before your tongue ends up like that," Bomi pointed to the meat sizzling on the grill.

"Anyone up for some cow's tongue?" Melissa asked as she placed a whole tongue down on the grill, it landed on the hot grill with a satisfying sizzle.

He gasped and covered his mouth with his hand and shook his head violently.

"That's what I thought," she then grabbed Cheolsu's hand and dragged him outside.

"Where are you taking me?" Cheolsu asked

I wonder where she's taking me so suddenly after the mention of my birthday, Cheolsu thought as Bomi let go of his hand and slowed down to a steady pace.

He wished to go back to holding her hand again and so as if his wished has been granted the sidewalk soon was crowded citizens, he quickly grasped Bomi's hand before he lost sight of her.

"Don't worry, you'll see," Bomi said with a smile and squeezed his hands as they pushed pass people.

"What are we doing here?" He asked again once they arrived to a bakery.

"Oh, why don't you just be quiet?" Bomi rolled her eyes and looked into the display case. "Oh excuse sir, can I have this cake right here," Bomi asked a male employee.

The cake she chose was a small cake about the size of rice bowl perfect for one or two to share. Covered in white whipped cream and decorated with purple whip cream flowers.

"Sure, one cake for the pretty lady," he opened up the display and grabbed the small cake Bomi pointed to and placed it in a small box.

Cheolsu balled his open hand into fist to calm him down; it popped up and bounced around his body like a spring: a spring of jealousy. He glared at the male worker.

"That'll be nine dollars, ma'am," the employee said with a kind smile.

"Here you go," Bomi handed him the cash, their hands touched for a moment which got Cheolsu shaking with anger. She took the box off the counter. "Thank you."

Cheolsu, calm down, he's just an ordinary guy nothing to worry about, But man, this guy should maybe think first before he calls a girl pretty because what if the guy standing next to her, holding hands, is – oh, I don't know – Her boyfriend! Cheolsu thought as he kept an eye on the guy.

Bomi then took Cheolsu back outside and sat down on the nearest bench they could find. "Here, Happy Birthday!" Bomi handed him the boxed cake.

"You didn't have to, you know," he took the box from Bomi's hands.

"No I had to, you are my best friend and best friends do things for each other like this," Bomi explained and Cheolsu started to feel the blood rushing up to this cheeks.

Luckily, it's cold outside so she can't see me blushing at just her little actions, Cheolsu thought.

I think Cheolsu is blushing, he's so adorable. I hope I don't start blushing. Bomi lifted her hands up and touch her face to make sure that her face wasn't warm.

Oh my! I think Bomi's blushing too, I could just kiss her! Cheolsu thought and smiled to himself.

"Thank you," he leaned over and gave Bomi a tight hug. "Now let's eat some cake!"

Chapter 14

~ Sunday, December 7 ~

CHEOLSU

"Happy birthday to you! Happy birthday to you! Happy Birthday, dear Cheolsu! Happy birthday to you!" Everyone sang as Wonwoo brought in the cake.

"How did you guys get into my house?" I squinted at all the boys.

"I have an extra key," Wonwoo said and placed the cake in my hands. I blew out the candles and everyone cheered.

"You guys got the cake free didn't you, I can tell you got it from my bakery," I said, narrowing my eyes at them.

"Hey Jasmine insisted she buy it for you," Hongbin said.

"Jasmine? Ah, Jasmine!" I had to think for a moment to remember who Jasmine was.

Jasmine is my co-worker at the bakery, she is dating my manager but she is rarely there since she is a trainee to be in a K-pop group called Affection.

"Yep, now let's eat some cake," Yeoshin said as he started to cut the cake.

"So where did Bomi take you yesterday?" Lucas asked.

"She bought me cake for my birthday," I answered.

"She didn't do anything to you right?" Hansol asked, checking my face and arms.

"What's that supposed to mean?" I questioned him.

"Girls can be very conceiving," he said.

"Dude, Bomi may seem like a sweet loving girl but she can be so scary," Lucas said, shivering. "She could be a viscous murderer for all we know!"

We all started laughing. "You guys you know how much she has threatened to kill me!"

"Whatever," I rolled my eyes.

AUTHOR

The first week of December has past and time is flying by. Bomi has once again starting hanging out with Bangtan but every so often hung out with Velocity and now the mood was lit up again. Jaesun was happy that Bomi was actually talking a lot more than she used to and smiles more and Doyoon was happy that Bomi was back by his side.

CHEOLSU

I'm really worried for today, what if everything goes wrong and I mess up? I paced around my room for a while.

"Yah, stop pacing around, you're making me dizzy," Yeoshin said.

"I'm sorry, I'm just worried about today," I answered, I squeezed my hands together; they were already feeling sweaty.

"What are you...? Oh, so you're actually going to do it?" Yeoshin questioned and I nodded. "Don't worry, you'll do great, lets head to school now," Yeoshin headed out the door and I followed.

I hope so.

BOMI

It's another week of December and the days are only getting colder and colder. I tried to walk faster to school but the cold air is basically squeezing the warmth out of my body.

Come on, I've been through this many times before, you can do this! I mentally cheered myself on and I finally made it through the schools gates and now all I have to do is walk up the school steps and into the warm building.

"You okay, Bomi?" Jaesun asked as I stepped in the school still shivering from the cold.

"Yeah, I'm fine," I answered, rubbing my arms hoping to create some friction for warmth.

"No, you're not," he then took off his jacket and placed it on me.

"Thanks." But I guess to him I still didn't look okay so he put his arm me and pulled me closer to him.

I blushed. "Jaesun, we're inside so I'll warm up so your jacket is enough." I was actually more worried about Dasom seeing us together or at least her spies who are everywhere and words gets around fast because of them.

"Oh really? Okay then," He let go of me but he looked a little disappointed.

I looked at him with smile and he smiled back.

JAESUN

Her smiled made me feel a lot better. I tried to do what Cheolsu did that one night that Doyoon apologized to her but I guess it didn't work out as well.

Maybe she doesn't like me after all, I thought as we walked to class together.

BOMI

Sorry Jaesun for hurting your feelings but it's still awkward around us and I don't even know if we can be together because I also like Cheolsu and having Dasom on my grill every day for liking you, it just won't work out, I thought as we stepped into the classroom.

The bell rang for lunch and Jaesun, Doyoon, Alex and I got up and headed toward the door and to my surprise, we found Cheolsu waiting outside the door.

"Hi Bomi!" He greeted me and bowed to the other boys.

"Hi," I gave him a big grin.

"May I talk to you in private?" He asked.

"Umm yeah, you guys can go first I'll catch up later," I said.

Cheolsu walked me to the empty school garden that rarely anyone goes to except me, of course. I go here when I have a hard time, even though, I prefer the rooftop better but anyway I'm curious to what Cheolsu wants to talk about.

"So what would you like talk about with me?" I asked.

CHEOLSU

Come on, we rehearsed this morning you can do it! I closed my eyes and took a deep breath.

I opened my eyes back up. I took Bomi's hand into my mine. "Bomi, you glow in my eyes and you're perfect. Honestly, when I met you I had no idea you'd end up meaning so much to me. So I was hoping... do you want to be my girlfriend?" I asked. She looked at me with a shocked expression.

BOMI

H-he wants me to be his girlfriend. I can't believe it, I like Cheolsu a lot but why don't I feel anything? What do I do? Should I say Yes or No? I don't know, I really like Cheolsu in all but...

"You don't like me do you?" He flat out asked.

"No, I like you but-" I started.

CHEOLSU

It crushed my heart to say those words and now I have to say more words that will shatter it.

"It's Jaesun, isn't it? I see the way he looks at you and the way you look at him," I said and she nodded. "It's okay." I tried to take like a man and act cool but I feel like everything is crashing down on me.

I stepped closer to her and hugged her tightly. "I just want you to know that I love you and I care for you." I let go of her but kept my hands on her shoulders. "Also, let's be close friends from now on, okay? And if anyone gives you any trouble come to me." I turned around and left the scene in tears.

BOMI

I was truly speechless; I stood there frozen. When he touched me, I was like a statue. He said all these kind words to me but in the end, I turned him down for something I might not even have to begin with.

He then left me standing there dumbfounded. When I finally realized lunch would probably be ending soon, I left and headed towards the cafeteria.

As I walked in, I caught Sungmin's gaze and it looked as if he cried a bit since his eyes were a little red. I feel really bad breaking his heart.

CHEOLSU

Bomi finally walked in and I guess she caught me staring at her since she looked directly at me. I looked away too scared to let her look at my heartbroken self.

It was never going to work anyway, nothing matter how close we got I felt we were still distant.

I hope you two work out because... he likes you too, I thought and continued to eat my lunch.

AUTHOR

Moments before Bomi walked in, Cheolsu roughly wiped away his tears and came into the cafeteria and went straight to Bangtan's table.

"Umm, Jaesun can I have a word with you?" Cheolsu asked, trying to keep his coolness as if nothing had happened.

"Yeah sure," Jaesun stood up and the boys walked into the empty halls.

"So..." Cheolsu looked down at his feet. "Do you like Bomi?"

Jaesun gave Cheolsu a weird look. "Of course I do, she's a wonderful friend."

"No not as a friend, I mean as a women."

"Yes as a women too."

"Good because she likes you too," Cheolsu said. Jaesun held his breath for a moment.

"What?" Jaesun choked out to make sure he heard correctly.

"Yes, she likes you," Cheolsu shuffled his feet around.

"How do you know?" Jaesun asked.

"Because I like her too and I confessed to her but she turned me down for you," Cheolsu explained.

"I'm sorry," Jaesun said he felt a bit guilty for being selfish when Cheolsu really liked Bomi.

"No, it's alright but if you hurt I will snatch her right back to me, you hear me!" Cheolsu said, firmly looking right into Jaesun's eyes.

"Don't worry, I won't hurt Bomi in any way possible," Jaesun responded.

During the time they spent talking to each other, Cheolsu told Jaesun things about Bomi so that he would know more about her.

"Just to let you know Bomi likes guys with nice soft hair with nice looking hair, good personality, good looking, and smart," Cheolsu said.

"Really, how's my hair?" Jaesun asked and tilted his head towards Cheolsu.

Cheolsu rubbed Jaesun's head and shrugged. "Mine's softer."

Jaesun then rubbed Cheolsu's hair. "How do you get your hair so soft?"

"Well, that's something I cannot tell you," Cheolsu shoved his hands in his pockets and walked away.

"Wait, tell me your secret!" And he ran after Cheolsu.

"It's baby shampoo," Cheolsu whispered.

"It's what shampoo?" Jaesun questioned.

"Oh, nothing," Cheolsu smiled and continued walking.

BOMI

I took my seat next to Doyoon at the table and just sat there not eating but staring blankly at the table.

"Are you okay?" Doyoon asked me but I kept staring at the table not even blinking.

"Are you not going to eat? Here eat." He put the sandwich to my lips but I didn't move an inch.

He then ripped off a piece and rammed into my mouth but I didn't chew I didn't care if it got all weird and squishy in my mouth; I'm just too shocked to do or feel anything at the moment.

I just hope Jaesun doesn't know I have feelings for him because what if he doesn't like me back or what if Doyoon likes me too? No, if he liked me he wouldn't do all those things he did to me, right? Hopefully Doyoon doesn't confess to me. I don't know, this is just too much for me to handle right now, I thought.

The bell rang indicating it's time to go back to class and I slowly made my way to class but I guess me moping around annoyed Jaesun so he took my hand and dragged me to back to class.

~ Later That Day ~

I sighed and leaned against the broom I was holding.

"Why so blue my little Bomi?" Collin asked as he wiped down a table next to me.

"I don't know?" I said slowly, staring at the table; it was like time has speed up around me so I couldn't have time to process what's going on in my head.

"Come on, no more daydreaming we have work to do and you need to be paid for actually doing something," he said, I shook my head and slapped myself in the face a couple of times to wake myself up.

"Bomi dear," Maybee cooed my name.

"Yes," I said with no interest at all what she wants to say to me.

"Sit down please," Maybee said, sitting down at the table Collin finished wiping. I did as she said and sat down. "Now tell me everything, I haven't seen you like this in a long time or at least ever since you met Bangtan."

I basically poured everything out to her but I kept on an emotionless face, I feel as of every system in my body is shutting down. It seem like Collin was listening as well.

“Tsk, tsk I knew that boy was up to no good,” he shook his head and slapped the wet, dirty towel down on the table.

“Yah Collin!” Maybee shouted at Collin for getting her wet.

"Anyway, it’s just so shocking that I don't how to feel anymore, is it because this is my first time being told someone loves me?" I questioned her.

"Yah, I told you I loved you," she crossed her arms and pouted.

"But that’s different," I said looking at her.

"Okay well, I guess it struck you so hard with shock that it basically caused you to be in shocked for the whole day," Maybee explained which is what I basically said.

"This conversation doesn't help at all but at least I got it out," I said, standing up again.

"You'll be better tomorrow for sure and then you'll be way better next week," Maybee said, patting my shoulder.

Yeah, hopefully everything is back to ***normal*** *and next week is good. Hopefully, nothing* ***bad*** *happens either,* I thought as I swept the floor.

Chapter 15

~ Friday, December 12 ~

BOMI

Today, we all decided we all just sit at one table today so lunch was packed with seven people from Velocity, another seven from Bangtan and there was one of me.

"So what are your plans for the weekend," Yeoshin asked everyone. "We're having a sleep over at my place; you guys can come as well my parents won't mind more company."

"Oh no that's okay," Kangdae said. "Our house is a mess and I think it was time we did some cleaning."

"Sleep sounds good to me," Minho replied and everyone nodded their heads in agreement.

"Work, the holidays are coming up, gotta prepare inventory," Cheolsu said. "Inventory is so hard."

"What about you Bomi?" Jaesun asked me.

"Me? I also have inventory to do at home to do," I answered. "Got to make sure everything is good and I make sure I have enough things to survive."

"I'll see you guys next week!" I waved goodbye to all the boys. I wasn't too surprised to see they all walked the same way back home while I walk in a different direction by myself. I sighed and continued my short journey back home.

I walked inside and slipped off my shoes and walked into my room. I lay down on my bed and thought about random stuff that kept floating around in my head when a thought I never really thought about popped in my head.

I'll eighteen in a week but that won't change the fact that I'm still living with the people that live in the room across from me since my money is going down and I have nowhere else to go.

I got up and walked over to my secret hiding place and grab the shoe box filled with my years' worth of savings.

"Only $4,000 left that means I spent... I spent $2000!" I said out loud. I quickly covered my mouth so my parents wouldn't barge in a take all my money.

"What was I doing?" I asked myself as I tried to remember how much I spent.

Then I remember school workbooks were twenty dollars each, five dollars a day for my lunch so that's about four hundred dollars for all my years at school, about three hundred dollars on dry cleaning, and then I bought some things for Aaron and Cheolsu but that wasn't much and other miscellaneous.

I rubbed my face in frustration. "Okay that's it no more spending, let's try not to ruin your uniform again and let's not spend so much on food," I nodded my head; this is the best choice I have.

"Nappeun Nyeon," My parents cooed my name and I heard the doorknob turning.

"No, no," I cursed under my breath and quickly tried to shove my money back into panel except all the money slip and enough most of it made it into the panel a lot of it didn't.

They opened the door. "Hi!" They happily greeted. "Ooh, what is this?"

I stood up and stepped in front of the scattered money but it was too late since they already saw what it was.

"Move," my father waved a stiff hand to the right telling me to move over. He bent down and picked up the money and after picking it all up he began to count it.

"Where'd you get all this money?" My mother asked with her hands on her hips.

"Work," I answered looking down.

“Are you sure you didn’t steal it?” She narrowed her eyes at me.

“Whatever it was, thank you for a $2000,” my father smiled widely and folded it up into his pocket. My heart stopped beating.

"So what we would like to talk about today is your new name, we were thinking it isn't fair to give you a name you didn't like,” my mother smiled. One moment she’s shooting me down with her eyes then the next she’s smiling like it’s the best day ever, not even the littlest incident made her mad.

Did they really have a change of heart after so many years? I thought but then the $2000 popped back up into my head.

"So we decided you would choose the name you like best," he added.

Damn! I would like Bomi as my choice but I don't think that will be a choice, I thought as they went on talking.

"The names we thought of are Byuntae (pervert) and Jiralhanae (Retarded Lunatic)," my jaw dropped when those names came out of their mouths. "So what you think?" They were smiling as if I just won an award and they are so proud of themselves for teaching me the right ways in life.

I then looked at them straight in the eye and smiled. "Let me think about it," I smiled through gritted teeth.

"Okay then, let’s go Honey," my father said to my mother and they both left. “What can we do with $2000?”

I wanted to scream but I couldn't. I wanted to throw things at them.

Why must they do this to me!? They probably forgot my real name too and I’m now left with $2000! I mentally screamed, I fell to my knees holding onto my heart and I let out a few tears.

For the next few days, all day long all I hear is my parent’s annoying voices ringing in my ears.

"Nappeun Nyeon, did you make up your mind yet?"

"Nappeun, should we call you Byuntae or Jiralhanae for a couple days to help you decide?"

"Did you choose yet?"

"Your birthday is coming soon; did you make up your mind yet?"

"Come on, you need to tell us what you want I'm getting tired of calling you Nappeun Nyeon."

Every time they try to talk to me I just ignore them. But this wasn't even the worst part, every day at school I'm getting pushed, tripped, and hit ever since I started to hang out with Bangtan again. This time it's more brutal, they don't push me lightly. No. They push me so hard to the ground that if my head were to hit the hard tile floor, I would be dead before any came to help me.

Dasom would stop me from leaving the bathroom and kick me around like a soccer ball, I have bruises here and there on my side and stomach and I'm sore. I'm trying to endure it even though it's hard to work because most of the times I have to lean down to wipe the tables, lean over to pick up heavy dishes and bring them over to customers, and get on the floor to wipe up spills. It's been tough all this week.

It's finally Friday and I finally get to get away from all the abuse but now I have to face my parents. I got home from school when my parents walked in front of me.

"So Nappeun Nyeon, did you do it yet, did you decide?" My mother asked, getting up all in face but I walked right passed her to my room.

Before I turned the knob to my door something hit me hard on the back of my head. I turned around and looked what lay on the floor: a slipper. I looked up and another slipper hit me square in the face.

"You're so useless, you can't even make up your own fucking mind for your own name," my mother said. “Why did I ever give birth to such an unintelligent daughter? I can't even call you my daughter.”

"You can't even do anything right," my father then added. “You're the stupidest girl I've ever seen.”

My blood started to boil as they went on and on how useless I was and that I can't decide correctly and I can't make any good choices in life. I balled my fists at my sides to keep calm but I couldn't hold it in any longer.

"I DON'T CARE! JUST LEAVE ME ALONE, DO YOU PEOPLE EVEN FUCKING REMEMBER MY REAL NAME?! MY NAME IS BOMI FOR BUDDHA'S SAKE, WHY CAN'T YOU BE LIKE NORMAL PARENTS?!" I took deep shaking breaths; my hands shook from all the anger that just escape from me.

"What did you say?" My mother asked and narrowed her eyes at me; her eyes were filled with the raging fires from hell.

I gulped, I knew I was wrong to yell at them but I said what I was feeling every time I got a new name every year and how I was sick of them treating me this way, I'm just done with this nonsense!

My father stepped closer to me with a stick in hand. "You have no right to talk to us like that Bomi."

I gasped as he lifted up the stick ready to hit me and I quickly turned the knob to my room and locked the door. I ran to the corner of my room where I kept a large suitcase.

This is my chance to get away but where would I go? My father banged on the door loudly, I knew right away after a few more blows that door will fall right down.

"You open this fucking door right now!" He yelled and I flinched. Rage filled his words.

I ran towards my secret panel and pulled everything out and shoved them in the suitcase, I shoved most of my clothes in the suitcase when I hear the door starting to give away.

No, no, no I need more time I haven't gotten all my stuff. Then the door burst open.

I zipped up the suitcase and stood up but I didn't grasp the luggage on time. My father barged in and pulled onto my hair, I screamed in pain and held his giant hands to release some the tension but it was no use.

He threw me out of the house. What came flying out of the house as well were my suitcase, my small blanket, my small pillow, and few more of my clothes.

"Park Bomi, don't you dare come back to this house, you hear me!" He yelled and slammed the door.

I quickly shoved everything into the luggage and got up and started to walk away quickly from that dreaded home.

I'm finally free! I thought but in the back of my mind I was full worried.

Where would I go? What if it rains or snows? The nights are only going to get colder, I thought as I walked into the busy night of the city.

I'm all alone, what do I do?

Chapter 16

BOMI

With every breath I take, it turns into a cloud of condensation. I shivered in the dark cold night and wrapped an arm around myself to keep warm.

Should I rent a room for the night? Do I even have enough money? I walked around the streets, only to find small shops.

Of course you do. I know but is it worth using? For Buddha's sake! Quit it, you have so much money and right now, it is so worth it! But- No buts! You better use half that money soon or I'm going to kill you myself. Ugh I'm done talking to you conscience, you do nothing but give me a headache.

Then clouds started to roll in, little drops of water fell one by one. I panicked; stores and shops were beginning to close for the night so I ran to find a safe place. I tripped along the way, my knee was scrapped. Blood ran down my leg and the pain burned at my skin. Tears coursed down my face and I roughly wiped them away.

I ran to the nearest ally way. I know it's not the safest place to be but right now, I have to find a place to take a cover and be dry.

I set my suitcase down on its back and sat on top of it. Instead of staying dry, I got wetter from the spilling water from the gutter above which splattered right down on top of my head.

Ugh my uniform is getting wet, how am I supposed to dry this by tomorrow? I questioned myself as it poured rain.

I'll be here all night, soaking wet, if I keep sitting here but I have nowhere else to go and the nearest hotel is a long ways away.

I looked down at my knee but it was no use, it was too dark to see anything. I put my head in between my knees and cried my heart out.

It was mix of tears of joy and tears of sadness. I'm finally free from my hostile parents but where am I to go on this dark, rainy, and cold night.

JAESUN

We just came out of the karaoke room after singing a variety of different songs for hours just for the fun of it and it was now time to go home.

"Looks like it's been raining," Kangdae pointed out to the wet ground and buildings that dripped water.

"We should go again sometime," Alex said and everyone nodded in agreement.

Then I heard sniffling almost like crying. "Wait, do you guys hear that?" I asked them.

"Hear what?" Leo asked, looking around to search for the sound.

"Listen," I whispered and we all listened in.

We all cupped a hand around an ear and listened in.

"I think it's coming from over there," Doyoon said and pointed to a dark alley.

"It could be just water," Minho said.

"What kind of water sounds like its crying?" I questioned, sarcastically.

"I don't know," he shot back and I just shook my head at him.

"Come on, let's go check it out," Ethan said.

As we neared the dark alley, I saw a small figure sitting there against the wall with their head in between their knees. I squint to get a better look at the sitting figure but it was just too dark to see.

Well this person is wearing a skirt so it's a girl.

As we walked closer I looked at the girl's outfit and it was a school uniform. I searched from a far any indication of what school she may go to.

Wait, I think that's our school uniform! Hold on, I think I recognize her now.

"Bomi, is that you?" I questioned as we got close to her.

She looked up at us and it was Bomi, I immediately ran over to her. "Bomi! What are you doing out here in the freezing cold? Are you okay?"

She didn't say anything but her eyes said it all. She stared intently in eyes as if she were trying to tell me everything that is bothering her but she couldn't. She then engulfed me into a hug.

"What's wrong?" I whispered to her. She responded by shaking her head.

BOMI

I heard someone call my name so I looked up and there was Bangtan looking at me as if I was a mystical creature.

Jaesun came running over to me and asked me a whole bunch of questions; I didn't say anything to him I just looked up into his eyes. I don't know what came over to me but I engulfed him in a hug and whispered a *thank you* to him. I just felt grateful that he found me to protect me.

"Bomi, you're all wet," Jaesun said and I let go.

"Sorry," I said and back away.

"It's okay, we need to take you somewhere to be dry," Jaesun said, getting up. "I'm taking you home with me." He took my hand and I got up grabbed my suitcase which was then taken by Doyoon.

"Bomi, are you bleeding?" Leo asked me. I hid my bad leg behind my good knee and looked away.

"Get on," Jaesun squatted down and I climbed onto him. The rest of the way Jaesun was giving me a piggy-back ride.

DOYOON

Since Jaesun took Bomi away with him (even though that should have been me), I might as well be generous and take Bomi's luggage which surprising isn't that heavy despite it being a large suitcase.

"Hey Minho, you want to carry this?" I asked him, already getting tired of dragging the large object behind me.

"You grabbed it so it's now your responsibility," he replied back.

I shrugged and thought; *if I take it for her she'll thank me and possibly go out with me, right?*

BOMI

It was at least a fifteen minute walk to Bangtan's house when we finally reached the small house.

"Sit down here first," Jaesun let me down on a small couch. "I'll be right back."

Jaesun came back with a small first aid kit; he kneeled down in front of me and cleaned off my wound with an alcohol pad which stung like crazy.

"It's only going to hurt for a bit so stay strong," he assured me. He then placed a bandage over the wound.

"Thank you," I quietly said. He took my hand and walked me over to somewhere in the house.

"Here's the bathroom so you can change out of your uniform," Jaesun said and handed me my luggage.

"Thanks," I said. shutting the door and locked it.

I looked at myself in the mirror and I was a mess; my hair was wavy and drenched in rain water, my eyes were red and puffy. I feel a bit embarrassed looking this way.

I stripped from my wet uniform and put on a pair of joggers and a t-shirt.

After changing, I just stared at myself in the mirror. *Should I ask if I can stay here for a few nights until I get my own place or should I ask to call Cheolsu?* I looked down at the crumpled number in my hands.

"Call me if you need me." Cheolsu's words went around my head. But then again I'm already here with Bangtan and staying with Cheolsu, (Someone I rejected for someone else that I might not have a chance with) I feel more comfortable with him.

"Are you alright, Bomi?" I hear Jaesun say behind the door. I walk over and opened the door which revealed Jaesun in a pair of gray sweats and a black V-neck t-shirt.

"Thanks for letting me change," I said and pushed back my hair behind my shoulders.

"No problem," he said.

There was an awkward silence. I closed my eyes for a bit, I have made up my mind on what I'm going to do. I crumpled the number into my pants pocket and looked up at Jaesun.

"Jaesun, do you think I can... Stay here for a few nights?" I asked.

"Of course you can," He said with a wide smile.

"Really, are you sure?" I asked still unsure. He probably needed to ask the others first before making the decision of me staying here is okay.

"Um, wait here, just let me ask the others first," He then left me still waiting by the bathroom door.

Maybe I should have called Cheolsu, maybe they won't let me stay here since they will have to feed another mouth. I sighed and waited patiently for Jaesun's return.

JAESUN

Bomi just asked if she can stay a few nights and I said yes automatically. It made me so jubilant to know she wants to stay here!

I walked into the kitchen which was where all the other boys were. They were huddled around the counter snacking on a bag of chips.

"Hey guys," I greeted as I walked into their little gathering at the counter.

"Hey," Kangdae greeted back to me.

"How's Bomi's knee?" Ethan asked.

"I cleaned and bandaged it up so it should be fine and heal quickly," I replied.

"Where is she now?" Leo asked.

"I left her waiting by the bathroom but... umm; do you think Bomi can stay here for a few days?" I asked and I see their eyes widen.

"What, she wants to stay here?" Alex questioned and I nodded. "But why?"

DOYOON

My eyes widen as I heard Bomi wants to stay here. *She's keeping her promise, she's coming back to me,* I thought, happily.

"I'm fine with it," I said, shrugging my shoulders acting as if I don't really care but in reality my heart inside of me is bouncing around.

JAESUN

Yes! The youngest one agrees with me but I'm not sure if he will treat Bomi right if she stays here, I thought.

"Hmm, I don't know," Ethan said, tilting his head to the side. "She will be living with just guys."

"It's either here or she might want to go see Cheolsu which this is almost like saying I'm not treating her right which Cheolsu will take her back and he gave me a chance to be with her." This would've been my answer but I wasn't sure if Bomi could hear us or not and I didn't want the others to know I like Bomi, especially, Doyoon since there's something fishy about that boy.

"I think this answer all relies on the oldest," Leo said pointing to Kangdae.

"Please Kangdae, I don't think she has anywhere else to go," I implored. I cupped my hands together and pouted my lips.

"Fine, she can stay," he responded and munched on a piece of chip.

"Thank you so much, Kangdae," I said and turned around to go tell Bomi.

"Wait," he said and I stopped in my tracks. "Bring her here first."

I nodded and walked back to Bomi and brought her into the kitchen.

"Bomi, you can stay here," her eyes widen with happiness. "But what are your reasons for needing a place?" He crossed his arms looking at her.

I never really seen Kangdae like this he's usually a chill guy and let's things slide; I wonder why he's being so serious? I looked closely at his face to find any hints but to no avail; Kangdae truly is one interesting guy.

BOMI

Kangdae sounds like a strict father right now so it scared me a little.

Why is he being so serious right now? I never really had seen him this way before.

I was happy that he accepted but now he was asking why I asked to stay.

Maybe I had better chances with Cheolsu, I thought as I bit lip thinking of the answer even though I already knew what it was.

"I got kicked out by my parents," I responded.

"What? Why can't you just go back?" he questioned obviously confused.

"Because I can't, they won't let me," I snapped through gritted teeth.

"Why?"

He actually making me a little pissed, I started to tense up. *Why can't he just understand my situation and that I don't want to tell him!*

"Hey, why don't we go see your room," Jaesun said, taking me away from the situation.

KANGDAE

It's not that I'm bothered by Bomi staying with us, it's-it's because I find it interesting why she wants to stay with us so suddenly and why she was there right when we got out of the karaoke room. So I thought, maybe if I pushed it a little she'd tell me why but obviously it was actually pissing her off. I let it slide but sooner or later she will tell us and I must be patient to hear her answer.

JAESUN

I can see Bomi tensing up from Kangdae questioning her so I decided to get her out of the tense atmosphere. I guess whatever happened between her and her parents it ended badly and it's not a good time to ask what happened.

"No one really uses this room so you can use is it for the time being," I said, opening the door and taking her inside.

"I know you said no one uses this room but how do you guys sleep?" She asked confused probably since our house is a small one story home. You kind of have to go on an adventure to find different rooms around the house.

"Well, a few of us share rooms like there's Kangdae and Minho, Leo and I, Alex and Ethan then Doyoon has his own room." I explained. "But just letting you know we actually have seven rooms in this house."

"What, really?" She questioned, shocked.

"Yep, as you heard me explain there are the five rooms and now the two other rooms were a little tricky to find until one little curious guy, Alex, found a sliding door in hidden within the wall then the attic counts as another," I replied.

"Wow, the things you find," she said giving me a small smile.

"I'll leave now so you can get some rest," I said but before I left, she engulfed me in another hug and I tensed up at the sudden skinship but relaxed getting comfortable in her hold.

DOYOON

I was about to visit Bomi when I saw those two hugging. My blood began to boil at the sight of them. I stomped my way into my room and shut the door.

She's mine, Jaesun! I thought angrily as I jumped into bed.

JAESUN

"Thank you so much and I promise I'll tell you everything later," she whispered in my ear and I hugged her back.

"You're welcome, now get some rest," we released. She stood on her tippy toes and kissed my cheek and with that I shut her door tightly and leaned against the door with a gigantic smile on my smile.

I touched my cheek and smiled again and giggled.

I can't believe she just kissed me! This must be a head start of having my chance, I just have to get around Doyoon somehow, I thought as I headed into my room and, of course, Leo would already be knocked out.

BOMI

I leaned against the wall and thought about what I just did.

I can't believe I just kissed him!

I slapped my cheek a couple times, I don't know what just came over me but I feel glad I did so. I slipped into the bed that was already in the room.

So this is what a bed feels like, I thought as I wrapped my blanket around me.

Soon my eyes started to droop down instead of forcing them to stay opened; I shut them tightly and fell asleep.

Chapter 17

BOMI

I've been staying with Bangtan for two days now and it's a little weird to wake up and then you see a bunch of sleepy boys walking around with either a shirt on or off except Jaesun, he always has his shirt on because he's the gentleman he is and respects their female guest but I guess I just have to get used to it until I find my own place.

It's now Monday and I really don't want to go back to school or I just don't want to see Dasom or Dujoon but more Dasom since Dujoon doesn't really bother me that much.

We walked out of the house and made our way to school which was only a twenty minute walk. We walked through the school gates and people started to stare and began to whisper to each other.

DASOM

"She did what!" I screamed my blood started to boil.

"Uh-huh, she walked right through the school gates with them and Jaesun had her arm around her too," some girl explained to me. "I heard she's living with them too."

"That's it! I'm going to get this girl!" I clenched my fists together; my blood was so hot if you touched me, you probably would've been burned.

I then stomped off to go get my girls.

BOMI

The day started off as usual: people trying to trip me, push me in the halls, and knocking my books out of my hands.

It's now time for lunch and I'm so hungry. *Wait NOOO!! I didn't bring any money so I can't buy lunch.* I closed my eyes in frustration. *I'll just wait till home.*

"Bomi, you ready?" Jaesun asked me.

"Yeah," I answered back.

"You okay?" He asked, concerned filled his voice.

"Yeah," I said not looking at him, I'm sad and pissed that I won't be eating today when I'm so hungry.

Once we got to the cafeteria I told Jaesun, I'll wait at the table.

"Wait, you're not going to be eating?" He asked with a worried look.

"No, I'm not hungry," I said giving him an assuring smile.

JAESUN

I didn't believe that girl one bit. Like always. I know she's lying, she didn't eat breakfast this morning and she's always hungry every day for lunch even if she eats slowly, she looks like she hasn't eaten for days.

So I grabbed a second sandwich for her. Now that I think about it, most students buy the sandwiches more often that they made the sandwiches a lot bigger with more stuff inside.

"Here," I placed the sandwich in front of her.

"I said I wasn't hungry, you didn't have to," she said, looking intently at the sandwich.

"Clearly if I could hear your stomach growling throughout the lessons," I laughed.

"What? Never mind, I'll just wait till home," she said and I froze a bit she just said *home,* she's only been at our house for two days and she already calls it her home.

"No, take it I already paid for it so you must eat it," I insisted and she finally gave in and unwrapped the sandwich.

"Thanks," she said, munching on it happily.

After a few minutes, she got up and excused herself to the bathroom.

Once she was out of sight I looked to over to the boys.

"Bomi's birthday is coming up soon, what should we do?" I asked them and they gave me a confused look. I think I said it too fast and they hadn't had time to process it through their minds.

"When is her birthday?" Leo finally spoke up.

"The seventeenth," I answered back.

"Umm, we could just surprise her in the morning with a small cake and breakfast," Kangdae suggested.

"I like that idea," I took out my phone and wrote Kangdae's suggestion down in my notepad.

"I do too," Doyoon said but the tone in his voice doesn't sound too excited.

"And you guys don't have to buy her presents, she might feel burdened," I said, sliding the stylus and putting away my phone.

"Why would you feel burden on your birthday? It's a day to celebrate you," Ethan questioned.

"Did you not see her reject a five dollar sandwich?" I questioned him and he shrugged his shoulders.

"Bomi's coming, we'll talk about this later," Alex said.

DOYOON

I can't believe I didn't know Bomi's birthday was coming up; I love Bomi more than Jaesun does, I should know this before he does!

I'll get her a present that makes her so happy, she definitely has to go out with me, well, that is when I have the courage to ask her but still, she will say yes.

BOMI

Finally it's time to go home and I'm so tired of doing school work, thank the Buddha that it's my final year of high school.

We walked out into the chilly air and I shivered.

One of these days it will snow and I will freeze to death, I thought.

I felt an arm wrap around my shoulder, I looked up and there was Jaesun. Being under the protection of his arm makes me feel happy.

~ Wednesday, December 17 ~

BOMI

"Happy birthday to you! Happy birthday to you! Happy birthday, dear Bomi! Happy birthday to you!" I woke up to the sound of people singing and when I opened my eyes I see Bangtan slowly creeping into the room with a small birthday cake, light with candles.

"How'd you guys know it was birthday?" I said with a smile and blew out the candles. I rubbed my tired eyes to get a good look at the boys.

"Well, we are your best friends now so why wouldn't we know," Alex said giving me a hug. "It's not going to stay a secret forever."

I yawned. "What time is it?" I squinted out the window and it was still dark outside.

"5:30 AM," Leo replied.

"What? You guys could've woken me up at six since that's the time I usually wake up," I said, stretching my arms up in the air.

"We take a long time to get ready," Minho said. "Plus, this hair needs to be perfect!"

"Okay then, we'll eat this cake later. Let's open up presents!" Ethan said, excitedly.

"Presents too?" I said.

"Of course, what's a birthday without presents?" Kangdae flashed a smile at me.

"Open mine first," Jaesun handed me a bag and I opened it.

I gasped. It was a jacket. My first jacket! I touched the soft fabrics with my hands.

It was a black and white varsity jacket; Seoul University was stitched in the small patch on the left breast plate. Seoul University is the most prestigious university in Seoul and is my dream school.

"Thank you!" I gave him a tight hug.

"But our gift is even better!" Kangdae said and handed me another bag. "This is from me, Ethan, Leo, Minho, and Alex."

It was another jacket but it was a bigger jacket. It was dark green winter coat with white fuzzy fabric on the inside. I started to tear up.

"Aww don't cry, it's okay," Jaesun gave me a hug another hug.

"I'm just so grateful that you guys would think of me this way," I said and wiped my tears.

"Doyoon, did you get anything for Bomi?" Leo asked and we all turned our attention to the younger boy.

"Oh umm, this is kind of awkward to know that you're older than me," Doyoon rubbed the back of his neck.

Ha-ha, I'm older than him, that's so hilarious!

"My birthday is on the 30th," he said.

"Oh okay," I said, biting my lip to keep myself from laugh out loud.

"Here's your present," he handed me a box.

I quickly opened it up and I really started to pour tears.

"How... How?" That was all the words I could say, my mouth hung open trying to find the right words to say.

"I got it so we could all keep in touch with each other," I looked up at him and it seems the others were shocked as well.

I held the smartphone in my hand; it was a black Samsung Galaxy Note 3. I let the sleek phone sink into my palm. *How can a phone so big, be so light?*

"Here, I'll put in my number in first," he took the phone out of my hands and typed in his number.

DOYOON

You are mine now! I thought as I typed in my number.

"Here you go," I handed her back her phone and her mouth was still agape.

I lifted up her chin and closed her mouth. “You guys should put your phone numbers in there as well.” Everyone just kept staring as if I committed a crime and didn’t get caught.

I shrugged my shoulders and smiled widely at Bomi. “I’m glad you like your gift.”

AUTHOR

After they put their numbers in Bomi’s phone, they all left so Bomi can get ready for school. They then all turned and looked at Doyoon with confused looks.

"When did you have the time to get her a phone and why didn't you tell us you were getting one for her?" They all asked him at once.

"Uh well, one, I got it yesterday and two, I paid it with my own money that I've been saving up myself," Doyoon explained.

"You must really like Bomi," Kangdae said and narrowed his eyes at the younger boy.

Doyoon slowly nodded his head, Jaesun walked away after seeing the younger one's action.

If this is your way of trying to get a girl to like you, you don't need to buy her expensive things. You need to show her, you love and care for her, Jaesun thought and went into his room to put on his uniform.

BOMI

After dressing into my uniform, I walked into the bathroom and I tried on my jackets; both were super warm and comfy.

"I see you like the jackets," Jaesun said as he leaned against the door frame.

"Yes, I love them so much," I walked over to him and hugged him tightly. "Thank you again, this means so much to me."

"You're welcome, you mean so much to me," he said.

"What?" I gave him a confused look.

"I-I mean what? It's just that-" he stuttered.

"I'm just joking with you," I punch him lightly on the arm. "Come on, we got school to go to."

I took off the green jacket because I'll be a walking marshmallow if I wore both jackets so it's best just to wear one.

We got to school on time and everyone kept staring at me. They would turn to their friends, point, and start to whisper things to each other.

"She's wearing a jacket."

"When did she get the money to buy that?"

"When did she ever have money?"

"Isn't it her birthday today?"

Those were the whispers I heard, I was kind of glad when someone questioned if it was my birthday today, I just wonder how they would know.

"I'll be back," I told Jaesun and went into the restroom. I looked into the mirror and my eyes looked a bit puffy from the crying this morning but it's going to be puffier with my tears right now.

"Well, well, well isn't it the birthday girl," that annoying voice said.

I turned around and there was Dasom and her *crew* right behind her with their arms crossed.

"What do you want?" I asked through gritted teeth.

"All I wanted to do is say happy birthday," she said, trying to use her innocent voice.

"Well, you did so leave me alone," I said coldly.

"Ouch, are you sure you're not the real bully," she said, putting her hand on her chest. "I haven't even given your birthday present."

"Present?" I gave her a confused look.

"Yes," she stepped closer to and I took a step back. She lifted up her foot and rammed her foot into my stomach.

"Who told you, you can be with my Jaesun, you don't even have a chance with him! You should've stayed with Cheolsu when you had the chance. For a moment, I was actually happy you found someone else!" She kicked me once more as I lay on the floor in pain.

"Get up!" I slowly used all my strength to push myself back up but she kicked me back down. I landed on my shoulder and I screamed in pain.

"If only you would listen, this would have never happened. I know you live with those boys, don't think you can hide your secrets from me."

I hid my face to hide the pain and my tears. "You're poor and ugly, how can girls like you get that many guys to like you! Let's see how old are you? Eighteen, right? So that means eighteen kicks."

"Wow, who knew you can do math," I painfully laughed and she kicked my again in the stomach. I felt like I was going to throw up all the food I ate.

"Dasom, I think that's enough," Chanmi said.

My vision was started to go out of focus and I coughed up some blood.

"Fine but I'm not done with you, why can't you disappear and stop ruining my life," she said as she walked away; the sounds of her heels clicking with each step.

I lie on the floor not moving a muscle. *Will anyone that cares find me in here? Oh my phone!*

I slowly slipped it out of my pocket and it landed with a clatter on the tile floor. *Who should I call Cheolsu, Jaesun, or Doyoon?*

I tried moving my phone close to my face but my arms was in too much pain so I tried moving my whole body towards it. With each movement I groaned as the pain shot up through my body.

I finally had my phone by my face and I made my decision who to call. I leaned over my phone and tapped the buttons with my nose.

"Hello?" he said. *I was happy to hear his voice even through the phone.*

"I-I your need help," I said weakly.

"Bomi, are you okay? Are you hurt? Where are you?" He asked. I can hear the worry in his voice.

"I'm in the bathroom, come quick please," I said.

"I'm on my way just stay put," he said and hung up.

"It's not like I'm going anywhere," I give a small weak laugh.

UNKNOWN

I just got a call from Bomi and it seems like she's in danger or in pain but either way she's hurt and needs my help.

Class was about to start but I ran off anyway, leaving my friends confused and the teacher.

"Yah, where are you going? Class is about to start!? Mr. Jeon called out to me.

I ignored him. I just needed to get to Bomi fast, when I got there I didn't think twice about entering the girls' bathroom.

There lay on the cold, hard tile floor ever so still was Bomi.

"Bomi, are you okay?" I lifted Bomi up so her head lay on my lap. "That was the most stupid question I ever asked of course you're not okay."

"Cheol... Cheolsu..." she said weakly, I can hear the pain in her voice.

"It's okay, I'm here, let's go get these wounds clean," I said and her eyes started to flutter close. "No, please Bomi, stay awake okay, let's go to the nurse."

"I can't stand, it hurts too much," she said and closed her eyes.

"No, no," I shook her and she opened her eyes back up. "Get on my back," I said but it was too late and she closed her eyes once again and was unable to open them back up.

"Dammit," I quietly cursed and hauled her up onto my back and ran as quickly as I could to the office.

"Hmm, she has major bruising on her stomach and legs and shoulder, I think she might have to go to the hospital," Miss Yoon said, tapping her pen against her clipboard. "What happened?"

"I don't know," I answered. "I found her by the... stairs."

"Maybe we'll figure out when she wakes up but for now, you must take her to the hospital, the students matter first before school," she said firmly and picked up the phone receiver.

"It's going to be alright, Bomi," I ran my fingers through her hair. "Why didn't you call Jaesun?"

"Ambulance will be here soon so that should give me enough time to dismiss the both of you," she said.

"Okay, thank Miss Yoon," I bowed down 90 degrees to show how much I appreciate her hard work.

"Ay, it's nothing like I said students before school or anything else," she said and nodded. "I informed your teachers about the situation so you're good to go."

After a while, the paramedics finally arrived with a stretcher and we were off to the hospital.

Chapter 18

AUTHOR

Bomi groaned and muttered odious words due to the pain as she moved around in the bed. “Ugh where am I?” She asked and rubbed her throbbing head.

“Bomi, you’re awake!” Cheolsu sat up straight and held Bomi’s hand. “We’re at the hospital.”

Bomi looked around the room surrounded by big white walls and deeply sighed. “I always knew I would end up in here someday.”

"It’s going to hurt just a little so just endure it," Cheolsu said as he applied the ointment to Bomi's wounds, there were a lot of cuts and scrapes around her body and bruises.

Bomi sucked into some air as the ointment started to sting. "There that's all the wounds," Cheolsu said, standing up from the bed.

"Wait, there's one more," Bomi said.

"Where?" He asked, getting ready to apply some ointment.

Bomi slipped her shirt off her shoulder and Cheolsu gulped down. But then what revealed on her shoulder shocked him.

"This one looks really bad Bomi, we should ask the doctor to look at it instead," Cheolsu gave Bomi a worried.

"I'll be fine, the ointment will help," Bomi said.

Cheolsu applied the ointment around the, hideous and painful, bruise that had formed on her shoulder. He traced his finger around the scar that etched itself onto her skin.

"There," he slipped her shirt back on her shoulder.

"Thank you for helping me," she said.

"No problem, anything for you," Cheolsu flashed a smile at her. “Let’s take you home.”

Cheolsu helped Bomi get up and they walked down the hallway towards the nurse's table. They signed the discharge papers and took a cab back to Bangtan's house.

"So you really are living with them?" He looked around Bomi's room.

"Yeah but this is just temporary until I can find my own place," Bomi said, playing with her fingers.

"You know you can always come stay with me, I don't live the other members, I live by myself so it gets lonely sometimes," he said and began to play with Bomi's fingers too.

"No, I don't want to burden you since you have to make meals for two and you just have to double everything," Bomi said with a concerned look.

"Oh okay," Cheolsu said with a disappointed tone.

But Bangtan has seven people so they have to feed an eighth mouth. Bomi, I don't understand you sometimes like seriously you make no sense at all when it comes to making decisions for yourself; Cheolsu thought and dropped Bomi's hand.

"You can leave if you want you don't have to stay here with me," Bomi said.

"Will you be okay in this house alone?" Cheolsu asked, standing up.

Bomi nodded her head. "I'll probably take a nap or something," she said and hugged Cheolsu before he left and he kissed the top of her forehead. "Plus school is going to be over soon, so Bangtan should be here by then."

"Bye Bomi," Cheolsu said and with that he left Bomi alone in her room waiting for Bangtan to return from school.

BOMI

I walked back into my room and lay down on my bed. I took out my phone and touched the screen. My wallpaper was a picture of me and Cheolsu when we hung out at the mall.

It was a perfect picture, just me and him. Nothing bad is happening between us but we're like perpendicular lines. We meet once and everything is stupendous but it's like we weren't meant to be since we must travel in different directions to get that perfect angle.

But the question is why did I choose Jaesun? Jaesun and I are like parallel lines if we meet then things get hostile so we keep our distance nevertheless we go the same direction in hopes of meeting someday.

I wanted to scream but I didn't have the energy to release any of my anger. I turned back around onto my back and stared at the ceiling.

For what seemed like forever (which was about two hours), I heard someone come inside the house.

"Bomi, are you home?" I hear Doyoon call my name. I sat up straight on my bed. He walked into my room followed by the other boys.

DOYOON

I was so worried about Bomi, I couldn't focus in class. So when school was dismissed, I left the others behind and ran all the way home. I never ran so fast before, however, there was this one time this dog chased me all the way home but that's not the point.

"Bomi, are you home?" I called out as I walked into the house and slipped off my shoes.

I walked into Bomi's room and there I saw her sitting on her bed but when I saw her face I was totally shocked.

I gasped. "Bomi, what happened?"

BOMI

Doyoon gasped when he saw me, he quickly ran over to me and cupped my face in his hands.

"Bomi, what happened?" He touched one of my bruises on my cheek; I turned my face away from him.

"I want to be alone, except, I want to talk to Jaesun," I told him. "Please,"

DOYOON

"Oh okay," I said and got up, I walked out of the room and glared at Jaesun whose face was clueless to the whole situation.

"She wants to talk to you," I said coldly.

"Me?" He pointed to himself.

"Who else?" I pushed passed him and went into my room but then I went back out to see the others huddled around her door.

AUTHOR

Jaesun walked into the room closing the door behind him.

While the other boys huddled around the door and placed an ear against it to listen to their conversation and to what Bomi has to say that is so private that she only wants to tell Jaesun.

They never thought her story would be so heartbreaking.

JAESUN

I was a bit shocked when she wanted to just talk to me. I sat down on the bed next to her.

"Can you help me put some ointment on please," she handed me a small ointment bottle; I gladly took the bottle from her small fragile hands.

She showed me a bunch of bruises she had on her back and a few cuts on her legs and a scrape on her face.

"Who did this to you?" I asked but she stayed silent. I sighed and made her turn around to look at me. "Bomi, you promised to tell me everything."

"Dasom," she answered.

That abhorrent girl did this to you! I thought angrily and clenched my fist.

As I finished putting on ointment on her, she stopped me from closing the bottle any further.

"Wait, I have one more," she started slipping her shirt off her shoulder.

I held my breath for a moment but to my surprise there was a big bruise on her shoulder and right by it was her scar. As I started to apply the ointment I feel her flinch everything I glided my finger across her skin.

AUTHOR

"So can you tell me why you're staying here?" Jaesun asked as he screwed the top back on the bottle and placed down on the table.

I guess since I did promise him, I'll just spill now, Bomi thought.

"The reason I'm here is because my parents kicked me out. So my parents they have totally forgotten name, every year for my birthday they would give me different name like slut, bitch, and gay. And so this year they gave me a choice on my name which was Byuntae and Jiralhanae. They have been bugging me all week if I made my decision yet and with that, I just exploded and I yelled at them so they just threw me out of the house," Bomi explained.

Bomi felt like crying but she just couldn't, she knew that her parents kicking her out was better than waiting until the next time then they just might as well "kill" her.

"Your parents are terrible people, my parents abandoned me when I was ten because all they cared about was partying and getting drunk," Jaesun said, fiddling with his fingers. "But how'd you get your scar?" The question was always in Jaesun's head.

Bomi took a deep and shaky breath. "Well, it happened about three years ago," Bomi started.

~ Flashback ~

It was around 9:30 in the evening and Aaron came over to spend some time with Bomi since he knew she was always so lonely. It seemed that Bomi's parents were a tad bit drunk and were having a fight about something in the living room but Bomi and Aaron just stayed in the room, ignoring whatever was happening between them.

"So I like this girl and I'm not sure if I should ask her out or not," Aaron said as he stared at his phone.

"Ooh Aaron has a crush," Bomi teased even though she disliked the thought of Aaron having a girlfriend because that would mean he wouldn't have time for Bomi but she wanted Aaron to be happy. "Are you gonna text her?"

"Yeah, I'm actually texting her right now," he said. "I was going to tell her today but she just left suddenly like she was nervous as well so maybe it'll be less nerve wrecking on the phone."

"Oh, I'll just tell her for you then!" Bomi snatched Aaron's phone and started typing in random stuff.

"No way! Give me my phone right now," He said trying to take his phone from Bomi but she dodged his moves. "Miss Park Bomi, you give me my phone!"

"I love it when you say my full name!" Bomi beamed.

"Oh, you'll love me for sure when I get you!" Aaron got up and started walking towards Bomi who was running away from him.

They chased each other through the house. The moment they stepped into the living room was when everything went horrible.

When they ran pass Bomi's parents, Bomi's mother lifted her hand up to smack her father but instead she hit the back of the TV which caused it to fall forward and fall onto the floor with a crash.

"Michinyeon!" Her mother yelled.

"How dare you break this TV, do you know how expensive this was?" Her father yelled. "Let me teach you a lesson!"

He walked into the kitchen and came back out with a small knife in hand. Bomi's eyes widen at the sight of the sharp object and backed away. Aaron stood there frozen not knowing what to do. He always knew how cruel Bomi's parents but never this cruel to bring out sharp objects.

"Come here, this won't hurt at all just a little scrap on his your arm and it will pay for the damage," her father stepped closer to her. Bomi furiously shook her head as she took steps back, soon her back hit the wall and there was no way out. Her father had the knife pointed at her.

"Got you," he said, closing in but before he touched her she ducked down and escape from being trapped but since the knife was pointed out at her it scrap her shoulder, it was a pretty deep cut that will turn into a bad scar if not treated quickly or properly.

"Why you little-" Her father ran towards Bomi and Bomi only ran into her mother who held her tightly.

Before Bomi's father can do anything else Aaron jumped in front of him and right there, the knife slid its way into Aaron's stomach. Bomi screamed and ran to Aaron who had fallen down onto the ground, holding onto the handle of the knife.

"That's what you kids get by not listening," her mother said and walked away.

"No, I'm so sorry, this is my entire fault I didn't mean for this to happen," Bomi cried. Blood began to seep out of his stomach and pool under Aaron.

Bomi immediately grabbed Aaron's phone and dialed 911. "911? There's an emergency my cousin has just been stabbed please send an ambulance!"

"Bomi, calm down please," Aaron's breaths were unstable. "I did this for you."

"Huh?" Bomi held Aaron's hand tightly. Her whole body was shaking in fear; it was like her whole world was shaking on its axle because her whole world **was** *dying beneath her.*

"Bomi... this isn't your fault... I wanted you to live to-to be happy.... I know someday you will find happiness and love."

"How can I find love? No one likes me, you're the only one I got," Bomi's tears started to pour down her face.

"Just be happy without me..." his voice was drifting away further and further.

"Don't say that! The ambulance will be here soon," Bomi said, stretching up her upper body, trying to see the flashing lights of the ambulance.

"But Bomi in the state I'm in, I might not make it," Aaron said, taking deep breaths.

"No, you will!" Bomi yelled. "You have to-"

Aaron's eyes started flutter as they began to close shut. "No, keep them open, Aaron Yang!"

"I love it when you say my full name," he whispered as he slipped off into complete darkness

"No wake up! Wake up Aaron! Wake up!" Bomi cried as she tried to shake him awake but there was no use. She bent down and leaned against Aaron's shoulder and cried, her tears soaking into his shirt not that it was already soaked with blood.

When the police and the ambulance, arrived her parents made up some excuse that a chaotic, mental man came in and tried to kill them and unfortunately they got to Aaron.

~ End of Flashback ~

After explaining this heartbreaking memory, Bomi's tear flowed out uncontrollably while Jaesun hugged her tightly; he was completely full of shock to hear how despicable her parents are. On the other side of the door, the boys were in complete shock as well.

Soon Bomi fell asleep and Jaesun laid her head down on her pillow and left the room silently. He walked passed the dumbfounded boys and sat down on the couch and stared blankly at the dirty white walls trying to comprehend how much pain Bomi has gone through and how she had such a vile childhood and she was only loved by one person.

Now it was in Jaesun's hands to protect and help her find solace so she can be the happiest girl you could ever know. He stood up, walked into his room and started planning in his head how he could fulfill his mission to fill Bomi's heart up with love.

Chapter 19

BOMI

It's been about two months since I told Jaesun everything and I guess the other boys knew about it as well but since that day, I felt like an enormous weight has been lifted off my shoulders.

I still have a plethora of money with me and so it was time to find a place of my own. I couldn't stay with the boys forever. I've already started looking for a place but not all of them were for cheap even the really ghetto places are expensive. I also asked to work on Mondays for now on in order to get more money.

"Hey, are you still looking for a place?" Collin asked as leaned against the booth and took a sip of his drink.

"Yeah," I replied as I counted the total number of chopsticks we had. "Maybee, how many did we have to start?" I called out to her.

"250 pairs so a total of 500," she called back. "Maybe but we should have about that much."

"Ugh, why do people love stealing chopsticks from us?" I ruffled up my hair in frustration and then started packing up the chopsticks in a napkin so they could be set on the table.

"Anyway, you know there's this old lady nearby, who is renting a place for cheap," he said and I looked up at him.

"Really?" I questioned.

"Yep, it's quite a nice place too. I think she's renting it for $50 a month," he added.

"How do you know this?" I narrowed my eyes at him. It's not that I don't believe him it's just he can be a very unpredictable guy and you never know what's he's up to. So I guess there are times where you can't believe him.

"I was looking a place for myself too but I found a better place instead of there," he said, leaning back against the booth.

"Can you give me the address," I handed him my phone and he gladly took it.

"I thought were living with Bangtan though?" He asked, slowly tapping on my screen.

"Yeah, but I can't live with guys forever," I said and continued packing in the chopsticks that needed to be finished before we get super busy.

"But you will be living with a guy forever when you get married," he said and I gave him a shocked look.

"Yah, whoever said I was getting married," I said and shoved a pair of chopstick in a folded napkin.

"Well, I would marry you," he said, smiling like a fool and leaning in close to my face, my eyes widen. "However! You're like my close friend and we're so close you could be my sister and I'm in love Park In-Soo."

I rolled my eyes. "Yah, don't lean in my face like that or I might as well punch your precious face!" I threatened.

"But it made your heart beat faster, didn't it?" He joked.

"Yah! Don't you have work to do," I yelled.

"I'm just joking. Well, this restaurant isn't going to run itself," Collin sat down in front of me and began shoving chopsticks into folded napkins.

Ding!

"Oh hello, welcome to Yong Su San," I stood up immediately and bowed to the incoming customers.

"Bomi, I got it, for how many?" Maybee took over and led the customers over to a table in her quarters. I love it when Maybee comes right in and takes over.

"Bye Bomi!" Maybee called out to me as I left the restaurant. I wrapped my jacket closer to me since it started to snow again.

I walked in the direction of Bangtan's house when someone stopped me. "Bomi, wait up!" I turned to see who was calling me and it was Doyoon.

"Hey, wait are you doing here?" I asked him.

"I came to pick you up of course. It's dangerous for a girl to be walking alone at night," he said putting his arm around me.

"Oh okay," I said and we walked in silence to the house.

I'll go look at the place tomorrow, should I take Jaesun or Cheolsu to go see the place with me, maybe I'll take Cheolsu, I thought as we crept closer to the house.

"Yah, where do you think you're going?" Dasom said as I tried to escape from her.

"Why can't you leave me alone," I muttered holding my books closer to my chest.

"What was that?" She questioned.

"Leave me alone please!" I begged.

"And what if I don't?" She question and I stayed silent. "That's what I thought." She then left and I let out a sigh of relief.

Can I even endure five more months, school is almost over and I can be free from all this abuse. I left the bathroom and headed to class.

Maybe I should stop coming to the bathroom in the morning and just go at home, before I walked over to Bangtan's table I made a quick stop at Velocity's table to go see Cheolsu.

"Hey, Cheolsu," I greeted as I stopped by where he was sitting.

"Oh hey," he greeted back.

"Can I ask you a question?" I asked. "In private."

"Of course," he replied, he got up and we walked into the empty hallway. "What's up?"

"Do you think after school you can come with me to check out a place?" I asked.

I don't know why I wanted to keep it a secret from the others but I didn't actually want Bangtan to know and I feel Velocity might tell them my plans.

"I'd be gladly to, I have nothing better to do anyway," he said with a kind smile.

"Cool, I'll meet you at the front of the school then," I said and left to go eat lunch with Bangtan.

CHEOLSU

"Sounds like a date to me," Lucas said with a smirk.

"She rejected me a long time ago," I said, playing with my empty milk carton.

"Well, maybe she thought, she was missing out so she's coming back," Yeoshin pointed out.

I looked over at Bomi who was happily smiling next to Jaesun.

Or maybe for a way different purpose that she doesn't want Bangtan to know, I thought as I took a bite of my sandwich.

BOMI

"Bomi!" I kept walking as she continued to call my name and threw wads of paper at me. "You better not be going home with him!"

"I'm not; I'm going home with Cheolsu!" I yelled back not even wanting to turn around but I can feel the smile creep on her face.

I walked down the stairs to the front and saw Cheolsu waiting for me.

"Ready?" I asked him.

"Yeah, let's go," he put his arm around me and we made our way to the place Collin recommended me. I texted Jaesun that I won't be home and I'll be out with Cheolsu so he doesn't need to worry.

"So where are we headed to?" He asked.

"Umm I'm trying to look for a place to stay," I answered, looking at my map on my phone.

"Why? You already have a nice place with Bangtan," He questioned.

"I can't live with the boys forever plus there are already seven of them and they always have to make an extra meal for me," I replied and pointed to the direction we need to go.

"You can still live with me, all you have to do is pay $30 which is half of the rent," Cheolsu suggested.

"No, it's okay, Collin told me the lady that is renting the place only wants $50 a month which is pretty good," I said.

"Come on, if you're living with me you only have to pay $30!"

"No, I'm almost an adult so I can take care of myself," I said, crossing my arms.

"Sure... Cheol-Cheolsu, I need your help," he mocked me.

"Shut up!" I said and slapped his chest which only made him chuckle. "Oh, I think we're here."

"Hey, the place doesn't look too bad," he said nodding his head.

It was short one story house, painted all white beside the door which was a dark cherry wood with a large rectangular window and two outer windows beside it. There was a black metal gate with a lock and then a stone walkway to the front door. Indeed, it is quite a nice place.

We knocked on the door to a smaller beside the house and a short old lady with gray hair came out. She wore a pink and white floral button-front shirt with a mix-matching pair of blue and green baggy pants. This was your casual Korean grandma look, especially, when she loves to farm.

"Hello, sorry to disturb you, my name is Park Bomi and I just wanted to check if this house is still for rent," I said with a bow and Cheolsu bowed also after greeting her.

"Oh yes, it's still open. Come on, I'll show you the inside," she said with a very soft but bold voice.

We followed from behind, her stride was a little unbalanced, and she kind of looked like a penguin waddling around. "Are you two a couple?"

"No, we're just really close friends," I said and saw Cheolsu pout. "Don't you know, you look ugly when you pout?" He grinned.

"Well, the house isn't big as you can tell but it's just like any other house," she said, opening the door and letting us in. We took off our shoes before entering the home and admired how nice the inside looked.

The house was bright; a good amount of sun came in through the windows. The house was neat and clean; wood floor were waxed and not a speck of dust insight but it was very empty, the rooms were quite big and had a lot of space, and the bathrooms were pretty nice as well.

"How much are you renting?" I asked, despite, already knowing the prince already.

"I'm renting it for $50 a month but how old are you, sweetie?" she questioned.

"I'm eighteen-years-old, Ma'am," I replied.

"Oh my, a girl, you're age living by yourself, your parents must be strict," she said, shaking her head in disappointment of my parents.

"Ha-ha, yes they are," I said with a small smile.

"Well then for you, you'll only have to pay $25," she said.

"Oh no that's okay, I can pay full rent," I said.

"Don't worry but if you become a rebel then I'll make you pay $35," she joked.

"Yes ma'am, thank you so much," I said, bowing down multiple times.

"So when do you think you'll move in?" she asked locking the door and leading us out to the front.

"I'm not sure but hopefully soon," I said.

"Please do call me when you made up your mind," she handed me a piece of paper with her name, phone number and address.

"Yes ma'am," and with that we left.

"Are you really going to move there?" Cheolsu asked.

"I have to," I replied. "I'll probably move out tomorrow."

"Oh, I'll help you," Cheolsu said.

"It's alright, I don't have much anyway and I can just ask Bangtan since I have to tell them I'm moving out anyway," I said.

"Oh okay then," he said with a sigh. "I'll see you later then, text me when you have settled in your new home and I'll come over."

"Don't worry I'll text you, bye Cheolsu," I said and walked in the house.

"Bomi, you're home!" Jaesun greeted as I walked in.

"Hi," I walk passed him and went into my room and sat down on the bed. It's been maybe an hour of me just sitting on the bed staring blankly at the wall across from me.

I took a deep breath and stepped out of the room and went to Jaesun's room.

"Jaesun?" I knocked on the door.

"Come in, Bomi," I hear him call from behind the door. I opened the door to reveal a clean, spotless room with Jaesun and Leo sitting on their beds staring at their phones. "What's going on?" Jaesun looked up from his phone.

"Can you get the other boys into the living room, I have something to say," I said and he nodded and looked over to Leo.

When all the boys were gathered into the living, there was a small awkward silence.

"Is there something you needed to talk about?" Leo asked me, breaking the silence.

"Oh, yeah umm... well, I just wanted to thank you guys for letting me stay here for so long when I just asked for a couple nights and that I found a new place of my own to stay at," I explained.

"No Bomi, you need to stay here!" Doyoon said, holding onto my hand.

I wiggled my hand out of his release but he held it closely to him. "I'm sorry Doyoon but I need to go, I can't stay here, I need to go on my own," I said.

"When do you move in?" Jaesun asked.

"Tomorrow," I answered and Doyoon squeezed my hand. I violently snapped my hand back from his grip.

"Can't you just stay here a bit longer until senior year is over? Huh?" He gave me those puppy eyes but I don't give in easily to puppy eyes. I shook my head at him.

"Well, I respect your decision and I can tell that anything we do to convince you stay, you will still decline," Kangdae said.

"Thank you," I said with a small smile.

JAESUN

It broke my heart knowing that I won't see Bomi every morning or every night but I can tell she wants to have her freedom and I totally respect her for that.

She walked back into her room and I followed her.

"So you really found a place?" I asked her, leaning against the door frame.

"Yeah, it's pretty nice actually. It has a gate, a stone walkway, a cherry wood door, two bedrooms, a kitchen, wood floors, and a floor heater too," she explained as she packed her items into her big suitcase.

"I see, do you need some help tomorrow when you move in?"

"Yeah, I could need some help carrying this heavy thing," she tried lifting up her suitcase but failed. I laughed and walked over to pick it up for her. "Ha-ha thanks."

"Bomi, what are you going to do without me?" I put my hands on my hips and shook my head.

"Umm, reaching for stuff on high shelves and picking up heavy things," she answered and giggled.

BOMI

After our talk, Jaesun headed back to his room and got ready for bed. I lay down on my bed and stared at the ceiling.

This will be my last night here, I thought as I drifted off to dream land.

Hopefully my life goes on happily from here.

The next morning, I called the old lady and told her that I would move in today. She was glad someone was moving in since she has tried for months but everyone just kept finding a better place.

I then thanked her and thought I go see what the commotion is that is happening in the kitchen. I walked into the kitchen to see six, sluggish and tired, boys standing around the counter. Jaesun was the only one not standing around being tired and lazy; he was here and there, preparing for breakfast on eight plates.

"Morning Bomi," Jaesun greeted as he flipped whatever was in the pan. I was guessing it was eggs.

"Morning," the others boys grumbled and yawned.

"My goodness," I walked over and smacked Alex in the back of the head.

"Ouch! Bomi!" Alex rubbed the back of his head, Doyoon burst out laughing and I slapped him as well.

"Awake yet?" I asked them and they nodded. "Geez... It's almost eleven o'clock; I've been up since three hours ago!"

"Same here, I woke up at 8:30," Jaesun said. "Okay, grab a plate."

I guessed correctly. Jaesun had made scrambled eggs with bits of chopped up vegetables and rice.

"So... You're moving out today?" Doyoon poked at his food and then looked up at me and I nodded.

"Jaesun and I are going to go see the place again today and help me out with stuff," I said and everyone turned their attention to Jaesun.

After brunch, I went into my room and started to prepare to leave.

JAESUN

"Ha-ha Jaesun, you really hit it big this time!" Leo patted me on the back.

"What's that supposed to mean?" I slipped on a gray V-neck shirt and a light blue button-front.

"What do you mean you don't know?" He crazily waved his arms in the air. "It's obvious you're in love with her and she's favoring you the most out of everyone."

"Oh on the contrary my brother, there's Cheolsu," I said, folding down the collar of the shirt.

"Pssh, she's been with you longer and she doesn't hang out with Cheolsu as often as she does with you," he pointed out.

I guess he has a good point; however, she could still have feelings for Cheolsu but is just too embarrass to see him since he did confess to her.

"Anyway, tell Bomi I said goodbye and I hope you have fun on your date," he said before scrunching up under his coverings going back to sleep.

"Geez," I was going to smack him but I didn't.

Gosh, he's so lazy!

I walked out of the room and knocked on Bomi's door. She opened it and came out with a light pink blouse and a pair of black skinny jeans and her suitcase.

"Umm, I think everyone just went back to sleep so let's get going, shall we?" I grabbed her suitcase and she led the way in her black polka-dotted shoes.

BOMI

"I had my son drop off a bed for you so you wouldn't have to sleep on the floor. Oh and there's even a desk to help you study for your finals," she said. "And here are your keys."

She dropped a pair of gold keys in my hand. "Thank you so much!" I bowed down (ninety degrees) multiply times.

"Ay, don't worry about it," she waved her hand. "Well, I hope you enjoy the place."

"Wow, it really isn't that bad looking," Jaesun nodded his head as we stepped inside.

Everywhere was lit up with sunlight but imagining how dark and scary it would be at night sent chills down my spine.

I took out my phone and dialed Cheolsu's number. "Cheolsu, I just moved into the new place."

"That's great but I can't come over today. Guess whose clumsy, chaotic sister is in the hospital like seriously who slips on squid?" He questioned over the phone.

"Yah Cheolsu, I can obviously hear you, you're lucky I can't walk over there and smack the silly out of you!" I hear Melissa yell.

"That's the point! Anyway, I promise I'll visit soon," he said.

"Oh okay, I'll see you later," and with that I hung up the phone.

"Let's go to the supermarket to buy some things that you need for your house," Jaesun suggested and I nodded.

After what seemed like hours, we purchased air fresheners, printed out pictures from my phone, picture frames, essential cleaning supplies, two floor chairs, and hangers. It's not much because we kind of just played around the place but at least we got some of my house needs.

We hung up many pictures on the wall; the majority of them were of Bangtan and I, a few with Cheolsu and Velocity, there was even one with all fifteen of us.

"This looks good," Jaesun rubbed his hands together and looked up at the wall that has been perfected to look artistic (in Jaesun's view that is).

"It's getting late, you should probably head home," I said to him.

"Oh, really? Okay well I guess I'll see you later," he said, putting on his shoes.

"Bye," I shut the front door and took a deep sniff of the house which now smelled like melons.

"I'm going to get used to this," I smiled and headed into my bedroom.

Chapter 20

BOMI

Time is going by quickly which is good. I will soon graduate and there will be no more bulling from others and I can live my life filled with happiness and the one thing I hope for to find – Love.

Every day after school, I would walk home with Bangtan and Cheolsu since my house was towards Bangtan's house but close to Cheolsu's as well. So I would walk with Bangtan when I go home but to school it would sometimes be just me and Cheolsu since we walk a different direction which is more towards Cheolsu's house and away from Bangtan's house. Confusing, I know but hey, it works.

Even though I'm not living with Bangtan anymore, I still get beat up for hanging out with them. Dasom would drag me to a bathroom or a dark hallway and kick me down into the ground until I can't move anymore. I tried to stay a little longer after school with Cheolsu so they could go on their own but it seems that Bangtan are always waiting to walk with me.

Finally spring was just around the corner. Spring is my favorite season since it doesn't get too hot and it doesn't get too cold, it's just right.

Today on my weather app, it says there's going to be plenty of sun today so there's no need on putting a jacket on.

I walked out into the fresh moist air; I took a deep breath and began my walk to school. Then everything went black. I panicked.

"Who are you?" I shook with fear.

"Hmm, guess?" He said with a small laugh.

"Yah, I nearly had a heart attack!" I shouted as I turned around to hit *Cheolsu* on his chest, he laughed.

"Sorry, say you're out early," he said walking along side me.

"Yeah, well, I just wanted to get to school a little bit early today," I replied. "What about you?"

"Oh um... Well, the air was nice so I thought I'd step out for a bit but I figured, hey, why not go to school now," I could tell he was lying but I just brushed it. "Wait a minute, look at me again?"

I gave him a confused look and he just stared at my face. He then cupped my face with his hands.

“What are you-?”

"Who did this to you?" He questioned with a serious tone but I was still confused so I took out my phone and looked at my reflection and I had a big bruise on the left side of my left eye. I gasped at the sight and hid my face.

"Who did this to you?" He questioned again, sternly.

"No one, I fell out of bed last night," I answered remembering what had happened yesterday.

"Try again," he said, crossing his arms.

"Fine, it was Dasom," I answered looking down. “Isn't it obvious?”

"Again!" I nodded. "I swear I'm going to teach that girl a lesson myself!" He marched off angrily.

"No Cheolsu, I don't want you to get hurt because of me," I begged, catching up with him.

"What? Me get hurt by Miss Perfection?" He laughed but I wasn't laughing.

"She knows people like Taejoon," I answered, clinging onto his arm as a tear rolled down my cheek.

"Fine, I won't but if she doesn't stop I will do something and you can't do anything about it," he crossed his arms and walked off.

This time I laughed since he was doing some weird catwalk. I ran up and caught up with him again.

"Why are you coming to school again with Bangtan?" Dasom yelled as she slapped me in the face, right where she slapped me last time that left a large bruise. "You think just bringing Cheolsu along is going to help!"

Tears flowed down my face; I couldn't hold it in anymore. "But you should be lucky to be alive now that I know you're not living with them anymore."

A teacher than walked in and Minah release her tight grip on me so I took a moment to take a deep breath.

"Aww Bomi, he wasn't meant for you, you deserve better," Dasom said and hugged me which I guess convinced the teacher and she walked into the Teachers' bathroom. "Like I said stay away from them," she whispered as she let go of me and with that I raced out of the bathroom.

"Bomi, are you okay? Why are you always like this in the morning?" Doyoon asked me as I took a seat down on my stool.

"I'm just having really bad nightmares in the morning," I lied and shook my head in annoyance over his stupidity.

"Do want me to stay over?" He asked and I stared at him, he then realized what he had said. "I mean do you want us to stay with you?"

"Oh no, that's okay," I said, shaking my head and giving a small smile.

"Ah okay," he said with a disappointed look. I don't know why but I feel nowadays I really dislike Doyoon.

I feel he's a bit clingy or obsessed with me. He's always trying to hold my hand (which I pretend that I don't feel his hand touching mine even if I do pull away quickly), he tries to squeeze his head next to mine when the boys and I are looking at something, he always says me or I and then changes it to us like what he just did earlier. It seriously does annoy me, not to be mean or anything but I wish he wouldn't be this clingy.

Anyway, I don't know why but during the lessons, I kept on tearing up. I'm not usually like this in the morning but the tears just kept flowing like a river. Mrs. Chan was beginning to worry but I just lied and said that I had seasonal allergies.

When it was time for lunch, we headed out of the classroom and headed towards the cafeteria. "Come back to the classroom, don't go to gym!" Mrs. Chan called out to us before we left.

"Are you okay?" Jaesun asked, putting his arm around my shoulders; I slid his arm off and took a step away from him.

"I'm fine," I answered. "I'm just going to go to the restroom first."

"Okay," he said and walked away.

I stared at my reflection in the mirror. I was pale and my eyes were red and puffy. I rinsed my face with cold water.

As I walked out, I was tripped by no other than *Miss Perfection.* I got back up and dusted off the dust on my skirt.

Why do I always go to the bathroom at the wrong time? I thought.

"I think Cheolsu is waiting for you to sit next to him," she said with a smirk. "Oh and by the way you still look terrible as ever."

I quickly walked away to the cafeteria. When I arrived, I looked around for Cheolsu or at least Velocity but they weren't there. My shoulders deflated and I sat down next to Jaesun.

"Are you sure you're okay?" Jaesun questioned again and I nodded. "Are you going to eat?"

I shook my head. "I'm just going to sleep." He nodded and moved his tray over. I put my head down on the table and slowly drifted off to sleep.

~ Bomi's Dream ~

"Hey, Bomi catch!" Aaron yelled and kicked the ball towards me.

"Oh hey, where am I?" I asked him as I caught the soccer ball in my hands and dropped it on the ground.

"We're home silly," he walked up to me and ruffled up my hair before picking up the soccer ball.

"Home?" I gave Aaron a confused look.

"Yeah, remember we said we would be together forever?" He questioned me.

"Yeah but..."

"But what, Bomi? We are finally free, you're finally free!" He spread his arms out and ran around the yard.

"Free?" I placed a finger in my chin and grinned. "I'm free, I'm free!" I then did what Aaron was doing and we both chased each other around the yard of our home. We then both collapsed on the ground.

"Wait, Aaron how did I get here?" I asked him out of breath.

"How am I supposed to know?" His voice trembled a bit.

I sat up and looked at him. "Because you're always watching me from above," I replied.

"Oh right... Um... well, the words you last said were I'll just leave," he answered. "But that doesn't matter at least we are together now right?"

I just stared at him confused.

"Bomi, Bomi!"

~ End of Dream ~

JAESUN

The other boys left and I stayed back to watch Bomi so nothing bad happens to her. As she slept I stared at her angelic face.

"Why'd you lie? It's obvious that you weren't crying because of nightmares unless you were trying to tell the truth to say that Dasom is the nightmare. And you can't hide your wounds from me," I whispered and pushed back her hair to where the bruise was hidden.

She moved her head the other way. I snapped my hand back and froze. She murmured the word *free* as she moved her head. "Are you thinking of the free candy from that old woman who sells the little toys and couple bracelets at her stand?" I laughed.

The bell rang informing students to head back to their classroom so I tried waking up Bomi.

"Bomi, Bomi!" I shook her softly. She lifted up her head and squint her eyes at me. "It's time to go to class."

"Oh okay, thanks for waking me up," she said rubbing her eyes which were still puffy.

I put my arm around her shoulders since from her sleepiness; she kept stumbling like a drunken person. I was glad that this time, she didn't push my arm away.

BOMI

As we walked into the class, I gently pushed Jaesun's arm away and sat down at my seat. I was still confused what my dream meant but I feel that whatever I did was good, thought, I'm not so sure about it.

I shook my head and turned my attention to Mrs. Chan who ordered us to skip gym and come back to class.

"Okay, I know you are supposed to go to gym now but we have to talk about exams coming," she announced and everyone groaned.

"Calm down, this is finally you're last exams until college at least but whatever. Anyway, for the rest of the remaining months of the school year, we still will learn new subjects and we will have practice exams and quizzes here and there."

I hate exams, they are just meaningless tests that you have to be taken in order to pass the grade and I guess I'm only saying this since the test are so easy (at least for me they are). After she talked about the exams for a bit, she asked us if we had any questions and there were none.

"Oh and I have even better news!" She said with a wide smile. "This year for our honors senior students, we are going on a camping trip!" Everyone gasped and started to whisper exciting things to each other.

"We are going in May so I am handing permission slips now since we have a hundred or so honor seniors and you know how hard it is to keep track of all those, especially, when you are the one to keep track of it. Also, I will hand out some index cards for you to pick out your camping cabin partners. There are four in a cabin so pick three other friends you want to be with, I don't care who you choose even if they are from a different honors class, I may have to move you guys around so I am sorry that you don't get that person you want and please girls choose girls and guys choose guys."

Well I am not going because no one ever chooses me to be their partner and all the girls basically dislike me so there is no use of going to stupid things like this, I thought as I doodled on the permission slip.

I can't get a parent's signature either.

"It's a two day and one night trip in the woods. Don't worry, there are cabins with beds. They're actually really nice cabins and not far from the beach too!"

"Are there rules?" Some kid raised his hand and asked.

"Of course, you guys have to follow the basic school rules like no smoking, drinking, bullying and stuff like that, however, you can do whatever else you want as long as you follow the school rules. What this mean is you can go to the beach without asking permission, go on a hike, sit and sleep in your cabin for all I care. There may be some special activities the staff and I have planned but I doubt it and then you guys have to make sure to come to breakfast, lunch, and dinner on time," she explained. "Now, please write down that you would like as your partners and place it on my desk. Afterwards, just do whatever you want. Oh and Jaesun, can you come outside with me for a moment?"

I watched Jaesun give a confused look and left the room. I stared blankly at my permission slip and index card.

"Who are you going to choose?" Doyoon asked me.

"I'm not going," I said.

"What? How come?" He asked.

"Because one, no one wants to be in a cabin with me and two, I need a parent signature," I explained to him.

"Mrs. Chan wants to see you, Bomi," Jaesun said returning to his seat.

I stood up and walked to Mrs. Chan. "Yes Mrs. Chan?" I said.

"So I recently learned about your family situation from the staff office when I was sending out report cards and if you want to go on this trip, I would be more than happy to sign the permission slip for you," she said with a kind smile.

"And I may not know what's going on with this school and you but I can tell you and the other girls don't really “click” together since I've never seen you hang out with any of them so if it makes you feel any better, I will allow you to pick boys in your group."

"Really, you will allow me to do this?" I questioned her.

"Yes, of course, anything for my favorite student!" She gave me a hug and I returned it.

When I got back in my seat and began writing down some names.

Jaesun
Cheolsu
Alex

I got up and placed my index card on Mrs. Chan's desk, she gave me a warming smile and I returned a smile back to her.

"Are you going to the trip, Bomi?" Jaesun asked as he filled out his permission slip.

"Yep, I’m going," and I did the same.

"What? I thought you weren't going?" Doyoon sounded a bit pissed since I said yes to Jaesun and no to him.

Well, I'm sorry that I can't make up my mind and then all of a sudden some opportunity pops up and then I make my decision.

"Well, I changed my mind since Mrs. Chan said that she would sign it for me," I said.

"Oh, who did you choose?" Jaesun asked.

"I don't know, I just left it blank," I lied and shrugged my shoulders.

"Oh okay," Jaesun said.

~ End of Class ~

"I'm going to walk home with Cheolsu because I have something to talk about with him so you guys don't have to wait for me, just go on ahead," I told Jaesun.

"Alright, I'll see you later," he said and gave me hug. I walked out of the classroom and headed to go see Cheolsu

"Oh hey Bomi," he said shoving a notebook into his backpack.

"Hey can we walk the other way to home?" I asked him.

"Oh yeah sure," he happily said, he slung his backpack onto his shoulder and took my hand and lead me outside. "Is it because of Dasom that you don't want to walk with Bangtan?"

I nodded and showed him that the bruise has worsened.

"I understand for some reason she leaves you alone more often when we hang out with each other," he said.

When I got home I bid Cheolsu goodbye and slipped my shoes off as I stepped inside. I started my homework in a matter of minutes, I pounced on my bed. Even though it wasn't planned I fell asleep.

I suddenly woke up with a jolt. I squinted at my phone to check the time, it was eight o'clock, I had the same dream that I had earlier today and it was completely the same no new information.

“Ugh, what the heck,” I shrugged it off once more. “Maybe I'll go take a hot shower to get my mind off it.”

I stood up from the bed and head into the bathroom. “Ahh... that's better!”

Once I finished I climbed back into bed and drifted off to sleep.

Chapter 21

BOMI

"Do you like one those boys?" Aaron randomly asked me.

We were lying down outside on the lawn looking up at the clear blue sky. I turned to my side to face him.

"Boys?" I gave him a confused look.

"Yeah, what were they called um...? Ah Bangtan, that's it!" He snapped his fingers and pointed at me as he sat up.

"Oh yeah," I said shyly and slowly sat up as well.

"So who is it?" Aaron questioned and gave me his someone-is-in-love look. He poked my sides which made me laugh.

"Jae-Jaesun," I answered, holding his hands tightly to make him stop tickling me, he pulled his hands back and rubbed them.

"Ah, Jaesun is a cutie! You do know that other kid uh... Doyoon I think likes you too," he said.

"Yeah but he's too clingy and he needs to control his temper, did you not see how he yelled at me when I drowned or when he gave Jaesun glares when I wanted Jaesun instead of him?" I explained to him and rubbed my temples.

"I understand, he doesn't really fit your style anyway," Aaron nodded his head.

"I have a style?" I raised an eyebrow.

"Of course you do, I made one up for you," he replied.

"When was this?" I asked him, crossing my arms.

"Ever since you started liking that asshole Dujoon," he answered, he slapped his soccer ball with his hand.

I woke up with a jerk due to my alarm going off; I laughed a little thinking about what I just dreamt. I still wonder what my dreams mean, it has no real meaning to it, is it a sign that I made some decision or is Aaron trying to say something to me?

I shook it off once again and prepared myself for school.

I stepped outside and made my way to school. "Bomi, wait up!" I turned around a see Cheolsu jogging towards me.

"Hi," I greeted him but without a smile.

"What's wrong?" He asked.

"I don't know," I answered, walking forward and leaving him behind, dumbfounded. He then ran and caught up to me.

"Fine, be like that!" He folded his arms and walked in front of me. I guess he was trying to make me laugh but it wasn't working.

CHEOLSU

"Fine, be like that!" I folded my arms and walked faster, I was hoping I would make her laugh but when I turned around, she still had her straight face on.

I wonder what's wrong with her she was totally fine yesterday, I thought.

As soon as we reached school I thought, I should start a conversation. So without turning around, I started to talk to her.

"So are you doing anything after school?" No answer. "So you're busy, what are you doing?" Still no answer, I turned to see if she was there but turns out she was gone. I sighed and walked away.

BOMI

Cheolsu started asking me question but before I could answer them, I was pulled away into the building.

"Leave me alone! I never even came with them!" I screamed knowing who it is.

"Even if you didn't come with them, I'm having too much fun pulling you out and seeing what a coward you are," she said laughing, she then kicked my side and I crouched down from the pain since she always end up hitting the same exact spot she kicked before.

When the bell finally rang, her friends dropped me and they left following their Queen Bee. I was left on the ground to get up by myself and walk to class.

I held onto to the wall to give me support as I steadily walked to class. Once I reached the door, I straightened up my body and tried to walk as normal as I can and walked to my seat.

"Hi, Bomi!" Jaesun greeted and I nodded at him.

"Huh, what happened to your smile?" Alex asked and pointed to my lips and I shrugged my shoulder.

I must've smiled a lot? I thought as I got up again to give my camping permission slip to Mrs. Chan.

"Thank you very much Bomi!" She said with a smiled, I bowed and walked back, of course, I couldn't just walk back to my seat safely.

I landed face first onto the ground; I sucked in some air through gritted teeth.

"Watch where you're going," Taejoon laughed out loud followed by others.

"Oh my, are you okay?" Mrs. Chan asked leaning over her desk. I said nothing and nodded; I dusted off my skirt and walked back to the table.

"Bomi, you're bleeding," Jaesun rubbed my face with his thumb. I slapped his hand away. I turned around and slipped out my phone to look at my reflection and there was indeed a small scratch of four red lines on my cheek.

Must have come from the backpack strap I landed on, I thought as I slipped my phone back into my pocket.

Throughout the whole lesson I was in pain, my whole face hurts, my hands are trembling, and my side feels like I've been stabbed thirty times. I was absolutely having a terrible day.

When lunch came, I scurried out of the classroom and hid myself in the library not wanting to seen by anyone and the library is the most peaceful place to be.

When I walked into the room full of silence, I hid in the farthest corner where no one usually hangs out by.

I lifted of my shirt and there it was the biggest and blackest bruise you've ever seen. It hurts so badly, even with the slightest move, it sends a sharp pain.

I sat down on the ground and cried. Crying that this would all end, crying to cover up the pain but crying wouldn't help at all and I soon fell asleep from crying.

JAESUN

Bomi has been acting strange today and I wonder why. I've been in deep thought when someone tapped on my shoulder.

"Hey Jaesun," Cheolsu stood in front of me with a worried look.

"Hey, what's up?" I questioned him and jerked his head wanting me to follow him out into the hall.

"Have you seen Bomi?" He asked.

"No," I answered shaking my head.

"Oh, have you noticed she's been acting weird this morning?" He asked.

"Yeah like she didn't smile at me and when I tried to help her, she just slapped my hand away," I explained and he nodded.

"I'm really worried for her," Cheolsu let a breath of worry.

"I am too, I just wish she wouldn't push us away," I said and ran my fingers through my hair.

"She probably needs some space right now," Cheolsu said. "Which is probably best for her but when she comes to again, make sure you keep an eye on her at all times."

I nodded and we then headed in different directions back to our tables.

BOMI

I woke up to the sound of the bell ringing and rubbed by tired eyes. I always liked this corner of the library I could fall asleep and then be woken by the loud bell since the sound box is right on the wall above the shelf I lean on.

As I slowly got up, I made my way to the nurses' office so I don't have to see all the people I want to avoid.

"Hi Bomi!" The nurse greeted me and I bowed down ever so slightly. "What do you need today?"

"Can you excuse me from gym please?" I asked her.

"Of course I can! But why?" She scanned me for any injuries and found none.

I guess she didn't the bruise on my face, however, at this very moment I don't really care anymore so I lifted my shirt and showed her my bruise.

"Oh my, how'd you get that?" She asked taking a good look at it.

"I was playing soccer with my cousin," I answered pulling my shirt back down.

"Ouch, did he kick the ball a little too hard?" She questioned on and I nodded. "Well here, take this."

She handed me a spray can of this medicine. "This helps with the pain it's like liquid salon pas. I'll call up your gym teacher right now and you just spray that on and relax."

I sprayed it on and, oh my goodness, did it feel good. It had an icy feel that just felt like heaven. I lied down on the bed and fell back asleep.

DASOM

"Dammit Bomi, you're missing out on the fun," I muttered as I held the balls in my hand.

"Dasom, throw the ball!" Taejoon yelled at me. I threw the ball and hit someone in the face. "I'm so NOT sorry!"

"Dasom, throw below the neck!" Coach yelled as he showed me where to throw the ball by waving his hand under his neck.

"Whatever," I whispered.

This is the stupidest game of dodge ball without Bomi. Where the hell is she?! I screamed in frustration when a ball slammed into my thigh.

"Ha, you're out Dasom!" Some kid yelled and I shot him a death glare. I hastily walked away and started texting Chanmi.

BOMI

"Are you having fun?" Aaron asked me.

"Of course, we're together aren't we?" I answered.

"Good," he said with a grand smile.

"Aaron why can't you tell me how I got here?" I asked him.

"Because it's a secret," he put his finger to his lips.

"But we never keep secrets from each other," I pouted.

"Well, this one is a little too big to tell you," he replied.

"Please tell me!" I begged.

"Fine, might as well because if I don't you'll haunt me in my dreams," he said, crossing his arms.

"You're already haunting mine," I muttered.

"Hey, I heard that," he said and I giggled. "Anyway, so you actually didn't..."

The bell rung. Awaking me from my dream, I reluctantly got up from the bed and made my way to class.

Stupid bell, I was about to learn what Aaron needed to say to me, I thought as I walked on.

Step, shlump, step, shlump. With every agonizing step a wave of pain shot through me.

Once I walked in, Jaesun and Doyoon immediately raced over to me.

"Yah, where have you been?" Doyoon asked.

"Are you okay?" Jaesun asked.

"I'm fine," I walked passed them and sat in my seat.

Throughout free period, the boys constantly tried to talk to me but I ignored them and put my head down and pretended to fall asleep. To make it even better, I put on my earphones and played music from the radio app on my phone.

The final bell rung and I sat up and deeply sighed. I took out a stack of sticky notes and wrote a small message to myself and shoved it into my pocket. I got up and quickly ran out of the class.

"What's the rush?" Dasom asked, pushing me back into a wall. I grunted as my back hit the cement wall.

Minah and another girl were holding me tightly by my arms. "You know I got a manicure during lunch from Mrs. Kim since I did her nails so I don't think I can beat you today but that doesn't mean I can't see you cry today. Girls!"

Couple girls came out of nowhere and start cracking their knuckles, popping their necks as if they would scare me.

Of course, I was scared to be beaten to death but their threatening actions didn't scare me at all for some reason. I just wasn't in the mood today to be frightened by useless acts of causing fear to people. Nonetheless, this is how I felt on the inside.

“Please, please don’t hurt me!” I could feel the tears brimming and sloshing inside me like water in a glass that is unsteady and too full.

"Go ahead, do your thing." Dasom waved her hand and I looked away.

The Minah and Chanmi released their grip on me. The girl with the pink shirt kicked me in the face which ached like a smoldering fire. I crumbled down to floor and hid my face away from another hit. The other girl started kicking my legs while pink shirt was slamming her foot into my stomach.

This continued on for minutes, maybe even an hour as my tears and blood spilled out onto the, cold, tile floor.

"Kay, I think that should be enough, thank you ladies," Dasom said and smiled at the two girls. I saw she handed the girls some cash.

I laid still on the ground as she walked closer to me; she then kicked me once more in the stomach. "Why don't you just die and disappear from this school forever. I never want to see your hideous face ever!" She hastily walked away.

Once she was out of sight, I slowly sat up and rubbed my face. I don't know why but when she left, I started laughing. I was literally going crazy.

I picked myself up and laughed even more but winced at the pain. I laughed some more but ended up coughing up drops of blood. I dropped back down to the ground. I got back up and used the wall for support as the world spun around me.

I must be going crazy.

I slowly, crept up the narrow staircase leading up to the best place to be right now. I pushed the steel door opened and took a deep breath feeling the cold, icy wind against my face.

I gathered up all my energy and stepped out onto the ledge.

Chapter 22

JAESUN

I waited for Bomi at the front of the school, yet, she never showed up and I know she still has to be here at school because Cheolsu was walking by himself.

As time passed by, I see some girls walking out. Sadly, it was just Dasom and few other girls.

Wait a minute! Dasom never stays after school.

I ran inside hoping to see Bomi anywhere but there was no sign of her. I walked along the halls calling out her name when I saw a little pink sticky note all crumpled up. I picked it up and unfolded it.

What would you do if I left without saying goodbye?

I gasped and covered my mouth. "No, Bomi..."

I noticed up ahead there were small drops of blood on the ground, there wasn't much but it was enough for me to follow.

Please Bomi be safe!

AUTHOR

Bomi stepped onto the ledge and looked down at the ground with trembling legs; she took a deep breath of the fresh, icy cold, spring air.

She looked up at the blue sky which seemed to be covered with light gray clouds.

She let out a small laugh. *So this is what you meant by saying that I'm now free, isn't it, Aaron?*

"You know, I can endure not eating three meals a day, I can endure the coldness of the winter but what I can't endure is the pain I feel every day from people who hurt me and burdening others because of me. So I don't feel pain anymore or burden anyone else I'll-I'll just leave," she let out a couple tears and took in a few shaky breaths.

"Bo-Bomi, what are you doing?" Jaesun's voice stuttered from the sight of Bomi. He walked closer to her.

"Don't come closer to me o-or I'll jump," sadness flowed through Bomi's words.

"Bomi, don't do it, it's not worth it," Jaesun implored on the edge of tears. "People need you in this world!"

"It'll be better if I died. Isn't that what everyone wants? Everything would be better if I was gone," Bomi looked straight ahead. Her hands trembled in trepidation.

"No... Please..." Jaesun's voice drifted away as he saw the wall building in between them before his eyes.

"I'm just not meant to be in this hateful world anymore," She closed her eyes. "I'm sorry Jaesun." One last tear ran down her cheek as she lifted one foot off.

With all the fear and adrenaline Bomi felt; she was drowned into complete dark and fell right down –

Into **Jaesun's** arms.

Jaesun sat on the floor with Bomi's head leaning against his chest. Bomi's breaths were uneven as her chest heaved up and down.

He caressed Bomi's cheek; tears dripping down his own cheeks. "Bomi, don't you realize the world isn't hateful, it's the people in it," raindrops patted down onto his head, he looked up to see the sky completely filled with crying clouds.

"I'm so sorry; I don't have the courage to confess to you yet. As long as I'm here, *you'll be safe in my arms*," he pulled Bomi closer to him and kissed her forehead.

BOMI

It was Saturday morning when I woke up to the rays of light shining through my window; I sat up to find myself in my bed – Alive.

"Why'd I wake up?" I asked myself. "I was supposed to be free from this hateful world."

I felt movement beside me. I looked over and there was Jaesun sleeping soundly beside me.

Why is he here? Did he catch me before I fell? Does he really care for me or is he just here to see me get beat up again by Dasom? I started to cry from all the sadness that came over me.

"Shh, it's okay," Jaesun sat up and wrapped his arms around me but I pushed him away.

I sprang up from the bed. "Why'd you do it? Why'd you save me? I could of been free, I couldn't been happy, pain free!" I said with tears coursing down my face. I was blaming him for saving a life. For saving my life.

"I did because I care for you," Jaesun said, staying calm. He stood up from the bed and reached out to me. I stepped back away from him.

"You don't know how much pain I'm going through, Jaesun!" I yelled and pointed at him.

"No, I don't but I'm here to change that," he said and again wrapped his strong arms around me, sitting me on the bed. "You're allowed to scream all you want. You're allowed to cry to your heart's extent but you are not allowed to ever give up."

This time, I didn't push away and let him hold me while I buried my face in his chest. I felt secure in his arms, his warmth radiated around us like a shield. I felt protected once again in his embrace and with that I fell asleep.

JAESUN

When Bomi fell back asleep, I let out a deep sigh. *I will try my best to stick by your side no matter happens, you will be safe.*

I laid her down on her pillow and got out from bed. I walked into her little kitchen and looked around for anything to cook with. Instead, I found empty drawers and cabinets filled with dust; I got out my phone and ordered some Chinese food.

I leaned against the wall and slid down onto the wood floor.

Will Bomi ever understand my feelings for her, when will she understand when I said, "People need you in this world" what I really meant was that I need her in my world. I sat there thinking quietly to myself until I heard a knock at the door.

The food has finally arrived. Bomi has only been sleeping for thirty minutes, I don't really think I should wake her up but the food might get cold. I took out my phone once more to check the time, 11:17 A.M.

Yep, I should wake her up now, I thought as I walked into her room.

"Bomi, wake up please, you have to eat," I called quietly to her.

"I'm not hungry," she buried her face in her pillow.

"Come on, you have to eat, you didn't have breakfast, lunch, or dinner yesterday and now it's late to have breakfast so you pretty much missed that too. It's almost time for lunch so you have to be hungry," I explained.

"Just leave me alone," she said with her face still in the pillow.

"No, you have to get up Bomi," I started to poke her sides.

"Fine," she finally got up and walked into the restroom to wash up. When she got out, she walked straight back into her room and lied back down on her bed.

"Yah Bomi, you can't just go back to sleep again," I was getting frustrated with her stubbornness.

"Yes I can," she replied with her eyes closed. I sighed.

Then a brilliant idea popped into my head. I grabbed my bowl of, still hot, Jajjamyeon (black bean noodles) and held it under her nose.

"Mmm, these delicious noodles will be such a waste," I said out loud, even though, she was just inches away from me.

"I will slap that bowl away if you don't get it out of my face," she said with her eyes still closed.

"You're making this way too difficult," I rolled my eyes. I climbed onto the bed and lay right on top of her.

"What the- Get off!" She yelled, squirming around.

"I will get off if you eat," I said.

"Fine, just get off fat ass!" She sat up angrily and blew hair out of face.

"Language, Bomi!" I scolded her as I gave her a bowl of Jajjamyeon.

"What is this?" she asked, staring contents inside the bowl covered with saran wrap.

"Jjajjamyeon, its Chinese food," I answered and started shaking my bowl around so all the sauce could go over all the noodles and did the same for Bomi's. "Eat up!"

It was now night time and I was still with Bomi. We sat in the living for hours in silence.

"What are you still doing here?" Bomi asked, tilting her head at me.

It was pretty cute I have to say. The way her face looked so innocent, the way her brown hair all flowed to one side of her head, and the way her big brown eyes stared into mine.

"I'm still here to keep you from doing anything weird," I answered.

"Well I'm fine now," she said, coldly. "So you can go home now."

"No, I'm staying." I said, crossing my arms. She then started pushing me towards the door with all her might.

Geez, did this girl get stronger? I thought as my legs gave away easily due to her strong force.

"Please get out," she said as we neared the door. "You're an inconvenience."

I quickly ran around her and settled myself down in the middle of the floor. I stared up at the ceiling and then back at Bomi.

"I'm not going and you can't do anything about it," I said and closed my eyes.

"Fine, good luck sleeping out here on the cold floor," she stated and shut her room door.

It's been about an hour or so, I was surrounded by complete darkness. My mind is telling me to sleep but my body doesn't want to obey.

I heard Bomi's room door open so I pretend to be sleeping still, she places a blanket on top of me and tosses a pillow onto my face.

Wow geez thanks.

"I hate you, Park Jaesun," she whispers sarcastically and went back into her room.

I love you too, Park Bomi. I smiled at her comment as I slowly drifted asleep.

Chapter 23

JAESUN

Every single day, I would stick by Bomi's side like glue making sure nothing bad would happen to her. There were a few times I lost my grip on her to Dasom but I always got her right back. I go over to her house every day in the morning and stay with her till night falls then I head home.

April has now come and there's only two or three months left in school. I just can't to graduate and be beside Bomi every day, though that might not happen if I don't have the guts to confess to her.

I just don't know why I can't do it, maybe by dating Bomi I will only hurt her more but already being with her is already causing her pain.

It was the finally end of the day when we were preparing to go home.

"I'm going to the bathroom, Jaesun," Bomi told me. "And you don't have to go with me, I'll be fine." She smiled at me happily.

"Okay," I smiled back. "I'll be waiting at the gates."

BOMI

I'm starting to like having Jaesun around. At first, it was annoying how he came every day to my house but then it just became a normal thing. I think I just smiled for the first time ever since attempted to end my life.

I walked into the bathroom and did my business. I got out of the stall and washed my hands when I heard the familiar sounds of heels clicking on the tile floor.

I need to get out of here! I thought but it was too late.

"Aww, look what we have here," Dasom said with an evil smile, Chanmi and Minah also had the same smile. "You know, I actually missed you!" She put her hands on her hips and tilted her head.

Click Clack, Click Clack the sounds of theirs heels bounce around the wall enclosing me into a tight space as she took a few steps closer to me and I took a few steps back. "Why so scared Bomi?" She laughed.

I limped my way out of the school; I went towards the back of the school where Cheolsu and I would always take when we walk home together. I didn't bother walking all the way to the front of the school plus it was the closet door to exit from the school.

It started to pour rain as my tears dripped down my bruised up face. I limped along the streets alone with no one insight.

I felt my legs beginning to give away with each step I took. I looked around the area for a place to relax and sat down on a nearby bench under the most beautiful, pink and white, cherry blossom tree.

Something so beautiful yet doesn't stay long when conditions get bad.

JAESUN

As time passed, I waited patiently for Bomi but she never came, it started to pour rain. I began to worried, I quickly walked around the school but there was no sign of her.

"Jaesun!" I turned around praying to see Bomi but it was Dasom. My heart dropped to my stomach.

"Where is she?" I asked her, malice filling and pushing out any calmness in my voice.

"Where's who?" She giggled innocently.

I scoff and bit my lip; I balled my fists at my sides to keep me from strangling Miss Perfection. "Don't give me that bullshit!"

"Jaesun, I don't know what you're talking about," she replied trying to look innocent.

"Ugh!" I pushed past her and ran off. I checked all the girls' bathrooms and hallways and still no Bomi to be seen.

I had to make sure she was home so I took the back way instead of the front since I was already at the back of the school.

BOMI

I looked up at the tree and smiled; petals danced around and landed on top of my head. I giggled softly. I love Cherry Blossom trees; they're so pretty and perfect to take pictures of. This thought did not cheer me up one bit.

I sat on the bench letting the rain drops sink into my clothes. I feel it running down my skin as I get drenched by the sudden rain fall. It continued to beat down on me like the hateful words people spat down on me.

Why'd I stay here? I shouldn't be here at all? The tears proceed to slide down my face alongside the raindrops. It seemed like the sky was crying with me.

I then felt someone sit down beside me. I didn't want to see who it was and I don't really care who it is either.

"What are you doing here, Bomi?" He asked. I looked up to the familiar voice. *Jaesun.* I quickly looked away.

"Did they hurt you again? Does it still hurt? Bomi?" Jaesun questioned with concern in his voice. "Bomi, look at me."

"I shouldn't be here, Jaesun," I said, not taking a glance at him. I sniffled and squeezed my hands together tightly.

"Bomi, please look at me," he sounded like he was about to burst into tears but I refused to look at him.

My heart beat slowly making my heart ache with pain. "Bomi, look at me!"

I flinched a bit, I never heard him yell at me before. He grabbed my shoulders and forced me to look at him.

I stared into his brown eyes with sad eyes. He leaned in closer to me as the space between us was decreasing. He then squished his soft lips onto mine; it was a gentle but passionate kiss.

After a while, we parted. "Jaesun..." I was truly speechless; I felt all my words have been just sucked out from me.

"Bomi, I love you. I care for you. I want to be with you, by your side. You are the most beautiful person I know and love. Please if you stay with me, you can be protected and safe," he pulled me into a tight embrace. Despite, being both drenched from the rain.

"I love you too," I finally choked out and hugged him even tighter feeling the safety and comfort in his arms.

The pain in my heart lessened as it started to beat faster and faster.

As we let out of each other, Jaesun looked at me with a kind and gentle smile.

"Let's go," He stood up and stretched out his arm giving me a hand.

I took it but as I stood up my legs were like jelly. Before I fell, Jaesun caught me just in time. He placed me back down on the bench, slipped off his backpack, and squatted down in front of me.

"Get on," I climbed onto his back and wrapped my arms securely around his neck, he stood up and we made our way back to my home.

"Get changed while I get something to eat," Jaesun told me. I nodded and walked into my room.

I shut the door and leaned against it. My fingertips suddenly reach up and gently traced around my lips.

He kissed me. He likes.... no, he loves me. Ah! I can't believe it!

For some reason, I couldn't help but smile because I'm just too astonished. I couldn't find the right words to describe the way I feel right now.

Does this mean I'm his girlfriend now? I thought as I changed into a sweater and shorts.

JAESUN

I touched my lips and felt my lips curve up into a broad smile.

I did it, I actually did it! You did well; you deserve an award, Jaesun! I praised myself in my head.

I grabbed my backpack, quickly unzipped it and clasped onto my gym clothes. I walked into the bathroom and changed in there. When I came out, I went back to my backpack and dug out a package of ramen.

I always keep a package or two in there for emergencies so don't judge me.

After I finished cooking our meal, I set down the pot on top of my thick math textbook and set two pairs of chopsticks beside it.

"Mmm, what smells so good?" Bomi asked, tiptoeing out into the living room.

"Look for yourself," I replied with a smile, waiting for her reaction.

She sat down and lifted the lid to the pot; her eyes glowed like two twinkling stars, though, her mouth didn't curve up to smile.

She rubbed her hands together and licked her lips. She stared at it like a small hungry child.

"Go ahead, eat," I said as I started to eat.

From time to time, I would look up and watch Bomi eat happily, however, her expressions never showed it.

"Bomi," I called her name. She looked up. "I have something to tell you."

I leaned over the pot and put my hand up as if I was to whisper something to her and as I leaned closer, I gave her a surprised peck on the lips. She looked at me with a shocked expression but soon she started to giggle.

"There's that smile I was looking for," I chuckled at Bomi's cuteness.

"You're weird!" She scrunched her face and threw her chopstick at me.

“I know.”

May

BOMI

Jaesun and I evolved into one lovely couple who love each other dearly. He takes care of me so much. I feel my heart has sealed up once again.

We announced to Bangtan the news and they were really happy for us and (surprisingly) Doyoon. I told Cheolsu and he congratulated us as well. Dasom or Taejoon don't know and I don't plan on telling them anytime soon but I honestly don't care if the word gets around.

Anyway, on some random day, Jaesun came over with a large bag in hand and he said the only way for him to see my precious face every day was for him to live together and that was what he was doing: moving in.

I was astounded at first but he's been basically coming over to my house every single day so he might as well move in. Now I get to see him every second, minute and hour of the day. My bed feels a lot more comfortable and warmer with him being in it too.

Today in school we're being told what the itinerary is going to be for camp since tomorrow is the big day.

"Okay kiddos so I will now announce your cabin roommates/group partners. Group number one is Gu Taejoon, Park Kyung, Aiden Ahn, and Lee Hyunshik. Group number two Hwang Dasom, Kim Minah, Bang Sooah, and Kwon Chanmi... Group number ten is Lee Yeoshin, Choi Cheolsu, Park Jaesun, and Park Bomi," All eyes were on me after my group was said.

"Mrs. Chan! Why does Bomi get to have guys in her group?" Sooah pouted with an angry look on her face. "This is so unfair!"

"Ask me again at the end of the year," Mrs. Chan answered with a mysterious smile on her face.

"Did you really not choose anyone?" Jaesun asked playing with my fingers.

"Actually, I chose you, Cheolsu, and Alex," I answered.

"You chose Cheolsu too?" Jaesun questioned.

“Uh-huh, what are you jealous?” I smirked at him.

"Of course not," Jaesun folded his arms and coughed to the side then pouted

"Whatever lover boy, you're so ugly when you pout," I laughed and touched his lips with my finger.

"So what you're saying is Cheolsu is better looking than me?" He asked, he looked pretty pissed if you asked me.

"Yes," I nodded making him angrier. He scoffed a couple times before looking at me in the eyes.

"How dare you say that? We live in the same house, you know I will get you," Jaesun threatened.

Ring!

"That's only if you can catch me!" I called out to him, racing out the door.

"You wanna bet!" I hear him call after me.

"Sure!" I yelled back without looking back. That’s when I crashed into someone.

“Wow, where are you going,” Taejoon asked me.

“I’m sorry,” I stepped aside and tried moving away but he grabbed both of my wrists and slammed me against the lockers.

“I think you need to repay me for the damage you have caused me,” he said and was only inches away from my face.

“Get away from her!” Jaesun yelled as he ripped Taejoon off of me. Taejoon easily pushed Jaesun like a measly ragdoll.

“Whatever, you guys are just losers anyway,” Taejoon muttered and continued walking through the crowded hallway. Jaesun quickly jumped up back onto feet and came over to me.

“You alright?” Jaesun asked me and I nodded. I then smiled at him and ran away as fast as I could.

“You can’t catch me!” I chanted.

After a while, I grew tired and slowed down. I didn't hear any footsteps behind me so I knew I was okay. Suddenly, I swept off my feet.

"I got you!" Jaesun smiled and spun me in circles.

"You caught me, now what do you want from me?" I asked him as he was still holding me up.

"Hmm, a kiss?" He questioned after thinking for moment.

"That's it?" I shrugged my shoulders and leaned in to kiss his cheek but before my lips touched him, he spoke once more adding onto his request.

"On the lips," he smiled like a fool. I just shook my head and pressed my lips onto his.

"You're a totally weirdo," I rolled my eyes as he carefully placed me back down onto the ground.

When we got home, I emptied out my backpack and started packing some clothes. Since I gained so much money throughout half the year, I finally had an actual shopping day!

I went to the shopping mall with Maybee who helped me pick out some clothes. We went to a variety of stores and tried on a plethora of clothes.

After I finished packing, I went out of the room to go see what Jaesun was doing. He sat down against the wall with his eyes closed and earbuds plugged into both ears.

He looked so adorable sleeping. I sat down next to him and just examined his beautiful, flawless face; his clear skin, to his cute, plump, kissable lips, to his cute little nose. Jaesun opened one eye, I scooted back in surprise.

"I can feel you staring at me. I thought you said Cheolsu was better looking than me?" Jaesun said with a sneer.

"He is but you have better features than him up close," I put my face close to his so there was barely any space between us.

"You know you changed so much ever since we started dating," he said, looking intently in my eyes.

"Have I really?" I raised an eyebrow and he chuckled.

"Yes, you have," he stood up and scooped me up in his arms. "Let's go to bed, we have to get up early tomorrow."

Chapter 24

BOMI

Finally, today is the day everyone who is an honors senior student is to meet up at school early with all their bags ready to go for our camping trip.

Instead of Jaesun and me walking, we took a cab o school. I refused many times knowing it was going to expensive. Nevertheless, being the gentlemen Jaesun is, he convinced me to take the cab and he will pay for it.

When we arrived at school, Jaesun handed the cab driver the money as we headed out to meet up with the other honor students.

"Oh look the slut here!" Someone called out.

"Oh yeah, isn't she in a cabin with a bunch of guys!"

"She thinks because there aren't any rules she can do whatever she wants!"

"What a slut."

"It’s okay, just ignore them Bomi," Jaesun whispered to me and he pulled me closer to him.

"What does she think she's doing?"

"Doesn't Dasom like Jaesun?"

"Of course, since Taejoon doesn't like Dasom. Jaesun and Dasom are like meant for each other."

"She's trying to seduce Jaesun. Who does she think she is a prostitute?"

"Oh my goodness, she's in a cabin with Jaesun!"

"Jaesun, can we go somewhere else?" I was on the verge of tears.

Obviously, if I was in a cabin full of guys, I would be called a slut, I thought as Jaesun and I quickly walked to an isolated area.

When we finally stopped, my tears started to fall one by one.

"Hey, hey just try to ignore them," Jaesun used his hand to lift up my chin for me to look up in his eyes.

"How can I when they're all talking all at once?" I questioned, I buried myself into his chest but he pulled me back out for me to look at him again.

"Listen to me, you need to be strong, don't show them you're weak," he then pecked my lips which made me smile a little. "But if you can't do that just tell them to shut the hell up."

I rolled my eyes and laugh. I love it when he does that, he says something really inspiring then makes a stupid plan B if the first one doesn't work.

"Does Dasom even know we are a thing?" He questioned as he fixed my messed up bangs.

"No why?" I raised an eyebrow.

"Interesting... No reason, it's because all those girls are saying that me and Dasom are perfect for each other and that you're trying to seduce me," he replied mimicking their high pitched voices which made me guffaw.

"You're not thinking of any of your strange ideas are you?" I narrowed my eyes at him.

"No, of course not," He voice drifted away, I soon grew even more suspicious.

"Bomi!" I see Cheolsu walking our way with his backpack and Jungwoo.

"Hi Cheolsu!" I waved my hand at him with a smile.

"So I heard I'm in your cabin," Cheolsu smiled.

"Same here," Yeoshin added.

"Yeah, I had no else really to choose," I explained.

“Eh, I don’t mind at all,” Yeoshin shrugged his shoulders.

"See I wasn't planning to go to this camp thing since if you don't go you don't have to go to school! But since I learned that I was chosen to be a cabin with you, I decided to tag along," Cheolsu said with a smile. "But you guys aren't going to do weird lovey-dovey stuff in the cabin right? Because I will jump out the window if you do and hopefully there is a window in the cabin."

"Oh don’t worry, you’ll be fine,” I assured him. “We aren’t that type of couple.”

"Okay then," He said still unsure of my answer.

"Okay seniors, gather over here please!" Mrs. Chan called out.

Mrs. Chan did attendance with our class as well as the other teachers also did their own classes. "This will be a two hour drive so let's hurry and board the bus. When we get there, I will give further instructions. Oh and sit around your cabin buddies!"

Jaesun chose a seat on the left side of the charter bus and so he sat by the window. While Cheolsu sat behind us with Yeoshin.

"Let's take a picture Bomi!" Jaesun suggested, already taking out his phone and tapping the camera application.

"This will be our first picture together so why not," I said.

He focused the camera on the both of us; I put up a peace sign with my fingers and curved up my lips. *Snap!* He then squished his face against my cheek and snapped a photo; he took a couple more of us acting cute together.

"Let's take one with my phone!" I took out phone as well and Jaesun held it up.

"Bomi, look over here!" He called my name and I looked over at him and to my surprise his lips were on mine. *Snap!* We both set our favorite pictures of each other as our wallpapers.

"Here," Jaesun handed me one side of his earbud and instead of me putting it in my ear myself, he leaned over and placed it in my ear for me. I blushed at his cute actions and placed my head on Jaesun's shoulder listening to the peaceful music and slowly drifted to sleep.

"Bomi, wake up we're here," Jaesun cooed in my ear and I slowly fluttered my eyes open.

The bus came to a complete stop and everyone cheered that we finally made it to our destination but as for me, I was too groggy to even make a sound.

"Grab all your stuff and let's head out!" Mrs. Chan ordered exiting out of the bus.

After we all got out we grouped together to hear more instructions from Mrs. Chan.

"So your cabins are listed over there on that board thing and then just do whatever you want. Afterwards at noon, meet at the lodge over there for lunch and we will then have some games and activities for you guys to do and yes you all have to participate," Mrs. Chan instructed, most people groaned and whined.

"Finally at 6 o'clock, meet back at the lodge for dinner. After dinner, there will be a bonfire and you can do whatever you want."

"Will we see you a lot?" Some nerdy kid asked.

"No, not really only at break, lunch, dinner, and the activities," she answered. "Kay, now go do whatever." She waved her dismissing us.

Sometimes I just really love Mrs. Chan, she can be really nice, cool, and scary but she really has the personality of a careless teenager that knows how to get things done to be done and get over with.

Jaesun, Cheolsu, Yeoshin and I slowly made our way to the board to see what our cabin number is.

"We are cabin three," Yeoshin informed us. "That way!"

When we arrived at our cabin, we stepped inside and were amazed how big and nice it was. It isn't an old shabby cabin; it's more modernized with painted walls and the cleanliness to it. There were two beds by each wall so four beds total, the bathroom was clean with tile floors and two sinks.

"I pick this bed!" I jumped on the bed in the far corner on the right side.

"Let's push the beds together," Jaesun suggested, I jumped back up and helped push the two beds together.

"We're only going to be here for today and then tomorrow do you guys really need to sleep together?" Yeoshin questioned us.

"When you get a girlfriend, you'll understand," Jaesun put his hand on Yeoshin's shoulder; Yeoshin shrugged his hand off his shoulder.

"As if I'll ever get a girl," Yeoshin returned to his bed.

During the whole four hours, we did make some conversation to one another but it soon dispersed and we were all staring at our phones.

"Oh, its twelve o'clock you guys, let's go eat I'm starving!" I said getting up from the bed.

We headed over to the lodge where the cafeteria is located. Jaesun and I were walking, hand in hand, as we entered the delicious smelling room. They were serving Green Onion pancakes, rice, and kimchi with a choice of water, banana milk, chocolate milk, or fruit punch. I picked up my tray and grabbed a chocolate milk carton but then it was all taken away by Jaesun.

"No, you already have your tray to worry about," I said trying to reach for my tray but Jaesun was one, taller than me by like at least 5 inches and two, we were already at our reserved table.

"Don't worry, I got this," he said and sat down, gently placing down both trays. "I once too worked at restaurant."

Later, Yeoshin and Cheolsu came over and sat down as well. "Cool ,we have a special table sign thingy," Yeoshin flicked the small paper that was attached to the a metal stick that read: **Cabin 3 - Park Bomi, Park Jaesun, Choi Cheolsu, Lee Yeoshin.**

"Ahhh," Jaesun held a piece of pancake in front of my mouth and I happily ate it.

"I thought you said you wouldn't do this kind of stuff," Cheolsu said, scrunching up his face in disgust.

"Don't blame me, blame him," I pointed to Jaesun with a shrug off my shoulders.

"Like I said you'll understand when you get a girlfriend," Jaesun pointed out once more.

Cheolsu rolled his eyes. "Whatever."

After lunch, we stepped outside in the open; I squinted and shielded my eyes from the bright sunlight. We headed over to the big grass field where Mrs. Chan was standing in the middle of waiting for us to arrive.

"Well, hurry up now!" She called out to us with a big wave of her arm. We all began to run towards her like a herd of cattle.

"Mrs. Chan, I'm in heels!" Minah waddled around the grass field trying to keep her balance.

"Does it look like I care, Minah? Okay then. So to start things off, we will have nice but intense game of soccer, alrighty?" She informed us. "So let's see Bomi and Dasom are going to be our team captains!"

I was a bit shocked since I'm never picked first or at least for team captain for anything, not even for mathletes!

"Bomi picks first," Mrs. Chan said and stepped aside.

"Jaesun," I immediately said and I hear Dasom curse quietly.

"Taejoon," Dasom flipped her hair to the side and side-eyed me.

"Cheolsu."

"Kyung."

"Yeoshin."

"Aiden."

And so on we went picking our team. I picked two other guys from Velocity as well as Alex and Doyoon while Dasom chose her crew and Dujoon's crew.

My team huddled together and started planning how we will defeat Dasom's team.

"Uh... to be honest, I'm not really good at soccer. I only played a few times," I scratched the back of my head and smiled. awkwardly. "But I will try my best to be in front playing."

"Are you sure, Bomi?" Cheolsu asked. "It's get really intense out there. When you have the ball, it's all on you."

"Of course," I assured him and clapped his shoulder.

"Bomi, Cheolsu, Doyoon and I will be up at the front playing," Jaesun added to the plan.

"I'll be goalie then," Alex said and stretched his body out and boy, can that boy stretch.

"So the rest of us will be defense then," Lucas said and we all nodded.

"After planning out, please play rock, paper, and scissor to see who gets the ball first and then enjoy your game!" Mrs. Chan yelled out then went over and sat down on a bench next to a man.

"Team Captains will decide who plays the ball first!" Taejoon yelled out.

"Hi, Miss Park Loser," Dasom greeted and stuck out her fist in between us. I glared at her but she just smiled.

"Rock, paper, scissors!" We both played. I chose rock while she chose scissors.

"Ha!" I yelled out. "We get to play first!"

Once we all got in our positions, I kicked the ball towards Jaesun who started dribbling it towards the other side. Which he then passed it to Cheolsu but quickly lost it to Taejoon who charged to our side. He pushed Doyoon, with his hand, out of the way causing him to land hard on his back.

"Yah, that's illegal!" Lucas yelled out and pushed Dujoon who pushed back.

“He was in my way!” Taejoon protested and folded his arms.

“That’s how you play, stupid,” Cheolsu rolling his eyes. “But not with your hands.”

“So what I play in the district soccer team,” Taejoon said in defense.

“Ha, more like your backyard soccer team,” Yeoshin joked which caused the other boys to laugh.

“Come on enough, we have to go see if Doyoon is okay,” I said, pushing past the boys. We all ran over to Doyoon’s still body.

"Are you okay?" I asked him.

"Yeah, I'm fine," He sat up and winced to the pain.

"I’m sorry but you can't play anymore," I said, helping him up.

"No, I'm fine I can't let this team down," he replied, slowly climbing up onto his feet.

"You can play when you feel better," Jaesun added and grabbed a hold of Doyoon’s shoulder.

"Fine," he said and sat on the bench Mrs. Chan was on.

"Jiseok, you're going to be offense but make sure you be defense as well when the ball gets near the goal," I directed him.

"Yes ma'am!" He saluted me and headed to the middle of the field.

"You want to play this way then let's play," I muttered to myself.

The ball was kicked and I ran for it. Dasom was also running for it but I was a minute or two faster because, come on, who runs in flats? Oh yeah, Miss Perfection over there does.

I dribbled the ball towards the goal; dodging everyone on the other team's attack. I passed over the ball to Jaesun who shot it right in the goal. We cheered in excitement, jumping up and down.

AUTHOR

"Minah, what are you doing?!" Dasom yelled and stomped her feet down in anger.

"I don't know how to be goalie, Dasom! I hate sports!" Minah whined. "And remember I'm wearing my heels!"

"Oh please!" Dasom ruffed up her hair but then quickly fixed it.

Why wear heels when we were obviously told we were doing an activity? Dasom thought and shook her head.

"Okay kids, last game and then you can do whatever you want. Just remember at eight o'clock, we are having our campfire!" Mrs. Chan called out after tapping the screen on her phone and talking to the man beside her for about an hour.

Bomi and Dasom's team were neck and neck, fifteen to sixteen; it's the most intense game out of everyone else who was playing soccer. It's so intense that everyone stopped what they were doing and gathered around the sidelines to watch.

Cheolsu had the ball in between his feet; he stared intensely over at where the ball's final destination should go. The ball was kicked and they were off, the ball was everywhere it barely reached any of the goals. The ball bounced off Kyung's head and landed right in the middle of the field.

Dasom and Bomi made eye contacted and sprinted for it like hungry savages.

BOMI

I ran as fast as my legs could carry but it seem like Dasom learned how to run faster in her flats. She stuck out her right arm and pushed me out of the way. We both fell but the force from her push was too much that I landed on my back. It felt like all the air was pushed right out of my lungs like a deflating balloon.

I fell into a deep abyss of darkness.

AUTHOR

Everyone gasped at the unconscious player, despite treating her like trash and beating her to pulp, they were shocked to her to see her knocked out like that.

"Ha, stupid girl," Dasom laughed and clung onto her side.

"Bomi!" Jaesun came running over to Bomi's side.

"Ow, Jaesun help me. My ankle hurts, Bomi tripped me!" Dasom whined and gripped her ankle but Jaesun just glared at her. Jaesun scooped up Bomi bridal style and carried her to Mrs. Chan.

"Jaesun!" Dasom screamed but Jaesun kept walking. "Taejoon..." But Taejoon just stepped over Dasom legs and proceeded to walk away.

UNKNOWN

It felt weird seeing Bomi so happy today, her smile looked so sweet and...

What are you doing you don't like poor, weak, and ugly girls! You like girls like Dasom or Minah or Insoo or at least hot girls! Why is my heart acting this way? I thought as I walked back to my cabin.

AUTHOR

"It's going to be okay, Bomi," Jaesun said, even though, he knows Bomi couldn't hear him. On arrival, Jaesun bowed his head down as a greeting.

"Oh my goodness, what happened?" Mrs. Chan asked completely dumbfounded to see her favorite student senseless in Jaesun's arms.

"She was struck by an arm and went unconscious after landing on her back," Jaesun explained.

"I knew someone would get hurt but I didn't expect it to be Bomi," Mrs. Chan shook her head. "Honey, we have another one."

The man who sat - mysterious and quietly - next to Mrs. Chan stood up from the bench and took a grand look at Bomi laying immobile in Jaesun's grasp.

"I've seen this many times when I go to high school soccer matches. She's unconscious from shock and the fact that she probably felt like all the air was pushed out of her lungs so she couldn't breathe properly. So I recommend you take her to her cabin, let her rest, and then when she wakes up in, oh, maybe an hour give her these pills because when she wakes up her back will feel sore," he explained.

He handed Jaesun a cup with a couple pills in it but Jaesun's hands were full so he held the cup in between his teeth. Regardless of having his hands full, Jaesun bowed his head once more and took long strides back to their cabin.

"Wow! Man, you're too good at this," Mrs. Chan hit her husband on the chest and he chuckled.

"I work at a hospital for a reason, Minjung," he said and wrapped his arm around his wife's shoulders.

"Psh... More like a clinic," she rolled her eyes and folded her arms.

"Same thing, it's in a hospital, okay! Plus, I work more than the hospital doctors, people always come in with minor injuries," he explained.

"Whatever you say, Steven," she slipped under his arm and walked away from the bench.

"Hey Jaesun, let me get that," Cheolsu took the cup from Jaesun's mouth and pushed open the cabin door.

"Thanks," Jaesun said, setting Bomi carefully onto the bed.

"So what did the doctor say?" Cheolsu asked, setting the pills on the window sill above Bomi's bed.

"Well, he said a lot of things but the parts I caught was she will wake up in an hour and that she will feel pain so give her those pills," Jaesun answered.

BOMI

I woke up with a strange pain in my back; it was a very sharp pain that ran up my spine at the slightest move.

Oh yeah, *I remember I got knocked out by Dasom.* I looked around and there was Jaesun sitting at the edge, tapping away at his phone.

"Oh hey, you're awake," Jaesun said with a smile. "Doctor says to take these for your back pain."

I inhaled sharply as I sat up; Jaesun put an arm around my waist and pulled me up into a sitting position.

"Thanks," I said taking the pills from the cup and handed me a water bottle.

"Feel better?" Jaesun asked after I took the pills. I nodded my head. "Good, we have four hours until the campfire. Everyone is hanging outside, do you want to go?"

I nodded my head and swung my legs over the bed. Jaesun lent out a helping hand and I gladly took it.

We headed outside and everyone was hanging out with their own little cliques. We scanned the area for our little group which was made up of Doyoon, Alex, Lucas, Yeoshin, Cheolsu, and Yano.

When we finally spotted them, sitting on the grass field, we quickly walked towards them and sat down.

"Oh hey, are you okay, Bomi?" Cheolsu asked.

"Yeah I'm fine now," I answered. "Thanks for your concern."

"Ay, that's what friends are for, they worry and care for each other," Lucas said, wrapping his arm around Yano which then turned into a chokehold.

"Oh, guess what Bomi? That man that's sitting next to Mrs. Chan is her husband and he's also the doctor that helped you and me," Doyoon explained.

"Really, wow they look really good together," I said nodding and looking at them from across the field.

"I bet that's going to be you two when you get married," Yeoshin pointed out to me and everyone nodded in agreement.

"Ha really?" I blush at his comment as I rubbed my nape.

We talked for some time, when the sun began to set behind the tall trees meaning it was almost time for the campfire.

"Hey Bomi, let's go somewhere," Jaesun said and grabbed my hand as I climbed up onto my feet.

"Where are you going?" Alex asked.

"They need some alone time Alex, if you know what I mean," Lucas said, making kissing noises which got everyone laughing. I walked over to him and smacked him on the head.

"Remember when the day of your competition and we went to go eat BBQ?" I asked giving him a you-better-watch-what-you're-saying look.

He gasped. "Just go!" he waved his hand and gently pushing me away.

"So where are you taking me?" I asked Jin as we walked with our hands intertwined.

"I don't know I thought, we could go on for a walk, just the two of us," he answered. We walked to an area where there weren't much people around but it was still crowded with people here and there. I had a strange feeling of someone watching us but I just shrugged it off.

We stopped midstride, Jaesun squeezed my hand. I looked up at him and he gave me a warm smile. "Finally, we could just be alone."

"There are still people around us, stupid," I said and pushing his head back.

"I know but they don't care," he leaned down and put his forehead on mine. "And I don't care." He cocked his head to the side and placed his soft lips onto mine.

A high-pitched was heard just seconds after our lips met but I shrugged it off once more.

DASOM

I watched as Jaesun and Bomi walked to somewhere alone hand-in-hand. They were talking about something; I couldn't hear them, when suddenly Jaesun put his forehead on Bomi's which made me gasp.

"No this can't be, don't you two dare do it!" But before you know it Jaesun turned his head and kissed Bomi. I screamed. "They're dating!"

"Who?" Minah asked me.

"Bomi and Jaesun," I said through gritted teeth. I wasn't necessary depressed by this turn of events, I'm more angry.

Minah gasped and clasped my arms. "Shall I spread it?"

"Do you really need ask? Tell the others girls too," I ordered and smiled.

UNKNOWN

Oh so she's dating that Jaesun guy. I snickered as I witnessed them kiss but why'd my chest have a weird sharp pain when I saw this happening.

She looks so precious when she smiles and looks so happy but I think it would look even better if I made her smile and made her happy. She will be *mine.*

Chapter 25

BOMI

As time went by, the sun seems to slowly seep away letting darkness take over. More people kept glancing our way and whispered things to each other. It's probably about us but we didn't care.

"You know, they actually look cute together."

"What are you talking about she's just some poor ugly girl, she doesn't even wear makeup."

"But to think about, she's actually pretty but not as pretty as us just like a level or two below us."

"Jaemi or Bosun, I think I like Jaemi better."

"Jaemi is so cute!"

"We should get to know Bomi better!"

"We can't! Dasom is going to kill us and treat us like Bomi; we can't let our image go down!"

"But she doesn't seem like a bad person what if she's not even poor?"

Their whispers polluted the air as they spoke, however, we can pretty much hear them since those girls are really bad whisperers. Their words made me happy but upset at the same time.

It was now time for the campfire and I'm so excited just because it's my first campfire. Students started bringing their blankets to cuddle with their boyfriends or girlfriend or with their best friends so Jaesun and I brought one as well. The fire was blazing hot on our faces but we still kept the blanket wrapped around us. Jaesun pulled it tighter around us and pulled me closer to him.

"Hasn't this been an interesting day?" Jaesun chuckled.

"It sure has," I said, leaning my head on his shoulder.

Everyone was talking and laughing around us, doing their own business, some people were being comedians or trying to show us their cool dance moves under the beautiful lit sky.

"Jaesun, look at all the stars!" I said and pointed my finger up at the sky. "Wow, they're so sparkly!"

"Not as sparkly as your eyes," Jaesun said and I snapped my head up to look at him.

"You're too cheesy!" I scrunched up my face and slapped his chest.

"But you love cheese," Jaesun replied.

"What? Okay then," I shook my head totally confused; I turned my attention back to the stars.

"Look there's the big dipper," Jaesun pointed out

"Where?" I asked, he took my hand and pointed to the constellation.

After seeing the constellation, our hands were still up in the air so I moved my hand so that our fingers enlaced together. We both looked at each other and smiled, we sat in silence enjoying each other's' presence.

"Jaesun, I'll be right back I'm going to the bathroom," I said, getting up.

"Do you need to me to come with you, in just in case?" He asked, standing up as well.

"No, I'll be fine and if they do get me, I'll try to ruin their makeup or hair before they touch me," I said with a smile.

"That's my girl but be careful they go crazy if you ruin their eye makeup," he said, playing along.

"That's where I'll ruin first!" I laughed, walking away.

"Wait, here take this," he handed me a flashlight. "It's dark over there."

"Thanks," I took the flashlight from his hands.

"Be safe and scream if you're in trouble, I will be there before you know it," he said and placed his forehead on mine.

"You worry too much," I said, pecking his lips and then walked away. I turned on the flashlight and let the light guide me to the bathroom house.

After doing my business, I headed outside to wash my hands. I found it weird how the sinks were outside the toilet but whatever.

I heard some shuffling and footsteps, I shined my flashlight around. "Jaesun?" I called out but there was no answer.

I began shake in fear since we were in the woods – the woods are always haunted with ghosts. The worst part was: I was *alone.*

Suddenly, I was picked up and carried off. I dropped the flashlight, which crashed to the ground with a crack but the bulb shining brightly.

I screamed but it was soon covered with someone with rough hands. My back smacked against a brick wall (the bathroom house) and was being held tightly to it. I couldn't make out who it was but I can tell this person was male, tall, and strong.

"Who are you?" I managed to say, with his hand still covered my mouth.

He then took his hand off my mouth but before I could even make the slightest sound, he rammed his lips onto mine. I started screaming but they were all mumbled because his lips moving around mine.

"I don't care if you already belong to someone, I just want to make you mine," he said his lips moving down to my neck and putting his hand up the back of my shirt, touching my bare back.

I know this voice but who does it belong too? I thought as I tried to escape his tight grip.

"Jaesun..." I tried screaming out but he just slapped his hand back onto my mouth.

"Say another word and my lips go back on yours'!" He threatened. "A little birdie told me you had a crush on me back in freshmen year so I thought you'd be happy finally having a kiss from me."

"You're just an asshole, *Taejoon!"* I said and I pushed his hand away.

"Am I?" I can tell he was smirking. I kicked him in the leg which made him cringe and I started running.

"Jaesun!" I yelled as loud as I can but I was caught by Dujoon. He started to put rough kisses onto my neck again.

"Jaesun!" I cried out as tears poured down my cheek.

"Get your hands off of her, bastard!"

I was dropped to the ground and heard punches being thrown and then someone running away. My guesses were, it was Dujoon running off.

"Bomi, are you okay?" Jaesun asked me as he helped me off the ground I engulfed him into a tight embrace.

"I was so scared, Jaesun!" I cried into his chest. "I didn't know what to do and... and..."

"I know, I'm sorry I wasn't fast enough," he rubbed my back to try to comfort me. "You were taking a long time to come back so I started walking towards the bathrooms when I heard you scream so I ran as fast as I could."

"I'm so glad you came," I wept.

"I know, let's go back to the cabin, it's getting late," he suggested and I nodded but then he bent down hinting he's going to give me a piggy back ride to the cabin, I hopped on.

When we arrived back at the cabin, it was still empty. I took a quick shower to rub off all the Taejoon on my body. I felt much better after scrubbing off every infected area of the disease.

I hopped into bed next to Jaesun. He quickly grabbed my towel to help dry my hair which kept dripping all over the bed.

"Feel better?" He asked as he rubbed my head with the towel.

"Yeah, a lot better," I answered, snapping my head back and gave him an assuring smile.

"What was he even doing to you? I couldn't see it was too dark but I know he was hugging you tightly," He said.

"He was talking about making me his and that he doesn't care if I had a boyfriend and he kissed me on my lips and he was putting rough kisses on my neck, he even put his hand up the back my shirt then he talked about when we first met and when I had a crush on him," I explained.

"He what?

That's I'm gonna go kill that sudden of a..." Jaesun stood up but I grabbed his arm.

"Jaesun, just leave it," I told him.

"Leave what, Bomi? That's basically sexual harassment," Jaesun explained to me. "I will never let you go through that."

I bit my lip. "I know but he's done it with every other girl, I'm just the only one who didn't like it."

"Fine but I will never forget what he has done to you," he sat back down by my side. "So did you really have a crush on him?"

"Yeah, that was freshman year. Then later on, he turned his back on me and started bullying me. That's why it was hard for me to trust anyone or at least love anyone," I replied.

"That was all in the past so you can forget about it. Now you got me," he leaned over and kissed my cheek. "So I heard tomorrow everyone is heading to the beach to hang out and then we go home at two o'clock."

"Really, I'm probably going to be the only girl wearing jeans to the beach," I said, lying down on the bed.

"You can borrow my shorts," Jaesun said, also lying down next to me.

"Uh I don't think so," I moved my head onto his chest and he started fiddling with my hair which I found relaxing. "But it's okay, I don't want to show too much skin anyway."

I closed my eyes and drifted off to sleep.

~ The Next Day ~

I woke up to the sun rays that shining down on my face, I turned around to see Jaesun's flawless face.

Once I got a good look, I slowly got up to wash up and prepare to go back home.

But then I was pulled back down. "Where are you going?" Jaesun asked with his eyes closed, holding me tightly.

"Where else?" I rolled my eyes. "I need to brush my teeth."

"Five more minutes we can brush together," he whispered, rolling me over to his side.

"You can sleep five more minutes and I can go brush," I said, pushing his strong arms away and walked into the bathroom.

When I finished, I walked back into the room to see all the boys awake and packing up their belongings.

"Oh Bomi, I found this by the door. I think this is for you," Jaesun said, handing me a neatly folded pile clothes: It was shorts and a t-shirt. The shorts were a beige color while the t-shirt was white with light black strips going across.

"Jaesun, you didn't have to," I said taking the clothes from him.

"I didn't do it," he said.

"What?" I gave him a confused look.

"They were by the door when I woke up," he said. I looked over to the other boys who just shrugged their shoulders.

There was a little pink sticky note attached on the top.

These were too small for me so I wanted you to have them. Please treat them well and wear them with confidence too!

~ Friends

P.S. Wear them at the beach so we know how cute it looks on you!

~ Last Night ~

AUTHOR

"Ahhhhh!"

"What's wrong, Yoojung?" Serin asked, running into the bathroom.

"I'm too fat to fit in my shorts!" Yoojung cried out as she tried to squeeze through the tight shorts. "I wore these last week!"

"Just throw them out and get new ones," Serin said taking it like it was no big deal.

"I can't just throw them out. They were expensive," Yoojung said with serious face.

"How much were they?" Serin asked folding her arms.

"Thirty-six dollars..." Yoojung said, biting her lip.

"Yah!" Serin was shocked knowing her friend was not exactly rich or poor. "Why'd you buy them?"

"Because they were so cute and they looked great with my legs," Yoojung said, pouting. "What am I supposed to wear to the beach tomorrow now?"

"Oh I don't know maybe the ten million other shorts and t-shirts you bought with you," Serin said, sarcastically.

"Not funny! What am I supposed to do with this?" Yoojung questioned, hold up the pair of shorts. "None of you guys are this size."

"I got it, give them to Bomi," Serin answered.

"But we can't be seen with her," Yoojung whispered.

"Who says we have to personally give it to her," Serin smiled and finally Yoojung caught on.

"Wait, she can't just have the shorts. She needs something to go with it," Yoojung pointed out and dug through her suitcase.

After searching the right shirt for Bomi, they folded the clothes up neatly and stuck a sticky note on top and wrote a small note.

"You sure we won't get caught?" Yoojung whispered as they walked through the dark forest towards Bomi's cabin.

"Yoojung quit worrying. Lights are out to be at eleven and supposedly Mrs. Chan and her husband are going around checking the cabins and so we will pretend to be them and sneak the clothes inside," Serin whispered the plan to her friend.

Finally when they reached Bomi's cabin, they shined the flashlight in through the window to make sure no one was awake. They then slowly opened the door and dropped the clothes in.

BOMI

I went into the bathroom and changed into my new clothes and they fitted perfectly. I walked out feeling a little embarrassed since I was showing a lot of skin. I know I wear shorts and a t-shirt to gym but these shorts were short like a lot shorter.

"How do I look?" I asked and all the boys looked up with shocked expressions.

"Wow, just stunning!" Jaesun said.

"Really, it's not too short right?" I asked, rubbing my bare legs.

"Not at all," he answered.

When everyone was ready, we all headed out and walked along the path to head to the beach.

The beach was so glorious with its golden sand, the waves crashing at our feet and the sun beaming down on our faces.

"Let's go!" Jaesun said, dragging me to the water.

"No! Jaesun, I don't plan to get these clothes wet!" I yelled, trying to bury my feet into the sand to stop him from dragging me any further.

He stopped dragging me. "Okay, I won't do it. Let's just walk alongside the water then."

We held hands as we walked along the crashing waters and since I was the one wearing sandals, I walked closest to the water. I think this scene would've been better if the sun was setting but I guess it doesn't matter as long we were together.

"You should wear outfits like this more often," Jaesun said.

"Ha, you wish," I replied. We stopped walking and he turned me around to look at him.

"Who cares anyway because you look beautiful with whatever you wear," I stared into his brown eyes.

"Even in a clown suit?" I asked.

"Even in a clown suit," he leaned in and kissed me gently on my lips.

"Okay, you kids have everything!" Mrs. Chan called out.

"Yes!" We all replied with our bags in hand and ready to get boarded onto the bus.

“You sure because I don’t want anyone crying that they left their eyeliner in their cabin,” Mrs. Chan said.

“We just want to go home, Mrs. Chan!”

“Alright, alright! Let’s get going!” She waved her hand and climbed up onto the bus.

We then boarded the bus and making our way back to Seoul.

Chapter 26

BOMI

There is only two weeks left until school is over and I'm so excited! The bullying became less frequent though I'm still called names here and there but I don't care anymore.

Anyway, another important event is this week on Friday is Prom Day and all the guys around the school are asking girls out. I didn't really want to go to prom just hang out at home with Jaesun but at the same time I do want to go and even though Jaesun and I are, you know, dating, I do wish he would at least ask me to go with him because (if there were any guys) what if someone does ask me to go. Of course, I would reject them but still you never know.

~ Prom Day ~

It was prom day; Jaesun and I were eating lunch together when Jaesun all of a sudden stood up from the table.

"Excuse me for a moment," he said.

"Okay," I said clueless to what was going to happen next.

After a few minutes of waiting for Jaesun, someone tapped me on my shoulder.

"Ahem, Bomi."

I turned around hearing Jaesun's voice. Jaesun was standing behind with a bouquet of flowers in his hands.

"I know this is a little late and obviously, we are already dating but it doesn't sound right if I didn't ask this question so will you go to prom with me?" He asked, holding out the flowers to me.

The cafeteria was silent and I can tell everyone was anticipating for my answer, despite, they already know that we are a thing.

"Of course, I will!" I said taking the flowers and stood up to hug him. Surprisingly, everyone clapped and cheered loudly for us.

JAESUN

I knew that her answer was going to be yes but I was just so relieved that she accepted.

I bought the tickets a head of time and thought of asking her later but then I kind of lost the tickets. But luckily, I found them so that's why I asked her on the day of prom.

BOMI

What am I going to do now; I don't even have a dress? I thought really hard on what I was going to do as Jaesun and I walked to my locker to put away my textbook.

I opened my locker and a small note fell out, I picked it up and read the note.

Meet us at the back of the school when school ends for a special surprise. Please come, I'm sure you will love it!

~ Your ~~guardian angels~~ Friends

"Sounds pretty sketchy to me so I'll come with you in just in case if this surprise is something that you won't love at all," Jaesun said, squeezing my hand.

"Okay," I said, shoving the note in my pocket. "I wonder why they crossed out guardian angels."

~ End of the Day ~

We walked to the back of the school and saw two girls standing outside.

"Oh, Bomi!" One of them greeted and I bowed a little. She was a little taller than the other girl and bigger. Not saying she's fat. No. Not at all. She's skinny but a good skinny (if you understand what I mean).

"Ay, no need to be formal," the other one said. She was the shorter one. I think we were about the same height she was also skinny, skinnier than the tall one though.

"I'm Yoojung," the tall one greeted first.

"I'm Serin," the shorter greeted next.

"We're the girls who gave you the shorts and the t-shirts," Yoojung said. "Or, at least, I did since they were my clothes that got too small for me for some odd reason."

"oh my goodness, thank you so much," I said giving them a kind smile. "So what's the meaning of you guys secretly putting a note in my locker?"

"Oh well, you know prom is tonight and we would like to take you shopping for your dress for tonight!" Serin said.

"Oh that's okay, I don't have any money anyway," I said, recalling all the random stuff I had purchased lately. So I thought it about time to stop and save it for important random stuff.

"Oh don't worry, I'll buy," Serin said.

"No, I can't make you do that," I said still refusing, no matter how much I really want to go with them.

"Hey, I have money. I'm not trying to brag but my parents own a company and I'm pretty sure buying you something won't hurt us at all," Serin said, taking my hand. "So will you come along, please?"

"I'm sure you want to look nice for your Prince Charming," Yoojung said and looked at Jaesun.

"Okay I'll go!" I said happily.

"Yay! Don't worry we will take her to prom tonight so you just arrive at school and be amazed!" Yoojung told Jaesun as Serin dragged me away to her car.

"Wait!" Jaesun called out and ran to me.

"Come on, love birds we don't have all day, prom starts in five hours," Serin said tapping her foot.

"Just one second," I said and turned to face Jaesun.

"Just be safe and I'll at the front of the school at eight o'clock, waiting for you," Jin said kissing the top of my forehead.

"Okay," I said.

"Kay, let's go!" Yoojung said dragging me away.

We hopped into the backseat of Serin's car and drove off.

"Austin, drive us to me mall please," Serin told her driver.

"Yes, Miss Park," I bowed his head through the rearview mirror.

JAESUN

After Bomi went off with Yoojung and Serin, I started walking home and then an idea popped into my head. I took out my phone and dialed the number.

"Hey Cheolsu, you want to go shopping with me?" I asked him.

"For what?" Cheolsu asked.

"Prom," I answered.

"I don't have a date plus I didn't buy a ticket," Cheolsu replied.

"Exactly, they are still selling tickets for thirty minutes at eight o'clock when you get in you try and score on a girl that is alone or with a group of friends especially a group of girls," I said.

"Okay I'll go with you," Cheolsu said.

"Yes! Okay I'm on my way to pick you up," I ended the call and quickly headed towards Cheolsu's house.

BOMI

We arrived at a dress store that looked and smelled expensive.

“We already got our dresses so this shopping will be focused all on you,” Yoojung said to me.

They shoved me into the dressing room and handed me a whole variety of dresses. I tried on dresses all shapes, sizes, and colors. I avoided anything too colorful and sparkly, anything too long or too short, and anything too poufy or skin-tight. Also, dresses that were strapless were a no go. Every dress I tried on, I had to walk out and show the girls.

Finally, when I found the perfect dress, I stepped out the dressing room and spun around showing the girls.

"Amazing!" exclaimed Yoojung, clapping her hands.

"Beautiful, Jaesun will love it!" Serin said.

"Really?" I smiled and spun around once more.

The dress I chose is a cute small pink dress with a black sparkly belt that wrapped around my waist. The dress length ended just right above my knees; the same length as our school uniform skirts.

"Here try these on," Yoojung handed me a pair of black flat.

"Perfect!" Serin smiled brightly. “Dear lord, I think I might cry.”

After I changed out of the dress, we headed to the cashier and paid for my dress. I was going to faint because it was so expensive. I was so grateful they would do this for me.

"Thank you so much, Serin," I will definitely cherish this dress forever.

"No problem, now we have... OH MY GOSH! We only have an hour till prom hurry let's go get our hair and makeup done before we're late!" Serin said, running to the car. “Austin, head to the hair salon and please step on it.”

JAESUN

“Here, try this on,” I handed Cheolsu a tux.

“Yah but this isn't my color,” Cheolsu whined.

“Oh my goodness, just try it on,” I rolled my eyes and pushed him into the dressing room. “We only have an hour left.”

I also went inside one of the dressing room to try on my tux. We both got out at the same time and admired our handsome selves in the mirror.

“I guess this dark red is my color,” Cheolsu nodded as he posed in the mirror.

“I told you,” I said as I ruffled up his brown hair. “Navy blue isn't that bad on me either.”

BOMI

Once we arrived at the salon, we dashed right in. We quickly got seated and the stylist got us all ready in just minutes.

I looked at myself in the mirror and was truly astonished at my transformation. It like looking at another dimension of beauty, I like the first dimension of beauty without make-up better.

My hair was filled with simple curls and my makeup was very, simple and natural, nothing too crazy. I had eyeliner, mascara and light pink lipstick to with match with dress. Since we didn't have much time, we were scooted to the back into a changing room and changed into our dresses. We hopped back into the car and made our way towards school.

"I'm sorry Bomi, we have to drop you off right here, I hope you understand," Serin said as we stopped a few feet before the school gates.

"I understand you did so much for me today and I thank you for that," I said, getting out and walked the rest to school. Good thing they didn't drop me off really far away, it was only a two second walk. I climbed up the stairs and I felt all pairs of eyes on me. I felt like a movie star in the movies walking down the red carpet except I was walking up stairs dull gray cement steps instead.

I see Jaesun talking to Cheolsu when he turned around and looked at me. I blushed and pushed my hair behind one ear.

"There's my Cinderella!" Jaesun walked over to me and pecked my cheek. I took a good look at Jaesun who was wearing a navy blue suit. It didn't really match my outfit but it still worked.

"And here is my prince charming," I smiled at him.

"Come on, let's go," Jaesun slipped his hand into mine and walked me inside but instead of going into the gym where the dance was held, we went up onto the roof.

"Why are we here?" I asked him.

"Look for yourself," he moved aside and revealed what he had setup. The roof was glowing with glowing lights and a table with two chairs and on the table was a bowl of salad.

"Salad? Really?" I raised an eyebrow at him.

"Well... you know... umm..." he rubbed the back of his neck.

"And I love it," I held both of his arms and made him sit down.

We ate some salad and talked for a bit. Jaesun got out his phone and played some beautiful orchestra music; he got and stuck out his hand towards me.

"May I have this dance?" He asked.

"Oh I can't dance," I said, waving my hands at him.

"Oh, really now? Not what I heard from Cheolsu," he grabbed my hand and pulled me up.

"But that was like pop music, I never danced to a slow song before," I explained.

"It's okay, just stand on my feet," I did as I was told and hugged myself close to Jaesun's chest.

"Jaesun?" I called his name

"Yes," he answered.

"Why of all girls did you choose me? I'm not pretty, I don't have a lot of money, and my life has been a nightmare."

"Well because I have all of that," we stopped dancing and I snapped my head up.

"Eh?" I have him a confused look.

Jaesun chuckled. "I'm good looking, I have a good amount of money, and well, my life isn't good. It's perfect now that it's filled with you," he said and returned dancing.

"You're too chest and weird," I giggled and leaning my head against his chest as we slowly swayed side by side.

"I love you too, Bomi."

Chapter 27

BOMI

I looked at my reflection with a wide grin. Today I decided to wear a plain white V-neck, a black cardigan, a black A-line skirt, and my black and white polka-dot shoes. It was a nice day to wear black and white or any day is always a great day t black and white.

"You ready for today?" Jaesun asked giving me a back hug. Jaesun and I were wearing matching outfits (of course, he was wearing black skinny jeans and not a skirt).

I nodded my head in response and gave him kiss on the cheek. "Let's get going before we're late for school."

Today everyone didn't have to wear their school uniform and basically wear whatever they wanted but must be school appropriate.

We walked up the school steps and into the school building, hand in hand, waving hi to the other students who waved back at us.

"Good morning, Mrs. Chan!" Jaesun and I bowed down.

"Ah, isn't it my favorite students!" She clapped her hands and hugged us both. "Please seat down, class should be starting soon."

The bell rang and everyone scattered to their seats, everyone sat down with large smiles plastered on their faces.

"My beautiful and handsome students, I am proud to say congrats on your graduation today!" She yelled and we all cheered. "I'm glad I got the chance to teach you all you."

Yes, you all heard correctly. Today is graduation day! The day we were all waiting for and now it has come.

"Today is a short day with our graduation ceremony and our hall of fame awards," she informed us. "Now, let's get your graduation gowns, shall we?"

Our graduations cap and gowns were royal blue and for honors students, we get a special gold ribbon to go around our shoulders with Honors stitched into it.

"Now that everyone is dressed beautifully in their gowns, let's head outside to the field on this beautiful day," Mrs. Chan called out.

"Welcome, parents and students of Junseo High," the principal, Mrs. Kim, greeted. She is a middle-aged woman with fair skin and little wrinkles. "I'm glad to see all these wonderful faces here today..."

She went on and on about the beauty and intelligence of this year's seniors. "I will now call each student from their classroom. We will start on the honors classes. From Mrs. Chan's classroom: Bu Minsung."

One by one each student went up and received their diploma. "Park Bomi."

Surprisingly, everyone cheered and clapped as I walked across the grass up to the stage. Suddenly, I tripped on someone's foot but I was luckily caught by a random male student. "Are you okay?"

"I'm okay, thank you," I smiled at him.

"Gu Taejoon, we had enough of your bullying," he yelled at Taejoon over the crowd.

"I don't care what you have to say," Taejoon smirked and crossed his arms.

I continued walking and walked up onto the stage. "Congratulations," I shook hands with Mrs. Kim and bowed down ninety degrees.

"Let's give a round of applause to our 2015 Junseo High seniors!" Mrs. Kim announced and the crowd went crazy, she then held her hand up to silence the crowd. "Now speeches from our teachers."

Mrs. Chan stood up to the podium. "Hello everyone, I'm Mrs. Chan, an honors teacher here at Junseo. I'm glad to have taught a class of such smart and unintelligent students," everyone gasped. "Don't get me wrong, they are very smart but I knew what went around in the classroom and this school and I am very angry. No, I am outraged with them! Now, I must reveal why I let Miss Park Bomi have males in her cabin are because all of you little kids are abhorrent little bitches!"

Everyone was in complete shock.

I can't believe she just said that, I thought and squeezed Jaesun's hand.

Then someone stood up clapping: Mr. Jeon. All of a sudden everyone was standing and cheering except for the students who knew they did wrong which was about everyone in the school. Even the principal was clapping.

"Now before I go on, I must say I will not be teaching here at Junseo anymore and I will be a professor at Ewha Woman's University as a journalist professor. Before I end this speech, I have one big shout out to my favorite students, congratulations to Park Bomi and Park Jaesun for getting accepted and received a two year scholarship into Seoul University!"

I was truly speechless and so was Jaesun. "Go up!" Serin yelled and pushed me and Jaesun out of our seats.

We got back up on stage and we were handed our certificate and scholarships. "Thank you so much!" Jaesun and I bowed down multiple times towards Mrs. Chan and Mrs. Kim.

We walked back down to our seats. "We did it, Bomi!" Jaesun whispered in my ear.

"Yes, yes we did," I squeezed his hand and smiled.

"Time to hand out awards, we have ten categories: Best Hairstyle, Cutest Couple, Best Dancers, Most Athletic, Most Popular, Most artistic, Class Clown, Most likely to Succeed, Most likely to become a K-pop idol, and Most likely to become a model. Please come up and stay on the stage." Mr. Jeon spoke into the mic.

"For Best Hairstyle, we have Hwang Dasom and Kim Leo, Cutest Couple: Park Jaesun and Park Bomi, Best Dancers: Velocity, Most Athletic: Gu Taejoon and Park Insoo, Most Popular: Bangtan, Most Artistic: Nam Daniel and Im Honey, Class Clown: Lee Alex and Seo Gooksu, Most likely to succeed: Park Bomi and Kim Leo, Most likely to become a K-pop idol: Warrior, and Most likely to become a model: Park Serin and Seo Yoojung, please give a round of applause to our award winners."

After everyone greeted one another, it was time to head home. "Mr. Hyung wants us to go to the restaurant for a surprise dinner," I told Bangtan and Velocity.

I raised my glass of sparkling apple cider in the air. "To surviving senior year!"

"To surviving senior year!" Everyone cheered and drank the fizzy drink.

"So what is everyone's plan for the future?" Kangdae asked.

"Well, Velocity has auditioned at an entertainment, we're still waiting for our acceptance letter," Yeoshin answered and we all clapped.

"I don't know yet, I guess wherever the road takes me," I said with a smile.

"Or us," Jaesun wrapped and arm around my shoulders.

"I still can't believe we graduated," Alex said and we all nodded in agreement.

"You know I can't believe Mrs. Chan cursed and Mrs. Kim agreed with her statement," Doyoon pointed out.

"You must really be her favorite," Lucas said.

"Hey, I did a lot for her. I graded papers, got 100%s on my test and quizzes, had perfect attendance, and did all my notes. It's not a lot to ask for," I shrugged my shoulders.

"So what do you guys plan to do with that scholarship?" Cheolsu asked.

"Emm like I said, wherever the road takes us," I said.

"Well, let's all hope in the near future we will succeed and have a wonderful life!" Yano raised another glass of apple cider and we all did the same.

"To a successful life!" We cheered.

That day was a day to cherish the memories we shared forever and ever.

Epilogue

BOMI

Four years has past now and Jaesun and I are still together living under the same roof. We both work at Yong Su San (the restaurant that I have been working at since high school). We both finished college and got our Masters' in Business since we clearly did not know what we both wanted to be as our dream jobs. Anyway, with the money we saved, we bought a new house that's much bigger than our first one with two stories.

It was a normal day in the house; Jaesun and I were relaxing and watching TV in the living room, when Jaesun started nudging my face with his face.

"What?" I questioned.

"Please?" He asked.

"Please what?" I asked laughed since he was tickling my face.

"Can I have a kiss, please?" he asked, pouting his lips.

"Geez, fine," I wrapped my arms around him and pulled him close to me. He started leaning in close to my face but before our lips touched the doorbell rang.

"Ugh!" Jaesun groaned.

"Yah! I kiss you every day, what difference does this one make?" I rolled my eyes. "I'll go get." He nodded his head. I walked over to the door. "Who is it?" I called.

"It's me," said a familiar voice.

No it can't be, it's not even possible, I thought and I slowly opened the door and who I saw brought tears to my eyes.

"Aaron..." I started crying. "Aaron!" I screamed and jumped on him.

"It's me, Bomi!" He squeezed me tightly.

"Bomi, is everything alright?" Jaesun came running

over to the front door. "I heard you scream so I came running."

"Jaesun, look it's Aaron!" I said letting go of Aaron.

"You mean your cousin but how?" Jaesun was also dumbfounded.

"How are you here?" I asked Aaron, wiping my tears away with his thumbs.

"Let me explain inside," Aaron said.

"Of course, come in," I said moving aside.

"You haven't changed much Bomi," Aaron said as he sat down on the couch and we sat across from him.

"You haven't either, I recognized you by your chicken legs," I laughed.

"Yah!" He yelled. "So who is this?" He pointed at Jaesun.

"He-he this is my boyfriend," I answered, holding onto Jaesun's arm.

"Eh?! Boyfriend! Full Name, Date of birth, Age, gender, do you drink, where do you work at?!" He threw a bunch of fastballs at Jaesun.

"Park Jaesun, December 4, 1996, twenty-one, I'm a man... No, I don't drink and I work at a restaurant with Bomi," Jaesun answered quickly.

"Interesting..." Aaron rubbed his chin.

"Anyway instead of interrogating my boyfriend, you have a bit of explaining to do," I said.

"Right... So prepare for a long one," he said. "Mmm... where to begin I'll start at the very beginning at that very moment."

~ Flashback ~

"We do not want to be contacted if anything happens, I'm sure his parents will do everything," Bomi's father said to the policeman.

"Yes sir, I understand," the policeman said.

They placed Aaron in the ambulance and were off to the hospital. The paramedics noticed Aaron was just unconscious from the blood loss so when they arrived at the hospital he was put into the Operating Room.

The surgery was a success and Aaron had lived.

"Brother! It's a miracle, Aaron survived!" Aaron's father called Bomi's father.

"Congratulations," Bomi's father said.

"Sorry for the trouble brother-in-law, we will make sure Aaron is a better nephew so we're sending him back to America," Aaron's father said.

"That sounds best for him. Congratulations again," Bomi's father said and hung up the phone. "What are we going to do?"

"What happened?" Bomi's mother asked.

"Aaron, he is still alive," he answered.

"No, we have to keep him away from Bomi," she said.

"I got it! Honey, let's go get ourselves a cat," he said with an evil smile.

They went on searching for a cat in a dark alley. When they found one, they fed it some poisoning and it slowly died. They ran to the nearest vet and had the cat cremated.

A few days later after Aaron had left the hospital; he headed over to Bomi's house, though, he was to stay at home to recover for a few more days but he needed to go see Bomi.

He rapped the door two times hoping Bomi would pick it but instead it was her parents.

"What the hell are you doing here?" Bomi's father asked.

"Hello to you too, Uncle," Aaron greeted with a bow. "Is Bomi home?"

"Of course not, she's at school," Bomi's mother answered.

"Oh yeah, is it okay if I wait here for her?" Aaron asked.

"It is NOT okay, you're not supposed to be at ALL," Bomi's mother replied through gritted teeth.

"What?" Aaron was feeling a bit scared because he

knows what her parents are capable of doing and could get away with it easily.

"If you ever come back to this house, we will hurt Bomi so why don't you do as you are told and go to America and never come back to see her, okay?" Bomi's father said firmly.

"Yes, Uncle," Aaron said and ran away as quickly as he could.

"America, what are they talking about?" Aaron asked himself as he ran home.

When he got inside, he called for his parents. "Mom, Dad!"

"Yes, son?" his father answered back.

Aaron walked into the kitchen and sat down at the counter where his parents were drinking tea.

"You want some tea, honey?" His mother asked him.

"No thank you, Mother," Aaron replied.

"I'll get you some tea," Aaron slapped his forehead as his mother got up and headed towards the teapot.

"So I went over to Bomi's house but I forgot there was school today and I was told something about going to America," Aaron explained, fidgeting with his fingers.

"Listen Aaron," his father put down his newspaper and looked at eldest son. "You've been in a lot of trouble lately..."

"What trouble?" Aaron questioned.

"Listen. So you can be more focused, we are sending you to go live with your little brother in America," he explained.

"My brother? You mean Andy, the one who ran away to go play soccer instead of following your rules to become a lawyer? Yeah sure, okay," Aaron rolled his eyes.

He didn't like his little brother one bit because one, Aaron was supposed to run away first and the younger sibling should stay with his parents and two, Andy never called back and it's been many years now. Though they are two years apart his little brother got first dibs on staying with their rich aunt in Washington.

"Yes, Andy. You will go to high school with him and

finish high school. Then when you finish high school, you're going to college and finish four years or more of college. You cannot come back to Korea until you complete these simple tasks. Understand?" His father looked at Aaron sternly.

"Yes, I understand," Aaron answered.

"Good. Start packing, you're leaving tomorrow," his mother said, placing the tea in front of him but Aaron hastily walked back to his room muttering odious words about his parents and slammed his door shut.

When Bomi arrived home her parents were in the living room waiting for her.

"Good, you're home. Here catch," her mother said and threw a box at her, luckily Bomi caught it.

"What is it?" She asked.

"Your cousin's ashes," her mother replied.

Bomi started tearing up and hugged the box. She ran into her room and burst into tears.

After all her tears had dried up, she stood up and grabbed a bundle of cash with her and left the house.

"How much is it?" Bomi asked the person at the front desk.

"Its $450 to put them in the displays and its $250 to buy the plot and be buried but also $50 for the stone," he replied.

"I guess, I'll bury him," Bomi said and hugged the box closer to her.

"$300 please," he said, Bomi pulled out her money and paid the man. He called some workers and they buried "Aaron's ashes" in the ground.

Bomi stayed for another hour standing up and looking down at Aaron's grave.

For the years Aaron has been "gone", Bomi went to Aaron's grave often especially on his birthday, Christmas, and other special holidays.

~ End of flashback ~

I clenched my fists at my sides in anger. "Why the hell would they do that?" I questioned with hot, fiery tears brimming at the edge of my eyes.

"Who knows but the good news is that you know is that I'm alive," Aaron said and leaned over and hugged me tightly.

"So when did you get to Korea?" I asked, letting go of him.

"Five hours ago," he answered.

"Did you eat yet?" I asked.

"Nope, I didn't have the time," he answered.

"Oh my, you must be so hungry from the long flight mmm... should we cook here or should we go out?" I asked.

"We should..." Jaesun started.

"Oooh, I know we should go out for dinner!" I said. "Let's go!"

"Did you see your parents yet?" I asked after we ordered our meal.

"No and I don't plan to," Aaron answered, putting his hands in his lap.

"What? You have to," I said.

"No I don't, they sent me to America to go live with Andy and I never got the chance to say goodbye to you or at least reveal that I didn't die," he responded.

"Still they must miss you," I said.

"Fine, I'll go but you have to come with me," he said.

"Okay then," I said. "So where are you staying if you don't want to see your parents."

"At a hotel nearby, it's a really fancy hotel, it's pretty awesome," Aaron answered.

That night was full of smiles and laughter.

~ Three months later ~

JAESUN

I went to the hotel Bomi's cousin lived at. I knocked on his door a few times until he came out.

"Oh, hi Jaesun," Aaron greeted with a small bow.

"Hello Aaron," I greeted as I did a 90 degree bow. Always got to be respectful to the people Bomi loves the most.

"Come on in," Aaron moved aside and I stepped in, taking my shoes off. "So what's going on?"

"Well, I have a request," I answered, turning around to face him.

"And that is..."

I explained my request to him. "You sure you are okay with this?" I asked.

"Of course, if you really love her and she loves you back, it's all good with me," Aaron said.

I smiled widely and engulfed him into a hug.

"Whoa, there buddy," Aaron patted my back slowly and I continued to hug him tightly.

AUTHOR

It was a beautiful summer day; the weather was extraordinarily wonderful with a cool breeze. Bomi and Jaesun were enjoying a small date walking in the park where little kids were running around, smiling and giggling, as the water fountain splashed water on them.

Jaesun wore a casual outfit of a pair of skinny jeans with a blue 3/4 sleeve button shirt with black converse while Bomi wore a cute white dress with black flats. They walked around smiling and holding each other's hand.

"Jaesun, can we go get ice cream?" Bomi asked pointing to the small ice cream stand.

Jaesun smiled and nodded his hand and walked over to the ice cream stand.

When they got the ice cream, they sat down on a bench that looked over the calm river, it was a crowded area but they didn't mind.

"I'll be right back Bomi," Jaesun said, getting up in a hurry.

"Okay," Bomi said and continued to eat her ice cream.

Bomi sat there waiting for Jaesun to return, listening to the people around her talk and the water splashing. She finished her ice cream and she waited patiently with her hands folded in her lap.

"Did her get lost?" Bomi tapped on her phone screen nervously.

"BOMI!" Jaesun ran towards her with a variety and plethora of balloons in hand but he tripped midway and released all the balloons.

"Oh my goodness!" Bomi ran over to help Jaesun up but instead of standing up, he stood there on the ground.

People started to surround them seeing the beautiful scene of Jaesun down on *one knee.*

"Bomi, we have been together for four years and every day I fell in love with you even more. You are my best friend, we've done everything together. We finished senior year, college and got our masters' degrees in business together. I wouldn't have chosen anyone else to accomplish all those things. For the rest of my life, I want to create more memories together. So I want to make today the most memorable. *Will you marry me?"* Jaesun pulled out a beautiful ring that sparkled in the sunlight with the many small diamonds and one big diamond crafted into the silver ring.

Bomi's tears coursed down her face. "Yes! Yes!" Bomi jumped up and kissed Jaesun passionately on the lips. The crowd cheered around them.

When they parted, Jaesun slipped the ring on her ring finger. "Now we can be together forever," Jaesun whispered into Bomi's ear.

~ April 15, 2020 ~

Bomi sat in her changing room for quite some time looking at her guest list.

"Seo Yoojung, Park Serin, Park Collin, Jeon Andrew, Shin Chanwoo, Choi Hyeontae, Moon Alan, Ahn Peter, Choi Cheolsu, Lee Yeoshin, Jang Lucas, Cha Yano, Kim Wonwoo, Oh Hongbin, Park Doyoon, Lee Alex, Lee Minho, Kang Ethan,

Kim Kangdae, Kim Leo, Maybee Kanemoto, Kiyoshi Ida, Hyung Henry, Hyung Sunny, Aaron Yang, Park Hyejin, Lee Jaekyung, Cho Mimi..." Bomi read out loud.

She then looked up at her utmost favorite wedding photo with Jaesun (that's why it was the one to be printed large).

They drove quite a distance (three hours) to take photos under the cherry blossoms trees. They traveled to Jinhae, a small town outside of Busan on the southeast coast. Thirty-four thousand cherry trees lined the streets, rivers, and train tracks so it was the perfect place to take pictures.

They took stunning photos with Bomi in her wedding dress and Jin in his black suit then they took some fun photos of Bomi dressed in cute party dresses while Jaesun wore different colored suits but they were all dark colored except for the light gray suit he wore.

But Bomi's absolute favorite was of her and Jaesun, Bomi was in her wedding dress and Jaesun in his tux standing in the middle of a bridge with his arm around Bomi's waist, glancing up towards the sky which was layered with cherry blossom crowns as the pink petals swayed and danced around them.

Tears ran down Bomi's face. "Hey, don't cry," Maybee said, wiping her tears. "You'll ruin your makeup."

"I know," Bomi said, sniffling.

"Stand up and let's get a good look at you," Maybee said and helped Bomi stand up in front of the full body mirror.

"Just beautiful," Maybee clapped her hands together as they stared into the mirror.

"Thank you," Bomi said, patting down her dress. Her dress was a white one-shoulder dress, sewn with little intricate flowers that designed the chest piece, a silver silk band that wrapped around her waist, and the skirt flowed out majestically around her leaving a small trail behind her.

"No, thank you, I had so much fun being maid of honor," Maybee said, putting down her clipboard and hugging the bride.

"Make sure to invite me to yours' and Kiyoshi's wedding and make me the maid of honor," Bomi said smiling.

"I will," She said. "Get ready; the ceremony will be starting soon."

"You ready?" Aaron asked Bomi as they stood in front of the huge oak doors.

"Yes," Bomi answered and the large doors were pushed opened. Jaesun and Bomi made eye contact with each other, both looked away flushing red.

Jaesun looks so perfect in his suit, Bomi thought as she walked down the aisle with Aaron by her side.

"You take care of my cousin, okay," Aaron whispered to Jaesun as they reached the small stage.

"I will," Jaesun nodded his head.

The pastor went on and on when finally the moment of truth came out. "Do you, Park Jaesun, take Park Bomi as your beloved wife?"

"I do," Jaesun answered.

"And do you, Park Bomi, take Park Jaesun as your beloved husband?"

"I do," Bomi answered.

"You may kiss the bride!"

Jaesun leaned in a kiss Bomi as everyone clapped and cheered for the two wedded couple.

BOMI

Afterwards, Jaesun and I went around the room greeting our guests. Seems like almost everyone was dating someone, Collin was dating a girl name Lee Boa and Doyoon was dating Cho Mimi while most people were still single.

"Congratulations to my best workers!" My boss, Hyung Henry, said and clapped Jaesun on the back.

"Thank you!" we bowed down.

"We have prepared a special wedding gift for the two of you," his wife, Hyung Sunny, said.

"Oh, there was no need for gifts," I said with a smile.

"Please you have been working at the restaurant for so many years now, we have to do something for you," Sunny said.

"As you know, I'm getting old and my wife is getting old too and we would like to just relax and enjoy our life while it lasts. Instead of closing down the restaurant, we want to give it to you," Henry said.

"Really?" I was shocked and touched that they wanted to hand over the restaurant over to me.

"You two are basically our grandchildren," she cupped my face in her soft wrinkled hands.

"Here are the keys to the restaurant," Henry dropped the keys in Jaesun's hand.

"We didn't want to close down because it's still a very successful restaurant," Sunny said.

"Thank you, thank you," I engulfed him into a big hug. "We will take very good care of it."

~ Two Months Later ~

AUTHOR

Bomi and Jaesun remodeled the restaurant to make it more modernized and so more young people came in and it became the hang out spot for them.

Jaesun was the head chef of the kitchen and Bomi was head waitress while Aaron helped with keeping the restaurant in good business by calculating the bills and how much they made.

They were also in need of more workers because Collin quit and became a K-pop star into their school name (Warrior), Maybee and Kiyoshi moved back to Japan to live and plan out their future together, Cheolsu wanted to help but he was also debuting as a K-pop group with Velocity, and the rest of the other students that worked there quit because the restaurant scene was just their first job to move on to their dream job.

After they put up the **Help** sign, many students and young adults applied for the job and some were even old classmates.

DASOM

"Yah, Minah I need a job," Dasom whined into the phone as she fiddled around with her make-up.

"Well, there's this restaurant I'm working at and they need help, they pay you nicely but I don't think..."

"I'll be right there, send me the address," I hung up the phone and grabbed my purse and my resume. "I'll show you father that I can actually do work."

"Dasom!" Minah waved her hand at me as I entered the restaurant.

"Hey, can you go get the manager for me?" I asked her.

"Okay... She's also head waitress so she might be busy," she said and left.

"Just go get her will you," I shooed away and fixed up my make-up some more because as you know you got to look nice to win big.

After a couple minutes, someone came up to me and I wasn't expecting to see her face again.

"Dasom?" I heard her say.

"Bomi? What the hell are you doing here?" I folded my arms in anger.

"What about you, what are doing here?" She asked me.

"I'm looking for a job," I answered.

"What, your father can't support you anymore," She laughed.

"He won't let me work at his company and he won't give me any allowance either," I explained. "But now since I learned you work here, I can't work here anymore!"

But then a few hot guys walked in that caught my attention. "Or I think you should quit so I can work peacefully." I stood on my tip-toes to get a better look at them.

BOMI

Is this girl serious? I thought.

"I don't think you should be talking to your boss like that," I said.

"B-b-boss!" She yelled and I nodded.

"What do you even have against me I didn't even do anything wrong to you? You know what; you're just wasting my time, you can leave now." I said, turning around.

"Wait, no, please I really need to this job," she pleaded. "I only treated you badly because... to be honest I really liked Taejoon and I got jealous and you were really pretty so calling you ugly made me feel more confident. But when Jaesun came along and Taejoon said he doesn't like clingy girls like me, I started to like Jaesun. Please forgive me!" she explained and got down on her knees. Everyone was staring at this unbelievable scene of Miss Perfection, Hwang Dasom, down on her knees apologizing.

"You started working now, go find Minah," I said with a straight face.

"Does this mean you forgive me?" She called out.

"No, now move along and Minah will train you," I said walking away.

DASOM

I let out a shaky breath of relief; I walked around to find Minah.

"How come you didn't tell me Bomi was the manager here?" I slapped Minah's arm.

"Ow! Because you didn't let me finish talking on the phone," Minah said, angrily.

"Ahh, she's so scary now that she's a higher level than me," I rubbed my face in frustration.

"Whatever, you know she's actually really nice once you get to know her. Here, get changed over there," she said and handed me my uniform. "Also, there's a lot to know about her. Before you make any mistakes, first things first, Bomi is married to Jaesun and Jaesun is married to Bomi, no questions asked."

"Figures," I rolled my eyes and trailed closely behind Minah.

"And second of all, quit your attitude!" Minah ordered.

BOMI

"We got a new worker," I said to Jaesun as I walked into the kitchen.

"Really? Who?" He asked, wiping his hands on a paper towel.

"Hwang Dasom," I answered.

"What?" He looked at me with an astonished expression.

"Yep, she didn't know I was the boss so she started having this attitude towards me and then when I told her that I was the boss, she begged for forgiveness," I explained.

"Wow..." Jaesun said, slowly clapping his hands. "The unexpected and crazy events that happened these days are unbelievable!"

~ Later that night ~

"Mrs. Park, you can go home now, don't worry we can close up," Loni said to Jaesun and I.

"You sure?" I asked her, grabbing my coat.

"You worry too much Mrs. Park, please go home and rest," Brendan waved his hand at them as he mopped the floors.

So with that, Jaesun and I let the students close up for the night and we walked home in happy silence.

"You want to take a break?" Jaesun asked and I nodded.

We sat down on a bench at a nearby park. "Man, a lot of crazy and amazing things have happened a lot this year hasn't it?"

"A lot," I replied. Even though it was sky was dark and filled with twinkling stars, there were a few little kids with their parents running around and playing on the jungle gym.

"Will we have kids some day?" Jaesun asked, following my gaze.

"Maybe but not now, I'm not ready to give up my freedom," I answered putting my head down onto Jaesun's shoulder.

When we arrived home, I immediately jumped onto my bed, inhaling the minty scent of eucalyptus spearmint that filled with air.

"Ah, finally home!" I said closing my eyes, Jaesun then lay on top of me.

"You tired, Bomi?" He asked me and I opened my eyes to see his faces inches from mine.

"Maybe," I smiled and wrapped my arms around his neck bringing him closer until our lips met.

"I love you," he said between kisses.

"I love you too."